D.M. Barr

EXPIRED LISTINGS

An Erotic Novel of Psychological Suspense

PUNCTUATED
PUBLISHING

COPYRIGHT PAGE

To my late mother, Sophie Bernice (Bunny),
whom I miss every single day:

You promised me that if I kept writing,
eventually someone, somewhere,
would want to read what I'd written.
So glad I was able to prove you right!

ACKNOWLEDGEMENTS

No BOOK IS WRITTEN IN a vacuum and this one is certainly no exception.

As a former business magazine writer and editor, non-fiction has always been my bailiwick, but fiction, my final frontier. I want to thank anyone and everyone who convinced me that I could actually plot out and complete an entire novel.

First, thanks to my family: the long-suffering Mr. Barr, the little Barrs, and the two hairy, four-legged, rescue Barrs, all of whom tolerated my abject neglect so I could concentrate on something so important to me. To my father, and to my brother, who never fails to make me laugh, even (especially?) at myself. To my fellow REALTORS©, who put up with my constant book yammering instead of talking about cold-calling, closings and everything else we normally discuss, and especially to Jennifer, who shared her agent contacts. To my encouraging accountability partner Rhonda and her friend Fran, who also liberally shared publishing advice. And of course, to Gayl, my BFF, who dutifully read everything I sent her and never judged.

To my journalism compatriots—Mike, Melissa, Mercedes, Bill, Phyllis, Les, Alan and my former editor Geri—as I fell into the desperate depths of commerce, you always reminded me that I was once and always one of you at heart, a writer. To the folks at Rough 'N Ready and my fellow members at the HVRWA and NJRWA, thank you for motivating me to write so I could belong to your elite circle. To my Facebook family—the writers I've known for a long time such as Chris G. and Carol B., as well as those who are newer to me such as Anne A. and Jeff S.—thank you for your unbridled generosity in sharing your publishing knowledge and expertise. And to Barbara N, my favorite Penguin, thank you for helping me with my police officer lingo, as well as keeping my competitive juices flowing, week after week.

To the members of the 'scene' who I came to know over the Internet as well as in person—thank you for your honesty, your humor, and your acceptance of someone who was just there to observe. I will refrain from mentioning first names or nicknames here out of respect for your anonymity, but you know who you are.

Thanks to my agent, Meredith Bernstein, for having faith and taking a chance; to Ellen, who taught me more than I ever wanted to know about mental health; to Jodi, who took a second look and gave me some invaluable advice; and to Kim Killion and the rest of my team at the Killion Group, for your awesome help and my amazing cover.

Finally, to those for whom I am most grateful: Marshall for encouraging me when I'd set my manuscript aside for good (and for warning me that the turkey might be slightly off), and to Jason, the world's greatest developmental editor and a sweet, patient friend.

PREFACE

S OME EXPLANATIONS...
According to the National Association of REAL-
TORS®, the term Realtor is be printed as REALTOR® which,
unfortunately, is clunky in prose and can get really jarring on
the eyes. Luckily, I have found several instances in journalism and literature where the author wrote the term as Realtor,
and I have followed their lead. Secondly, and more importantly, please note that every real estate agent does not au-
tomatically qualify as a REALTOR®, which is why the term
is never to be used interchangeably with 'agent' or 'broker.'
Actual REALTORS® must adhere to NAR's strict code of
ethics. Fortunately, every fictional agent in the fictional town
of Rock Canyon has pledged to adhere to this code, which
permits me, as author, to refer to them as Realtors. One must
assume, however, that their fictional MLS board will immediately retract their status after reading this book.

Please note that any mention of actual commission
amounts and commission splits is arbitrary, and not indica-
tive of any 'standard' or 'typical' practice in the real estate
industry. All commission amounts and splits in real estate
are negotiated on a per-deal or per-agency basis.

I know some agents will contend that this novel tarnishes
the public's perception of the real estate industry, a profession that sadly has a 17% public level of trust, according to a
recent Gallup Poll. This means it currently ranks just below

lawyers but a smidgen higher than advertising execs, used car salesperson and politicians. To those protesters, I say, relax and get over yourselves. It's a satire. I wrote it to be so over the top, no one could possibly imagine that agents kill off their problem clients or mourn the faked deaths of colleagues, just to garner public support. And if they do actually believe such fabrications, the profession's rep was irreparably besmirched long before I set pen to paper.

I also want to reiterate that the real estate characters described in *Expired Listings* are fictitious. I have worked in real estate for nearly two decades and I can assure you that 99.95% of all the agents I've met have been honest, hardworking and ethical. Thank goodness for the other .05%, who inspired some of the more outlandish exploits concocted herein.

Finally, you might notice that throughout this novel, while I have capitalized titles such as Dom, Top and Sir, I have also capitalized the names of bottoms and submissives. The first is common BDSM convention and I wanted to stay true to the culture of the community. The second is actually counter to that protocol, but I felt a lack of capitalization might be too jarring to readers. My apologies.

WARNING: This book contains sexually explicit scenes and adult language and may be considered offensive to some readers. This book is intended for Adults Only, as defined by the laws of the country in which you made your purchase. Please store computer files and books wisely, where they cannot be accessed by under-aged readers.

DISCLAIMER: Please do not try any new sexual practice, especially those that might be found in a BDSM title, without the guidance of an experienced practitioner. Neither Punctuated Publishing nor its authors will be responsible for any loss, harm, injury or death resulting from use of the information contained in any of its titles.

PROLOGUE

Dungeon: March 12

THE FIRST "WHAT THE FUCK?!" is always the sweetest. The impassioned pleas and expletives that follow have their own particular charm—it's true—but nothing beats that first moment when the chloroform wears off and prey senses predicament.

The makeshift dungeon is brightly lit for my viewing pleasure, but not my guest's, whose blindfold ensures both darkness and disorientation. The closed-circuit camera captures the delicious onset of adrenalin dump: the tensing muscles, the primal struggle against the leather ankle and wrist restraints, the mounting desperation as the brain registers there is no give, no escape. Ah, yes.

I turn up the speakers, return to my overstuffed recliner, close my eyes and savor the serenade of screams, the verbal pageant of anguish that fills my cozy viewing chamber. It's orgasmic, this frantic, intoxicating journey from indignation to resignation, marked by hoarsened throat and slackened struggle. The scene underlines the primary lesson du jour— namely that today, for once, I am the one in charge.

Realizing there is no imminent chance of rescue, the body finally goes limp, the clamor ceases. A good time to make my grand entrance. I switch on the mic, and the room fills with the crackle of static.

"Hello?" the voice calls out, weak, straining. "I'm here, I'm here, help me…"

"Not so high and mighty now, are you? Not so sure, so full of yourself today."

My voice distorter creates an inflection more automated than human, unrecognizable.

"Look, there's been a mistake. I'm not like the others. I try to do right by my clients. It might not always seem like that, but it's true. I know the others were sleazy. I know they hurt many people. But I'm not like that. I'm not—"

"Don't give me that horseshit, you goddamned hypocrite," I interrupt. "I'm not some shlub condo buyer you're sending on a one-way trip to the poorhouse, so shut up and listen. You've got 24 hours. During that time, I want you to think. Think long and hard over this life of yours. You've got until tomorrow evening to recount your sins and prepare to atone for them. One day to cleanse your soul. The next time we speak, I expect some heartfelt confessions. Otherwise, better drum up whatever catchy slogan you'd like written on your tombstone. Clear?"

Silence.

I don't like to be ignored. This is my domain and when I speak, I expect to be acknowledged. After all my trouble, all my preparations, I deserve at least that.

I march down the hall, fists clenched, floorboards creaking underneath the weight of my sneakers. The door squeals as I enter the torture chamber, barren except for the long wooden table that holds my captive hostage and my implements of persuasion hanging from hooks on the walls and scattered along the floor's perimeter. I stop about a foot away and watch my captive flinch.

"I repeat, have I made myself clear?" My glance lingers upon the naked skin, a blank canvas awaiting my signature, scribbled in bruises and blood.

Still no answer. My face grows hotter, spurred by this obvious insurrection. I pull back my arm, and with an open hand, slap my guest's right cheek so violently, the head jerks all the way left to the point of neck dislocation. My guest rewards me with a prolonged shriek of distress. I can see the spot swell and throb. I wonder if there are tears forming beneath the blindfold. I regret not being able to tell.

Still no answer. Insubordination bordering on the suicidal.

I yank a cane off the wall with such force the hook comes along with it.

"Tongue-tied? I think this may loosen it a bit." I slam the bamboo against the soft flesh between the rib cage and hip. That does the trick, inspiring several deep moans followed by a satisfying, guttural rasp, "Clear."

"Good. Now get to work." I saunter out, leaving my guest to shuffle through years of memories and missteps, trying to figure out exactly which one would be the most critical to nominate for atonement before I deactivate one last real estate license for good.

CHAPTER 1

November 6th (Four Months Earlier)

BILE MAKES FOR A LOUSY lunch. Dana Black swallowed hard as she blinked twice, dug her fingernails into the leather-wrapped steering wheel, glanced at the clock, and tried desperately to orient herself. Then it hit her, where she was, why she was there. Suddenly, the gray ambiguity of the past few hours didn't seem like such a bad alternative. She reached for her spring water—a constant cup holder companion for just such occurrences—hoping to eradicate the bitter taste, but she knew it was less gastrointestinal, more foreboding about what awaited inside. She had to go in; it was expected. But her body didn't always buy into logic. Or duty.

The noontime chill was typical for November in the Hudson Valley, but the slovenly woman who answered Cassandra Beckett's door warmed Dana with a welcoming hug.

"I was just making your mother a sandwich. Can I make you one as well?" She took and hung up Dana's jacket, and then led the way through the cavernous foyer of the McMansion into its space-age kitchen.

"No, I'm good, but thanks," said Dana, still feeling queasy.

"Well you must be thirsty then. Do you want some hot cider to warm up? If not, I made your favorite."

"The lemonade would be fine." Despite fear of aggravating the reflux, Dana rarely refused the specialty drink.

Cassandra's caretaker, Lorelei Simpson, had the patience and kindness of Mother Theresa, trapped in the body of Spongebob Squarepants. Her short, black hair could have been styled by the local butcher, ragged and uneven, framing a hardened face highlighted by bright red, perpetually smudged lipstick. She never donned an apron, so there was always some sort of gravy or pie-filling stain adorning her size eighteen, Alfred Dunner polyester blouse or pants. But none of that mattered because unlike her mother, Lorelei always made Dana feel accepted and wanted.

The caretaker returned with a wine glass filled with the yellow elixir. Hand-squeezed lemons, as always, with the perfect amount of sugar, then topped with sweetened coconut. Dana felt an uncharacteristic rush of affection for the caregiver, one of the few people currently in her life that truly seemed to give a damn, minus some secret agenda.

"How is she, Lorelei?"

"Ah, in rare form today. Go in and see for yourself." Lorelei pointed to the living room and then disappeared back into the kitchen.

Dana hesitated, gripping the glass so tightly, it was a miracle it didn't shatter. She forced herself to visit every few weeks, partially because she felt a certain responsibility for Cassandra's condition, but mostly because she knew that no one else would. Even though her older sister Melanie lived next door, she certainly couldn't spare the time out of her harried schedule, and her brother-in-law Reid, clearly not Mom's favorite, avoided the place like the plague.

After debating for a minute or two, she forced herself over the ropes and into the ring.

"Hey, Mom, what's going on?" Dana asked the seventy-year-old near-skeleton sitting in a recliner, watching Cartoon Network. Her light blue housecoat was a far cry from her real estate power suits of yesteryear. Mom had regained ninety percent of her speech post-stroke and could still walk but rarely did so, preferring others to wait upon her like royalty.

"What the fuck do you care?" Cassandra grumbled, without glancing up from *Adventure Time*. "What are you looking for, a handout?"

"Mom, that's not fair. I've never borrowed money from you."

"I seem to recall you running up my credit card to the tune of $5,000."

Fuck, that again. Like a playlist on eternal repeat.

"Back when I was fifteen. That was twenty years ago. Look, I didn't come to argue. I came to see if you needed anything."

"Yeah, I need the last fifty-four years of my life back. Anything you can do about that?"

Cassandra's vitriol was a tsunami, drawing back the surf into a titanic wall of water before crashing down and submerging the shoreline. Caught up in its lethal force, Dana felt the oxygen being sucked out of the room, her earlier wooziness returning as the couch and end tables began to spin around her. Thankfully, as if by divine intervention, Lorelei chose that moment to invite her back into the kitchen for a refill of lemonade.

"I warned you."

Dana nodded in grateful recognition; Lorelei was her lone ally on the front lines of the Battle of Cassandra and the sole reason she didn't have nursemaid duties herself.

Cassandra's opulent kitchen, however, was less shelter than second battleground. Dana was embittered as always as she observed its cherry cabinets and granite countertops. It was like a page out of *House Beautiful*: Viking chef's stove, Bosch convection wall oven, Sub-Zero fridge/freezer. All the frills. Some people had so much while others so little.

"I know my mom's sick, and I know it hasn't been easy for her, but that doesn't give her license to make everyone else's life miserable."

Lorelei nodded, trading Dana's empty glass for a new one. "Melanie's been talking about selling the house and moving somewhere smaller. Says your mom doesn't need this big place in her condition and it's true, we don't even use the rear nine rooms. All this chatter is making Cassandra more agitated than usual. Speaking of which, how's the real estate business? Catching up with your sister?"

Dana sighed, tired of Melanie—Rock Canyon's number one Realtor—being used as her perpetual measuring stick of success.

"I'll never be that busy, thank God, but it really has been crazy. I skipped Broker's Open Houses today so I could stop by."

"Well, since you *are* here, why not take a breather, rest for a bit?"

"Thanks, I think I may take you up on that." She retreated down the hall.

Over the past few years, Lorelei's bedroom and her computer had served as Dana's solitary refuge in hostile territory, especially since the house's lack of a wireless router rendered her iPhone and iPad practically useless. Even its color, a still water blue, invited relaxation.

Dana plopped down on the bed and glanced at the photos scattered atop the adjacent dresser. The snapshots captured Lorelei during what Dana imagined had to be happier days: one at her nursing school graduation, another from the top of the Empire State Building, a third posing by the Hudson with Lady Liberty proclaiming freedom in the background. *Give me your tired, your poor, your huddled masses…* Dana smiled at the irony. She imagined that the Lorelei in that photo had no inkling of the huddled mass that awaited her years later in the form of Cassandra.

After a few deep, restorative breaths, Dana checked her email and online agenda for any urgent messages, forgotten tasks, or—*please, God, no*—a last-minute cancellation of her long-anticipated, 2:00 pm appointment. Nothing. *Whew!* Then she closed her eyes and prayed for an hour of glorious, nightmare-free napping.

She ended up with half that, her peaceful slumber interrupted by an invasive explosion of animated bickering. Steeled for another sparring session, she emerged from her haven into the harsh reality of the living room, where Lorelei plumped Cassandra's pillows, in spite of her patient's slew of invectives.

"Lovely as it's been to see you both, I've got to go. I've got some prospecting to do."

"You should be going to therapy, not pestering potential home sellers." Cassandra kept her eyes glued to the screen, which was now televising a repeat of *Ed, Edd n Eddy.*

"Yes, how is that going, Dana?" Lorelei interjected,

before Dana could react to her mother's advice. "Is Dr. Lawrence helping you with your nightmares?"

I wish it were only nightmares—and not the blackouts. That would be bearable.

"I've only had one session, but another is scheduled later in the week. Thanks for asking."

"Go back, back to Centralia. More important than some lousy listings," snarled Cassandra.

"You're one to talk. When did you ever, and I mean ever, put anything before the almighty house sale?" Dana wanted to kick herself as soon as the words left her lips; why fan the flames and raise her own blood pressure?

"Stop your squabbling, both of you. Cassandra, your daughter's got a trying day ahead and took precious moments to visit and make sure you're well. Now tell her thank you."

Cassandra remained silent, not acknowledging Lorelei's admonishment. Dana shrugged, gave her mother a kiss on the cheek and bolted. Lorelei hurried after her and helped her on with her coat. They shared a tight hug goodbye. Dana nearly tripped over her own feet trying to get to the sanctuary of her Honda Accord and to the spring water that would hopefully dilute the returning acid she felt inching up her esophagus.

Once inside, she yanked the door shut, slunk down in her seat—as if that could possibly shield her from Cassandra's venomous residue—closed her eyes and counted to twenty. Then she headed over to her empty listing on Gangi Court where her prospecting date awaited. And where she planned to challenge herself in a much more pleasant way.

CHAPTER 2

November 6ᵗʰ

FORTY MINUTES LATER, DANA FOUND herself bound, spread-eagle, to a four-poster bed—flushed and bathed in sweat—and mere moments from a game-winning orgasm, when her telemarketing prospect brought up the frigging commission.

"Good question. I charge 3%," she half-huffed into the microphone of her Bluetooth headset, trying desperately to modulate her breathing and suppress any auditory clues to her predicament. "Together we'll decide what to pay the buyer's broker—Yes, that would be *ahhh-*ditional but—No, 1% wouldn't leave me enough money to market—" *Click.* She let the cell phone fall from her right hand to the floor, thwarted. "Goddammit!"

"He hung up, didn't he?" Dare, her lover, switched off the giant vibrator and theatrically plopped it down beside her on the bed.

"Yes," she pouted, her breathing slowly returning to normal.

Dare—average in height, weight, actually in every way other than his sadistic imagination—walked over and pulled the left speaker of her headset an inch from her ear. "Could you speak up?"

"Yes," she repeated, louder this time. *Sarcastic prick.*

"That's five disconnects in a row, you know."

"Yes. Thank you. I know."

"Five more and you've lost."

"Again, thanks for the recount."

"Kind of unsatisfying, huh?" Dare blithely let go of the earpiece so it snapped back with an annoying thud. He slowly surveyed her fit, naked body with his palm, pausing over her ample breasts and pinching each nipple for a beat or two before moving down to her belly, patting it twice. "I mean, you came kinda close that time. Or should I say, you *almost* came kinda close?"

"Fuck you! Stop gloating."

"Ahem?"

"Oh forgive me. Fuck you, *Sir.*"

She gave him the finger but the effect was muted since both of her wrists were secured firmly to the head posts of the bed they were 'borrowing' for the afternoon. She couldn't even kick him since her legs were also drawn far apart, ankles tethered to the foot pillars. This positioning gave him and *Mr. Awesome*, the crown prince of vibrators, easy and unobstructed access to her most private parts. He had purposely propped Dana's head up with a pillow so she could watch him mercilessly tease her—but only as long as the call remained in play.

At first, the exercise had sounded simple enough: keep the potential home seller on the line long enough to achieve orgasm *and* get the listing appointment, all while staying on script and maintaining a steady voice that wouldn't tip off the prospect as to the conditions surrounding the call. It was typical Dare, designing an experiment that required extreme concentration and self-control, one where her fate hinged almost completely on her own competence. Unfortunately, today's results were leaving her frustrated, both sexually and professionally. Still, it was a hundred times better than the hour she'd spent with her mother earlier in the day.

"I hate this fucking list. Where did you get these names?" she asked.

"They're the new For Sale by Owners that came out online today."

"Well, then of course they're not going to want to talk to me. They haven't even tested the market yet. I never call FSBOs until a few months in, after they realize they can't sell their house themselves."

"Dana, you were the one who proclaimed yourself the queen of real estate cold callers." Dare picked up his favorite crop, the one with the royal blue handle. He studied it, turning it over and over again in his hands. "You were the one who accepted the parameters of this challenge. One appointment for every ten dials—that's what you agreed you could achieve. You never specified a particular type of call." He looked her straight in the eye. "Are you telling me you're giving up and blaming it on the list?"

"No, I am most certainly not." And to emphasize her strengthened resolve, Dana gave a defiant tug against her wrist and ankle restraints. She knew there would be no give but always enjoyed the chaotic feeling of being temporarily out of control.

"No, of course not. You never give up." He ran the crop's leather tongue over her short, straight auburn locks and then brushed it lightly against her right cheek. "That's one of the things I like best about you. I get to watch you struggle through some elaborate scene, trying to prove yourself. The moment you finally realize your ego's written a check your body can't cash? That's the sweet spot."

"You're wrong. I can do this, you, you big…"

"Really? A former journalist and you can't come up with a decent insult?" He playfully swatted the side of her left breast.

"It was only a trade magazine." She shrugged.

"Fair enough. I certainly hope you succeed, Your Telemarketing Highness, especially now, because that little *Fuck You, Sir* comment is going to cost you big time. I'm upping the stakes."

"You can't change the rules mid-scene."

"I believe I can do anything I want." He traced her body's contours with the crop. "And short of safewording, I don't think you're in any position to protest. Are you?"

"Do you change the rules like this with your other subs?"

"Other subs? First off, I do not classify you as a submissive. And that's a compliment, because if you were one, you'd be the world's worst. All you think about is how you can gain control, take the upper hand. I can't think of anything I suggest that doesn't get pushback. At best, you're a PITA bottom."

"Okay, I'll rephrase. Do you change the rules with your other Pain in the Ass partners?"

"We're not discussing me, Dana," he said, again skirting her accusation of promiscuity. "So here are the new rules. As usual, when you're reciting your sales spiel, your voice can't give away the fact that I'm working you over. But now, I'm going to crop you as well. If you let it affect you, if you break the cadence, forget your script or drop the phone, game over. Agreed?"

Deep dramatic sigh. "Fine."

"And what are the consequences if you lose?"

"I spin the Wheel." She rolled her eyes. Dare had

perverted a miniature carnival wheel into the Wheel of Misfortune, with each space's legend indicating a rather unpleasant outcome. He brought it along every time they played, to whatever empty listing she could snag for their rendezvous.

"Good girl. And remind me, what is our motto?"

"Cumming is for Closers."

"That's right. Perfect. Let's begin."

Dare repositioned Dana's headset so that the noise-cancelling microphone wouldn't pick up the hum of *Mr. Awesome* or the thwack of the crop. Then he scooped the cell phone off the floor where she'd let it drop.

"Hmm, let's see …" He scanned the FSBO list with mock concern. "Ah, here we go. Terrence Douglas. 425 Jeremy Court." He punched in the number and placed the cell phone back into her open palm, positioning her thumb over the Disconnect icon. She couldn't even fake the conversation; the fucker had downloaded a call recorder app onto her phone.

Three rings. Then a click and a groggy "Hello?" Mr. Douglas sounded like he had just woken from a deep sleep. *Great.*

"Hi, this is Dana Black, and I'm an agent with Rock Canyon Realty." Dare switched on the vibrator and set it on its designated course. She squeezed her eyes tight, clutching the phone, determined to concentrate on the call.

"So?"

"So I saw you were advertising your home for sale…"

Dare's pulsating intruder found a good spot. A very good spot. The sudden shock jolted her, causing her breath to come out in short spurts, like a Lamaze demo. She clenched tighter, trying to forestall the inevitable explosion long enough to get the appointment that would win her the game.

"And…I was wondering…" A wave of almost stifling warmth overcame her as *Mr. Awesome* continued to romance its ultimate target. With his other hand, Dare started to whack the side of her hip with the crop. So much stimulation was difficult to absorb all at once. She prayed that she could keep the conversation going as her arousal rose to a fever pitch and her juices drenched the bed.

"…I was wondering, if for some reason it doesn't sell…how long you would wait before you'd consider… ahhhh…"

"Miss, are you okay?"

"What?" Her eyes shot open and she violently shook her head back and forth to grab Dare's attention and urge him to stop. He ignored her signals and increased the torment, now rubbing the vibrator up and down against her crotch and moving the crop to her breasts, stimulating her in all directions at once. She kissed her concentration goodbye.

"You sound like you are in pain and out of breath. Are you having a heart attack?"

On top of everything else, at that moment, Call Waiting interrupted with an annoying click. Damn. She was going to lose the challenge *and* the orgasm.

"HEY!" she screamed at Dare and then lowered her voice back to a professional level. "No…I'm fine… excuse me…I'll have to call you back." She disconnected the call with her thumb, effectively conceding defeat.

Her sharp tone convinced Dare to switch off *Mr. Awesome*, his expression a mixture of disappointment and triumph. She gulped and took a moment to moderate her breathing before pressing the button that allowed the new caller to come on the line.

"Hello. This is Dana."

"Dana, it's Endie." Endicott Coxwell was her colleague, closest friend and confidant, as well as her safe call.

"What is it? What's wrong?" Since Endicott knew she'd be spending the afternoon playing with Dare, it had to be an emergency for him to intrude.

"You sound weird. Did I catch you in *flagrante delicto*?"

"Something like that. Can I help you?"

"Wow, answering a call mid-scene. You're becoming as bad as the agents in *Glengarry Glen Ross* who'd sell their own mother for a deal."

"Endie," she said, exasperated, "is there a point to this call?"

"Oh my God, yes. Honey, you will not believe what's happening here. I would have called you earlier, but things have been so, so crazy…"

"Okay, so would you like to share?"

"It's Annika." Annika Henderson-Goldenblatt was one of Rock Canyon's most powerful agents. Second only to Melanie.

"What'd she do? Pull her usual stunt of sending the listing agent a mortgage prequal and binder for one set of buyers, and then bringing a completely different couple to the closing?"

"Oh she won't be doing that anymore, I guarantee it. So picture this: late this morning, the office caravan stopped by her open house on Cranberry. You know, the cute split with that awful green paisley wallpaper, the one that came on last week?"

"Okay, so?"

"We walked in and there she was, slumped over the dining room table. Dana, I can't believe it. She's dead!"

CHAPTER 3

November 8th

TWO DAYS OF SOMEWHAT SNARKY press coverage later, Dana's first glimpse at the meager crowd at Dennison's Funeral Home confirmed her suspicions that no one particularly minded the loss of a real estate broker. True, she had not been to many funerals in her life—really only her father's when she was very young—but she couldn't imagine one more poorly attended. There were only five other mourners present: Endie, Annika's husband Drew, and a few administrative assistants from the brokerage, probably there to get a few hours' reprieve from work. Most noticeably absent: Deborah Lee Decker, the agency's owner.

"That's some tie." She squeezed Endie's shoulder and sat down beside him, his somber charcoal-grey Armani suit brightened by a fanciful black, purple and gold vintage necktie which featured Mickey Mouse in various poses.

"Like it? Anniversary present."

"Lovely, but somewhat inappropriate, sweetie." It was a rare and delicious opportunity for her to turn the tables and criticize Endie's outfit for once.

"Hey, had to do something to get this party going. This place is dis-mal with a capital Dis. Why the hell are they having it here, anyway? Aren't most of the Jewish services held across town at Levin's?"

"I heard Deborah Lee ordered Drew to keep it close to the office," Dana said. "Didn't want people away from their desks for too long. Word was, if he didn't agree, accounting would have withheld Annika's last commission checks."

"Typical."

Annika had been raised Lutheran in her native Sweden, but converted a few years back to court the town's underserved Jewish market. Well, her version of converted, anyway. She hyphenated her name to add the most Jewish-sounding surname she could muster, constantly tossed around Yiddish words like "kvetch" and "kvell," and convinced Rabbi Tannenbaum that she'd completed her Talmudic studies elsewhere—something he deemed imminently plausible in light of the discounted commission she agreed to charge for his home purchase.

They sat silently, lost in their thoughts as the rabbi entered and walked to the front of the chapel.

"Do they even know what happened?" Endie asked after a bit.

You know, Mr. Trivia, you should turn off *Jeopardy* once in a while and watch the news. They rushed the autopsy through, and best they can figure, she died from eating poisoned shrimp at the open house. Cyanide, apparently. But no one can figure out how it got there. The mortgage broker who provided the food claims he knew the house was kosher, so when he dropped food off around 10:00 am, he only brought what was appropriate: bagels, lox and cream cheese."

Endie surveyed the chapel. "Couldn't have felt too broken up about it. No mortgage brokers here. Not even Scott, that hot guy from Canyon Mortgage, and that cute butt of his."

"Down, boy. Whoever it was is probably keeping a low profile and anyway, I hear Scott is sneaking around with some hotshot broker. But what do you care? Aren't things hunky dory at home?"

"Same old. Same old. Grayson's constantly on me for working late. But he didn't complain last week when I brought him home a Rolex."

"He got a Rolex, and you got a tie? Kinda lopsided, no? Still, better than back at college when we used to crash weddings to get a decent meal."

Dana cut short her reminiscing. She was becoming more and more disconcerted by the sparse mourner attendance. If part of the measure of a person's life was the size of the audience at their funeral, then Annika had had no life at all. Where was the validation of her existence? Had she not affected others, been part of something larger than herself? Dana fought back nausea and tears; showing weakness or vulnerability was a no-no in her world.

"You'd think that even if she didn't have close friends, the homicide rumors would have lured some curiosity seekers, no? And where are the police? I mean, what if the killer comes by to check out the results of his handiwork? Shouldn't they be here, monitoring the, err, crowd?"

Endicott shook his head. "Dana, Dana, Dana. You know that after the Merriweather Stevens incident, no one in town is going to believe there really was a murder. None of these folks—especially the police—give a rat's ass about real estate agents anymore. To them, the murder was a public service. Hell, they're probably bidding on who gets to kill one of us next."

"I thought we were past all that." Apparently, old grudges died harder than the pews underneath their butts.

Kerrianne Cooper, a British, fair-haired newer admin and the sole mourner in the next row forward, turned to face them. "I keep hearing that name. Who exactly is this Merriweather Stevens, anyway?"

Endie's eyes grew wide with excitement. "You don't know?"

Kerrianne shook her head. Endie, the consummate gossip, was practically shivering in his seat.

"She was a long-term associate broker with the firm. A few years back, Deborah Lee held a press conference to tell the world about her suicide. She explained how Merriweather wasted nine months showing a couple over 100 homes. Then they bought a For Sale by Owner without her. Instead of the $10,000 commission she would have earned, they sent her a $25 flower arrangement and a note saying *sorry*. After that, Merriweather supposedly fell into a deep depression from which she never recovered."

The young intern looked skeptical. "If she was that despondent, why didn't anyone reach out to help?"

"Great question, Kerrianne. No one reached out because no one in the office had ever heard of Merriweather Stevens. And it's not really all that surprising, considering there are over 2,000 agents in town, many of whom work out of home offices. But thanks to a slow news week, the media grabbed the story and ran with it, printing column after column about how useful real estate agents are, what an important contribution we make to the economy, blah, blah, blah. It played beautifully on the public's collective guilt over the suicide. Soon everyone in Rock Canyon felt almost unpatriotic buying or selling a house on their own, as if they were cheating a fellow American out of a paycheck."

Endie paused and nodded at a late arrival who walked past. She smiled back as she left business cards on the empty pews, in case any mourners needed a replacement agent for the deceased. The card bore an insignia engraved in florescent purple, casting an odd, glow-in-the-dark hue that contrasted sharply with the dim lighting in the chapel.

Endie leaned in closer to his audience to avoid being overheard. "The one person who wasn't happy was Melanie Wright. She was handling 60% of the business before the media blitz, but afterward? It fell to around 20%, as buyers and sellers struggled to spread the wealth. Even the worst of brokers were getting rich."

"Melanie obviously did something to turn things back around since she's still on top," Kerrianne countered.

"She did something, alright. She killed the golden goose. Went to the press and told them there was no Merriweather Stevens and never had been. She was a total fabrication, the entire suicide story a massive publicity stunt concocted to shore up business."

"That must not have gone over well…"

"Worse than you can imagine," Dana chimed in, making no excuses for her older sister. "Most people hate to appear foolish, but that's especially true in Rock Canyon. Everyone here has a chip on their shoulder because they can't afford to move across the river to Westminster. They're already defensive about their income; they weren't about to put up with being called 'suckers' and 'chumps' as well."

"Not surprisingly, a terrible anti-Realtor backlash

arose," said Endie, reclaiming the spotlight. "Suddenly, everyone started marketing their homes themselves. It wasn't until a few months later, when nothing had sold, that business began to slowly trickle back to the top agents, like Melanie."

"So now everything's back to normal? Good agents get the business?"

Dana and Endie nodded. Kerrianne, whose ambitions clearly extended far beyond her current position of admin, turned around to listen to the beginning of the service, seemingly satisfied that the hoax wouldn't negatively affect her future income.

"I get it about the public not showing up," said Dana, underneath the eulogy's drone. "But how about all the other agents and brokers? Her co-workers. Where are they?"

"Hell, they're happy as clams," said Endicott. "Less competition."

"How shellfish of them."

At the end of the service, they murmured their condolences to Drew and then headed out, Endicott back to the office, and Dana off to her therapy appointment.

"Sweetie, one word of advice." He pulled her close into a conspiratorial embrace. "If you plan to make a play for the Jewish market, better be quick. I hear that Aisha Singh is already answering her phone 'Aisha Singhowitz.'"

CHAPTER 4

November 8th

DANA HAD A FEW MINUTES to kill before therapy so she made a quick pit stop at Starbucks, grabbed a Venti Tea Misto, and then wandered down to Wild Thing, the exotic pet store at the far end of the strip mall. She loved to watch the puppies in the window. Two English Bulldogs, maybe eight weeks old, were wrestling a Kong chew toy away from a Chinese Crested which, at half their size, was clearly the underdog. Her heart ached for the bullied little guy who ultimately lost his valiant struggle. Undaunted, the Crested turned his attentions to a knotted piece of rope in the opposite corner. She silently cheered his resilience.

The storeowner gave Dana a nod of recognition. Dare often brought her into the shop based on the results of the Wheel of Misfortune, where he'd drape a snake around her neck or perch a cockatoo on her shoulder while she closed her eyes and tried not to scream or vomit. He claimed that facing her fears made her a stronger person but deep down, she knew how delighted he was that she had so many of them.

Dr. Eleanor Lawrence was Rock Canyon's leading

therapist. She operated out of a ground level office on Noyes Drive, in the town's newest corporate park. The office itself resembled a cozy living room. A long, blue, oversized sofa dominated the space, covered in a soft, velour-like material, and flanked by two tan leather recliners, equally inviting. End tables positioned between the sofa and the recliners held bowls of various mini-sized chocolate bars—100 Grand, Milky Way, Three Musketeers—along with bottles of water and boxes of tissues. A black, tan, and red hand-knotted Persian rug tied the whole room together. Matching blackout drapes ensured darkness when needed.

Dr. Lawrence reminded Dana of a slightly chubby Ellen DeGeneres. She had straight, platinum blond hair that fell to her shoulders, bright blue eyes and a friendly expression that immediately engendered trust. During their initial meeting, Dana had joked incessantly, as she often did to mask her nerves, alternating between "What's up, Doc" and references to Dr. Frasier Crane on *Cheers* and Dr. Jennifer Melfi from *The Sopranos*. The doctor's easy laugh had immediately set her at ease.

Starting therapy had been her older sister's idea. But neither Melanie nor the rest of her family knew the true extent of Dana's issues. Though she'd initially been wary of Dr. Lawrence, the therapist had made her feel safe enough to admit she needed help.

Dana relaxed into one of the recliners and closed her eyes.

"Dana, when we initially spoke, you said the nightmares and flashbacks were occurring more frequently. But you also mentioned blackouts. Any more lately?"

Dana shook her head. "Not sure. The problem is sometimes I know when I've blacked out because I wake up somewhere unexpected and can't remember how I got there. But other times, people mention seeing me out someplace or doing something, and I have no recollection of any of it. It's really scary."

"I can imagine. Are these episodes precipitated by stress?"

"I wouldn't be surprised. Between my real estate career and wrangling with my mother, I'm usually pretty stressed out anyway." She strategically left out any mention of Dare and their sex games. If those antics didn't cause stress, she didn't know what did. But it was fun stress, her way of proving herself.

"When was the last time this happened, that you are aware of, anyway?"

"Umm…a few months ago. I woke up in one of my empty listings, but I'd had no reason to go there."

Dana hoped her answer sounded credible. The actual last time was far more recent—the morning Annika was murdered. She couldn't recall anything between finishing breakfast and showing up at her mother's doorstep. The thought of it shot a chill through her entire body.

"That's frightening, clearly dangerous. Are others in your life aware of this? People who can watch you at night and make sure you don't get into trouble?"

"No, and I'd prefer it if we kept it just between us. In this business—and with my family in particular—you don't want to advertise any vulnerability. It can work against you."

"Huh. Sounds like a tough crowd."

You don't know the half of it.

"Any idea about when the problems started or what initiated them? Anything traumatic in your past?"

"My dad died when I was six. I don't really remember much before his funeral, but I consider that pretty traumatic." She stifled a sob and reached for a Milky Way Mini. Ah, the magical, restorative powers of chocolate.

"Hugely so," agreed Dr. Lawrence, "especially at such a young age. Do you want to talk about that?"

"I'd love to, but I don't know much. They told me he'd played the stock market, but other than that…no one talks about him in my family. It's almost like he never existed. After a few years of having my questions shot down, I stopped bringing it up. My Grandma Gloria—she's the one who raised me—said to put the past out of my mind and concentrate on the here and now."

"Do you remember anything about him at all?"

"I remember that I adored him. He was fun to be around, always making silly puns and jokes—oh, how my mother hated that—he never seemed to take life too seriously. He played show tunes and sang and danced with me like we were on stage. But that's about it." Dana's voice started cracking as she fought back the tears. "They say he died on my birthday. Sometimes, in my dreams, I get glimpses of our last day together. Party hats. Balloons. Music. It's fuzzy…and it never plays out all the way."

The tears won out and Dr. Lawrence waited as Dana sat up, grabbed some tissue and dabbed her eyes as she fought to regain her composure.

"Can we change topics?" she begged.

"We can, but I really think this is important stuff that ties into your issues. Think you can go a wee bit further?"

Dana sat silent, overwhelmed by the irony. She proudly projected strength in every aspect of life. She donned a strong crust in real estate negotiations, she endured countless playtime tortures at Dare's hand. Yet here, the mere mention of her family brought her to her knees. She would have none of that.

"Sure, why not?" She hoped her flippant tone would help to mask the pain.

"Thank you. I wouldn't press on if I didn't think this all tied into your blackouts. And I promise, if it gets too hard, we'll stop, okay? So back to your dad, did you go to the funeral?"

"Yes. As a matter of fact, I was thinking about that today because I went to Annika's. You know, the agent who was poisoned?"

"Yes, I heard about that, I'm sorry for your loss."

"Thank you. We weren't close or anything, but her funeral was just as poorly attended." She reached for another tissue to wipe the returning tears from her cheeks. "I remember pleading for them to open the coffin so I could see my father's face one last time. But no one would listen."

"Why not?"

"I don't know. Maybe my mother wanted to forget who was inside. She spent as little as possible on that funeral. That much I remember. She said that since no one was going to see my dad in the ground, what was the point of an expensive casket? Instead, she buried him in a plain, plywood box and used what was left of his money to help her and my sister Melanie move out of town."

"Melanie is the sister who suggested you start therapy?"

"Yes. Melanie Wright, big-time real estate broker. Maybe you've heard of her?"

"Yes, of course. Everyone in town has seen her signs. So they moved out. But what about you? You stayed?"

"Err, no. She dumped me on my grandmother."

"Why? Why not take both of you?"

"I've been wondering that my whole life," Dana said through gritted teeth. "Why she took Melanie and not me. Why she made me change my last name so there wouldn't be any connection between Cassandra Beckett and Dana Black. Why I grew up never feeling wanted or that I belonged. Maybe you can wheel her in here sometime and get her to enlighten you because she refuses to explain it to me. Especially the part where I didn't see or hear from my sister for 24 years."

Dr. Lawrence fell silent for a few moments. Dana guessed it was a pause to allow her hostility to abate.

"Anyway, I lived with my grandmother until I was eighteen."

"Tell me more about that."

"What I remember most was the sickening smell of sulfur and the hot ground. You couldn't walk outside barefoot. The snow would melt almost as soon as it hit the asphalt."

"Why? Were you living in hell?"

That's what I like about Dr. Lawrence. She's my sarcastic doppelgänger.

"Close. I grew up in Centralia, Pennsylvania."

"That sounds familiar. Isn't that the town with some huge, underground fire that couldn't be snuffed out?"

"Yup. That's my hometown." Dana beamed with mock pride.

"I thought I read that it was deserted."

"Now, pretty much yes. A few hangers-on, that's all. But back then? For a while, it was bearable, but eventually poisonous gases vented up through people's basements into their homes and offices, and turned the town into a death trap. People bailed in droves. By the time my mom left me with my grandmother, it was already a ghost town, about 70 percent deserted.

"What a terrible way to grow up. Why did you stay?"

"My grandmother was poor and stubborn. A winning combination. We couldn't afford to move and even if we could have, she didn't want to leave that old hovel; it had been in her family for generations. She'd even turned it into a boarding house to supplement her income, and didn't want to displace her tenants or lose their rent money. But around 1992, the uproar over the fire went national and the government condemned all the affected homes and offered to buy them—eminent domain. It took a few years but by the time I was eighteen, we got the payoff. My grandmother used it to send me to college and then move to Ashland where she'd spent years cleaning office buildings, and where I'd gone to high school."

"You and your grandmother were close?"

"Very. Other than what I remember of my father, she was one of the very few people in my life who ever truly loved me. Or at least ever showed it. We had very little, except for asthma, thanks to the poisoned air. Gloria sacrificed for me, was always there when I needed her. She spent everything on me, nothing on herself. As soon as I was old enough to get hired, I picked up some part-time jobs to help out—babysitting, shoveling snow in nearby towns where snow actually stuck, bagging groceries at the supermarket. Whatever I made, I contributed half."

"And your mother? Where was she all this time?"

"She was living up in Rock Canyon, making her millions. She occasionally visited me, but never allowed me to come see her or Melanie. Said it would disrupt the flow of things. I guess that meant her schedule. She'd usually fly into Scranton on a Friday night, stay at an airport hotel, spend Saturday with me, then take off again that evening. She'd joke about it, saying it was 'About time to hotfoot it outta here!'"

"How did you spend your time together?"

Dana grew quiet.

"Please bear in mind that the things hardest to discuss are likely what's closest to the root of your problem."

Dana debated a minute longer before continuing.

"It was always the same," she sighed. "Around three or four times a year, she'd pick me up, exchange pleasantries with my grandmother, then whisk me off to brunch at the Lehigh Valley Mall, far away from the fumes. She'd ignore me for the entire meal, as if she didn't even want to know anything about my life. Instead, it was always all about her—her blossoming business, her problem clients, their shaky deals. Usually punctuated by about ten calls to clients and lawyers, which she'd make on her prehistoric cell phone, much to the dismay of nearby diners. We'd shop for a few hours so she could buy some business clothes. Then, poof, she'd be off."

"Wow, not particularly quality mother-daughter time."

"Nope, but it was classic Cassandra. When she pulled it on my 15th birthday, I'd had it. She got so involved in her conversations that she simply handed me her credit card so I could go shop by myself. On my birthday. The anniversary of my Dad's death. I was so pissed, I went into Macy's, and in about a half hour, I spent $5,000 on clothes for myself and my grandmother. All non-refundable, I made sure of it."

"How did she react? Surely she could sense your resentment?"

"I arranged to have the stuff delivered so she wouldn't see. When I got back to the restaurant, she was still on the phone so I sat myself down and ordered a piece of cake. Happy fucking birthday to me." Dana's voice broke. These were old wounds, but picking at scars, even when healed, could still draw blood. "I don't know how she eventually reacted when she got the bills. We never even discussed it. Pretty much because on that day, I cut my mother out of my life. I told my grandmother I never wanted to see Cassandra Beckett again, or her favorite daughter, who never once tried to contact her baby sister."

"But that didn't last. You've said you currently work with your sister and still see your mother."

"It's a long story, one I don't want to get into now." Dana hung her head. The silence in the room became palpable.

"I can see how upset you are. Many of us mourn relationships that aren't the fairy tales we grew up watching on television. I'm curious, have you told your mother how you feel? Is this a relationship you want to rekindle?"

Dana shrugged. "I'm not sure. At this point, I'm numb to it. I have no illusions."

"Maybe that's enough for today. Do you feel well enough to go?"

"It is what it is." She sighed as she stood up to leave. "I'll be fine."

Dana didn't want to tell Dr. Lawrence how pivotal that particular incident had been. She'd learned three important life lessons that day. First, risk was exhilarating. Second, bucking the system could be profitable. And third, sticking it to her mother could be very satisfying.

Three lessons, each of which had provoked its own set of serious repercussions. And none of which had any place for discussion in future therapy sessions.

CHAPTER 5

November 8th

AS DANA WALKED OUT OF Dr. Lawrence's office, she felt a sudden surge of nausea. She made it halfway to her car before she fell to her knees in the parking lot and regurgitated tea, Milky Ways, everything she'd consumed up to that point. Once she felt a little better, she got into her car and took a swig of spring water. Though it washed away the sour taste, nothing could douse the bitter feelings she still harbored or drown the unearthed memories that gnawed anew at her psyche. She closed her eyes and tried to relax but flashbacks forced their way to the forefront of her consciousness:

"Tell me about you and Dad."

Cassandra scowled as she set down her Motorola. This was clearly not one of her favorite topics, but Dana knew her mother had a few hours of downtime before she needed to return to Rock Canyon and Melanie. "What do you want to know?"

"Absolutely everything. I really don't know much about my own parents. How did you meet?"

"I was auditioning for roles in New York City," she

said in her businesslike voice.

"Grandma could afford to send you to New York?"

"Hell no. Ran away at 16 and never looked back. Hitched rides all the way to Manhattan. I was determined to be a star on Broadway."

"That sounds...exciting."

"Yeah, it sounds a lot more romantic than it was. Like every actress, I had to get other work to make ends meet—coat check girl, waitress, whatever. Eight years of ketchup sandwiches, of landlords banging on the door demanding the overdue rent, of roommates who..." Cassandra's voice trailed off, lost in memory.

"But then you hit it big?" Dana struggled to get her mother to focus.

"No. I tried out for Hello Dolly, Funny Girl, and Fiddler. Nothing. 1965 was supposedly the golden year of musicals, and I couldn't even land a spot in the chorus. It finally hit me—the star of Centralia High was obviously not going to cut it on the Great White Way. So I went out and found a fairly decent-paying job as a bank teller. That's where I met Brent. He would come in every week, make big deposits and flirt a little. He asked me out, and I went."

"Was he rich?"

"Sometimes. He was a stock market speculator. When the market was good, he was rich, and the deposits were large." She took a moment and lowered her voice, and then continued in an angrier tone. "At other times, they were very small."

"Did you fall in love right away?"

Cassandra's eyes clouded over, and her face relaxed slightly as she thought back. "He was very handsome in that Irish kind of way. Black hair. Blue eyes. Very charming. Loved to make these stupid puns all the time.

He made everybody laugh. Everyone liked him."

"And you got married."

The dreamy expression vanished.

"Yeah, we got married. We moved to the sticks. Drysdale. His idea, not mine. And then your sister Melanie came along."

"Melanie!" Dana was always excited about any mention of her big sister. "Why don't I ever get to see Melanie?"

"She's busy working, Dana. She doesn't have time to come all the way to Pennsylvania."

"Too busy to write? I send her letters every week but I never get an answer. I miss her."

"Well, you wouldn't have missed her as a baby. She was a pain in the ass. Colicky. Always crying."

"Don't all babies cry?"

"Not like that." Cassandra shook her head in disgust. Dana winced. She recalled how her mother would treat her whenever she'd cry and wondered if she had spanked Melanie as hard for doing the same.

"How did you hear the crying if you were at work?"

"I wasn't working back then. I stayed at home, and your daddy worked. Until the market started falling apart." Cassandra shook her head, as if Dana's father had caused the crash singlehandedly. "It was December of 1968, and your sister was a toddler. The market was in the mid-1600s. Then it went into freefall. By the next year, the Dow Jones closed at 753."

"Is that why you used to say, 'That's another 753, Brent,' to Daddy whenever he made a mistake?"

Cassandra ignored the question. Her face turned crimson with fury as she continued the story of how her bright future had flickered dim. "The market continued to fall, sweeping our life savings along with it. By 1974, there was no money left, and your dad couldn't find a job. I grabbed the one thing I could find that didn't require a high school diploma and offered decent pay. I joined a new real estate agency, Foremost Realty, as an assistant."

"What did Daddy do?"

"He stayed home and took care of Melanie. She was 7 years old by then."

"Did he like it?"

"I don't know. I didn't care."

"Did you like working?"

"It didn't matter if I liked it or not. I did what had to be done. We needed food. We needed clothes. We needed to move to a house in a better neighborhood where Melanie could go to school."

"So when was I born?"

"Three years later. I was at the top of my game. Had an assistant, lots of clients, a shelf full of awards. Was the top agent in town. We lived in Drysdale's best neighborhood. And then I got pregnant with you." Cassandra practically spat out the words. "Are we finished with our trip down Memory Lane? I have some calls to make."

"Sure. I apologize."

"And wipe your eyes. Christ, you're a teenager. I would have thought you'd have outgrown those tears by now."

A horn of a passing car yanked Dana back from the past, and she used her sleeve to wipe away the same tears she'd been chastised for years before. *That settles it. No more therapy. Never again. I'll deal with my issues the way I deal with everything else in my life. Alone.*

CHAPTER 6

January 16th

LIFE REMAINED RELATIVELY QUIET IN Rock Canyon for the next few months following Annika's funeral, both in listings and in murder count. Always the optimist, Dana had naively hoped the agent community would rally together in an 'Us-Against-The-Murderer' linking of hands and hearts. Instead, the only thing the surviving agents rallied fairly aggressively for were Annika's clients.

Listings normally belong to the real estate company and not the individual agent, so it fell upon Deborah Lee Decker to distribute them. Surprise, surprise. Despite several private meetings between various top agents and Decker, Deborah Lee turned all of the orphaned listings over to Melanie. Her fellow agents resented the obvious favoritism and discussed revolt.

"Agents are revolting, fancy that," Dana texted Endie.

But it went no further. None of the local brokerages even bothered to institute new safety precautions in light of Annika's death. They simply wrote off her poisoning as a personal attack, the tainted shrimp symbolic of a *goy* unwanted in a Jewish world.

January 16th was to be a special day for the firm.

Deborah Lee had requested all agents clear their calendar and be present at Rock Canyon College's auditorium where the school's marketing department was scheduled to present Dana's sister with an honorary doctorate. To her amazement, none of her fellow brokers questioned how a high school dropout qualified for such a prestigious award or why the school was graduating anyone mid-term.

According to Lorelei, who had shared a discussion she'd overheard between Melanie and Cassandra, it was all one big publicity stunt. The college dean had agreed to the diploma in exchange for some no-fee rental housing for his administrative staff. To capitalize on the event, Melanie's team had already erected billboards around town with a picture of the new 'doctor' holding a stethoscope up to the side of a home. The ad read, "To cure the headache of selling your home, call Dr. Melanie Wright, PhD, the Wright Agent for your real estate needs."

Since Dana had known about the ceremony weeks in advance, she'd made her own plans to celebrate her sister's achievement. Dare had been extremely receptive to the suggestion of spending several uninterrupted hours together at her empty listing on Vincent Street, one that was temporarily off the market until the owners replaced the 70's brown shag carpeting with hardwood. She eagerly anticipated whatever kinky scene he had in store.

The day before, Dare had advised her, via e-mail, to prepare for her own graduation day, as long as she passed the requisite final exam. He instructed her to dress appropriately: a black gown, garters, a pair of nylons, and black patent leather shoes. She complied, not because she ever paid much attention to orders, but because she loved to visit thrift stores where she'd find these sort of items cheaply and discreetly.

And since Dare hadn't mentioned anything to the contrary, she planned to wear a little something extra when she met him, something forbidden that would teach him not to forget anything in future directives. She smiled to herself as she dressed, anticipating his mock displeasure and her prospective punishment. Topping from below, where the supposedly less-powerful player tried to control the scene, was one of her specialties, or so she'd been told.

What Dana enjoyed most about Dare was his concept of foreplay—games of torture meshed with games of chance. This unique style was probably why he was so in demand at their club. Unlike typical submission scenes, she played with Dare less for sexual fulfillment and more to challenge herself and see what she could endure (or how she could outwit her partner).

She'd select remote homes for their rendezvous, far from the gaze of nosy neighbors. Even so, Dare, a paragon of discretion, would usually park several houses away. Dana would leave the front door unlocked and he'd ring the bell twice before entering. That was her signal to assume the required pose and not to speak until spoken to.

So, at noon, Dana tried to set aside her angst that yet again, for the third time that week, she had absolutely no recollection of anything that had happened earlier in the day. Instead, she took a deep breath and waited for the doorbell to ring. As she stood in the middle of the bedroom clad in gown, garters, hose and heels, eyes closed, hands clasped behind her head and legs spread apart, she felt deliciously warm, flushed with anticipation, floating. Posing always influenced her consciousness, transporting her into the trancelike state BDSMers called "subspace." To Dana, it was sexual crack.

She heard his steps as he entered, followed by a crinkle and clump, as if he had dropped something heavy onto the floor. She pictured him circling, inspecting her appearance. His finger grazed the side of her face and then went to her mouth, which she opened as she had been trained to do. He traced the inside of her lips, and then he left his finger there, her cue to slowly suck it. "Nice," he whispered. "So far, you're passing."

Dare left his finger in her mouth as she worked it in and out, swirling her tongue around it temptingly. With his other hand, he slowly unsnapped the front of her gown. When he reached the fourth snap, he stopped, obviously having discovered her little surprise. Dana wore pasties on her nipples. From each hung a little black tassel, like the ones on graduation caps.

"What's this?" he asked, feigning incredulity.

Dana stopped sucking. "Well, you *said* it was graduation, so—"

"So you thought you could violate code?"

"I—Uhhhh—" He cut her off by adding his thumb to the other finger in her mouth, slowly wrenching her upper and lower jawbones apart until they could separate no farther.

"I think you've said quite enough."

"Uhhhh," she moaned, fearing dislocation. "Ewww ewa ed ooh ahal." Her attempt to remind him that he'd never said, "No tassels."

"Hope you're happy. You just flunked your final." Though her eyes were closed, she could picture him smiling, glad she had given him an excuse to put her through her paces. "Well, Miss Tassel Tits, for being such a smart ass, I'm going to make sure you smart all over. If you want to earn enough credits to graduate, that is.'

"Aaaah," was all she could say in response.

"I'll take that as a yes." He removed his fingers from her mouth. "Hands behind your back."

Why not? This is going to get good. Really good.

He moved his hand up, grabbed a handful of hair and pulled it back. She gasped in pleasure.

"Normally, your professor would instruct you to hit the books. But in this case, sweetie, the books are going to hit you. I'm going to ask you a series of questions. For every one you miss, five whacks."

He let go of her hair and ordered her to take off the gown. She broke pose and complied. When she heard him laugh again, no doubt in spite of himself, she surmised that he had spotted her other surprise: a white thong with the words "Graduates do it with class" written across her crotch. This was an even more extreme violation of code; thongs or panties restricted access.

"Make that ten whacks. Take it ALL off. Now."

Again, Dana obeyed, shivering with anticipation.

"Lean forward, hands on knees."

She knew this position well. Not a problem at first, but as time passed, she'd be challenged to keep her balance. Falling forward would be another punishable infraction.

Eyes still closed, she heard him step backward and the crinkle of what she assumed was a paper shopping bag.

"What was your worst subject in college?"

"Uhhh…. Science, I think."

"Science. Okay. You have ten seconds to respond." She heard him flip through the pages. "Ahhh, here we go. What is a bruise, and how long does it take for one to fade?"

Ah, bruises. Black and blue marks were trophies, fond souvenirs of their time together that sustained her during the weeks they often spent apart. Dana knew he had many partners but tried not to play with any of them too often; it smacked of commitment. On occasion, he'd mention the unfortunate, self-sacrificial "I do" he'd vowed many years earlier, and how he'd never again repeat that particular mistake.

"A bruise is a contusion, evidence of broken blood vessels from an impact with the body." She lifted her head slightly, proud of her precision.

Silence.

"I'm waiting, Dana."

"For what? The train to 'I've already answered' has left the station." She couldn't help it. Whereas most partners would never dream of answering back, she knew her sass was what kept him returning for more.

The first whack threw her completely off balance, and its impact caused her to stumble forward. She struggled to regain composure and resume her position, but the next whack came even harder.

What's he fucking hitting me with, a textbook?

"You *whack* never *whack* said *whack* how *whack* long *whack* they *whack* take *whack* to *whack* fade *whack*."

He administered the last two to the back of her upper thighs, which might have been an issue if miniskirt and bathing suit season hadn't been a good six months off. Still, that was previously untouched flesh, and it hurt worst of all.

"What have we learnt?" he asked.

She opened her eyes and looked over her shoulder to address him directly.

"Textbooks fucking hurt."

He sighed. That was clearly not the answer he'd been

waiting for.

"Obviously, oral quizzes aren't your forte."

"Oh, I don't know about that." She winked and licked her lips. They both knew her qualifications in that particular area were beyond reproach.

Dare shook his head in resignation. "Okay, turn around and get on your knees. There will be plenty of time to earn your degree later this afternoon."

Several extremely satisfying hours later, Dana picked up her phone and checked in with Endie to see if she had missed anything at the office. He covered for her whenever she had…commitments.

"Thank God you're okay," he answered before she could even utter a hello.

"You knew I had plans."

"I did. And today's event being required attendance and all, no one was particularly surprised when *you* didn't show. Penelope was quite another matter!"

Penelope Randolph-Purser was one of the up-and-comers at the office, another of Melanie's most aggressive rivals. She would have been first in line to show up at anything that would earn her brownie points with Deborah Lee. Dana stared over at her own up-and-comer, decided he was going to continue to sleep for a bit, and that she had time to chat.

"You're right. Knowing Penelope, she would have hit up the Dean for a listing *during* the ceremony. What gives?"

"Best we can figure, an 'opportunity call' came in about an hour before she was scheduled to leave for the ceremony, someone requesting a tour of homes priced at $500,000 and up."

"Penelope must have been thrilled. That's what she

needs to beat out Melanie this year."

"Right, so you can imagine why she shot out of the office after that call. The receptionist heard her say she had a rule about never meeting new clients anywhere but at the office, but this one time, she'd make an exception."

"And?"

"She took off in her little red Porsche hours ago, and no one has heard from her since!"

CHAPTER 7

January 17th

"**H**OW HAVE THINGS BEEN GOING?" Dr. Lawrence asked Dana when she arrived for her morning appointment. "When you disappeared over the last few months, I was concerned I'd scared you off."

"Thanks for seeing me on such short notice." Dana plopped herself down in a tan recliner this time. "I have to admit that our last meeting stirred up a lot of memories I hadn't dealt with for a while. But I've been having more…flashbacks lately, so I guess sitting here is the lesser of two evils."

"A left-handed compliment if I ever heard one, but I'll take it, if it means we can move forward." Dr. Lawrence checked her notes. "When we ended last time, you were describing life with your grandmother in Centralia. Do you want to pick up there?"

"Sure." Dana grabbed a Three Musketeers mini. A little self-medication never hurt and, as painful as this was going to be, she had to get to the bottom of the blackouts. They were occurring more frequently, and with the recent real estate agent deaths and disappearances, she needed to be doubly alert, both for her own safety and… possibly that of others.

"Right after the giant blowup with my mother, I realized that the library, my favorite place to escape, was also my ticket out. I put down the mystery novels and started to research everything I could about the stock market—like father, like daughter, I guess. I took the money I'd earned at odd jobs and through my grandmother, made some investments that paid off big time: Nature's Bounty, International Game Technology. Bought a used car, split the rest with her. In my senior year, the College of Gresham awarded me a partial scholarship, and we used some of the eminent domain money to cover my room and board."

"Was it difficult to leave your grandmother?"

"I definitely missed her, but I knew my stock dividends would help to cover her expenses. She wrote weekly about how happy she was in her new Ashland digs. I figured she deserved some quality alone time, without looking after me or anyone else."

"How was the transition to college? Happier times?"

"Not bad, I guess. I tried to fit in, I really did. I joined various clubs, even a sorority, but nothing ever felt right. Everyone was into such fluff—clothing, make-up, the latest fads. My adolescence had been so different, no one ever seemed to be on my wavelength. But I did make a great friend in Endicott. We met during my second semester and we've been close ever since."

"Romantically so?"

"Hardly. Certainly hot enough—he could double for Taye Diggs—but unfortunately, I'm totally not his type. Still, we did everything together—have sleepover parties, watch old movies, cry into our Häagen-Dazs over the men that broke our hearts. If it had been romantic, it would never have lasted this long."

Dr. Lawrence smiled. "And what did you study?

Investments? Finance?"

Another laugh. "Hardly. I majored in English and creative writing. After all, when I was younger, I'd spent most of my spare time with my nose in a book, trying to pretend I was anywhere but Centralia. I wanted to give others that gift of escape."

"What happened after graduation? You became a writer?"

"I wouldn't go that far. I never finished college. I got through two years and then…"

"And then?"

"I began to explore Internet chat rooms. And I met this guy."

Dana grew quiet, wondering how well this next bit would go over. It all hinged on how open-minded Dr. Lawrence turned out to be. She had no desire to defend her morals or justify her sexual choices, and this was one aspect of her life she had kept hidden for exactly those reasons.

"You're safe here, you know. Oath of confidentiality and all that."

"His name was Harrison. He was my…my introduction to kink."

Dr. Lawrence nodded, no speck of judgement in her face or demeanor.

"What part of kink interested you in particular?"

"BDSM: Bondage, Discipline, Sadism, and Masochism. Those were the type of chat rooms that piqued my curiosity."

"Which flavor? Dominant? Submissive?"

"It's weird. Neither, really. For some reason, it was the danger of not knowing what could happen that really excited me."

"Fear play? Predicament play?"

"Kind of a combination of both," Dana smiled, impressed. *Dr. Lawrence actually knows some of the lingo.* "More like fear play plus turning the tables. How can I explain it?"

She thought a moment. She crumpled the candy bar wrapper and absentmindedly rolled it between her thumb and forefinger. "Growing up, I had all these fantasies based on cartoons, like Snidley Whiplash tying Penelope Pitstop to the railroad tracks. And horror movies where people would try to fight their way out of quicksand. I found their struggles stimulating."

Dana fumbled and the balled-up wrapper fell to the floor. She took a moment to retrieve it and noticed with surprise that her hands were shaking slightly.

"Then when I was in high school, I sneak-read *The Story of O* in the library, afraid to let anyone see me check it out. And I'd fantasize I'd be bound and blindfolded, whipped and insulted, all of my begging to be released, ignored." She paused again, stared down at her fists, and squeezed them tightly to stop their juddering. "But it didn't end there. I'd find some way out of my predicament. I'd turn the tables and force my captor to acknowledge me and beg for mercy."

Dana inhaled deeply. She'd speed-rapped the last few sentences as if breakneck tempo would diminish their impact. She looked back up at the therapist, expecting to see a look of revulsion or disdain but Dr. Lawrence seemed unfazed.

"So less about power exchange and more the reclaiming of power?"

"Exactly. Is that really crazy?"

"Not in the least. Have you heard of endorphins?"

Dana heaved a sigh of relief. "Oh yes. Endorphins and I are close friends."

"Yes, I'm sure." The therapist laughed. "Well, while acts of masochism result in pain, which causes the body to release endorphins, fear play causes the adrenal glands to secrete a hormone called adrenalin. Are you familiar with that term?"

"The rush you feel when you sense danger?"

Dr. Lawrence nodded. "It's highly addictive. So I'm not surprised you would find that type of play pleasurable and worth repeating. As for your fantasies, most children don't have control of what happens in life, but in your case, that was especially true."

"One parent dead, the other casting me aside, busy elsewhere. Not exactly Disney movie material. Unless you count *Bambi*."

"For you, those out-of-control moments were probably especially traumatic. And in our fantasies, we try to right the wrongs we have experienced in our past."

Dana sat back, tilted her head and thought for a moment. "Are you saying that sexually, I search for situations that feel comfortable—like being ignored, invalidated, and humiliated—and then I attempt to reverse the outcome? That I would feel pleasure in controlling as an adult what I was unable to control as a child?"

"Exactly!"

Dana took a moment to absorb this new revelation.

"I'd always chalked it up to bad wiring, but you make it sound almost normal." She was torn between relief and regret over the many years she had second-guessed her own sanity.

"Bad wiring? Not at all. You adapted to your situation in a very understandable way. I am guessing you are a person who strives for control in all situations?"

"You could say that, yes."

"BDSM,   from   what   I   understand,   requires participants—and especially subs and bottoms—to have a tremendous amount of trust in their partners. After all, you *are* handing over power and they're putting you in positions where you could be very vulnerable. But it sounds like by demanding control as you do, you lack a certain amount of faith in others. Is that fair to say?"

"It's true. Anyone I've ever relied on… let's just say it hasn't worked out well."

"Aren't trust and control two conflicting mindsets?"

Dana reached out and grabbed two Milky Way minis, taking a moment to unwrap and then savor each one, as she carefully mulled over Dr. Lawrence's theory.

"Now that you put it that way, I realize I've always played with partners that ultimately *could* be controlled. In the early days, I'd vet them carefully, ask them lots of questions before meeting. Verify their stories via social media and the Internet. Maybe it was naïve but the safest partners seemed to be those who had the most to lose, either important jobs or sterling reputations. I figured they were people who had too much at stake to screw up.

"Once I became part of the 'scene,' it became easier, safer. I could ask others in the group about prospective partners, and even learned I could request references from the Doms and Tops themselves. Anyone who ignores a safeword or puts a sub in a dangerous situation? Their name turns to mud and everyone is quick to spread the word."

"I see. Dana, I'd love to hear more about your relationship with Harrison but unfortunately, we've run out of time. Next visit?"

"Sure. I'm actually feeling pretty good right now. Maybe all this soul-searching and confession will keep my demons at bay, and finally let me sleep at night."

CHAPTER 8

January 17th

DANA ARRIVED HOME, FEELING NOSTALGIC for the first time in years. She switched on her computer and pulled up a copy of her initial online encounter with Harrison.

It had been a typical, lonely Thursday night during her sophomore year, and she'd been surfing the chatrooms on the web. A skittish, BDSM virgin, skirting the fringes of the scene, posting an occasional sarcastic comment or pun as her alter-ego, 'This.' The nickname itself was a joke. Some chatters loved her humor, but others, more serious kinksters who took their Master and slave personas terribly seriously, hated her cavalier attitude. She didn't care. That dour mindset wasn't hers and never would be.

She'd scrolled through the feed, filled with its discussions of food, flame wars, philosophical arguments over scene etiquette and, of course, nonstop accusations of subs being doormats. (The conclusion being, a doormat was anyone who was more submissive than you.)

Welcome to Dungeons and Drag Queens. This is a lifestyle channel, not a pick-up room. Please respect your fellow kinksters.

Webtart: That is ridiculous. People at Ren Faire have every right to wear their collars and leashes. They are exercising their right of free speech!

Velvetsub: I respectfully disagree. Children go to those events. Seeing people in fetish garb is an inappropriate and premature introduction to kink for younger Ren Faire attendees.

You have a private message

Pornfree: You look frenzied. You look frazzled.

This: Peaked as any alp.

Pornfree: Hey, good call. Now you've *piqued* my interest.

This: I love Pippin! My dad used to play that recording all the time when I was little. But, Pornfree? That's some nick. What are you doing, protesting dirty pictures? Or hawking them free of charge?

Pornfree: Neither, I just like soundtracks. I'd be lion if I said I didn't like Elsa and her story.

This: *GROAN* That was bad.

Pornfree: I am bad, honey. A very, very bad man.

This: Intriguing. I bet you were the black sheep of your high school glee club.

Pornfree: Don't let an innocent love of show tunes fool you. I'm more than I appear. As are you, I'm sure. I've seen your name on channel, plenty. I've watched you make jokes, Thissie. I wonder how many jokes you'll tell when I string you up to a St. Andrew's cross and flog you.

Rereading the scroll, Dana let out the same gasp she'd let escape years back, and a familiar shiver ran up her spine. She remembered how she'd pictured herself that day, bound and helpless, at the mercy of this anonymous, albeit amusing and obviously intelligent, digital intruder.

Pornfree: You still there?

This: Yes, I'm just not used to someone speaking to me quite so presumptively. You do take liberties, Sir.

Pornfree: Is that a bad thing?

This: I'm not sure yet. What do you do, PF, when you're not punning or quoting lyrics or stringing innocent girls up to crosses?

Pornfree: Can you keep a secret?

This: Yes.

Pornfree: You sure?

This: Yes, I'm sure.

Pornfree: Then I'll tell you. Shhh. Ready?

This: YEAH, I'M READY. Come on. Sheesh!

Pornfree: Okay, okay, no need to shout. Here goes. I rescue them from their boring, vanilla existence.

This: I was hoping for something a little more concrete.

Pornfree: I'm sure you were. It's a shame that pretty little subbie girls don't always get what they want, isn't it?

This: It is. But this pretty little girl isn't necessarily a sub, and certainly doesn't chat with people she doesn't know, so nice meeting you.

Pornfree: So get to know me. What are your plans for this evening?

This: I'm going to read, take a long bath and go to sleep.

Pornfree: As riveting as that sounds, why not meet me

in the city instead?

This: New York City?

Pornfree: No, Johannesburg. Yes, of course, New York City. How far away are you?

This: About 40 minutes by car.

Pornfree: Perfect. Meet me at 9:00 pm. That even gives you an extra hour to get gussied up.

This: Gussied up? Where did you grow up, Petticoat Junction?

Pornfree: Cute. Get yourself ready and meet me outside Art is Anal. It's at 2 Park Avenue.

This: Art is Anal? What the hell are you inviting me to? An ass-painting exhibit?

Pornfree: No silly, Artisanal. It's a fondue place. You like fondue?

This: I've never had fondue.

Pornfree: Well, then I'm going to introduce you to the best. Of everything. You up for an adventure?

She recalled her apprehension. Adventure was one thing; this could be suicide. Was she really going to let this seemingly charming man get her to lower her defenses and lead her into the great unknown? But then again, wasn't interest in the 'unknown' what had brought her to sites like this in the first place?

Pornfree: Are you still there?

This: I'm thinking. I suppose it's a public enough place that if you're an axe murderer, I'll be safe.

Pornfree: Sure. As safe as any blind date. What's the worst that can happen?

This: I hope I don't find out. Tell me your name and what you do.

Pornfree: Sounds like you're apprehensive.

This: If it were a blind date, I'd know at least that much.

Pornfree: Point taken. My name is Harrison Wilder. Google me. You're going to find my name under a lot of photographs in travel articles. Read some of them. I'll expect a review of three when we meet. Or else!

This: I'll do the research, don't worry. But I also want a phone number so I can call you if something happens and I'm delayed.

Pornfree: My home number is 212-555-3235. Be sure to Google that too. You'll find it circles back to my name. And address. My cell is 212-555-3414.

This: Fine. If things check out, I'll meet you. I'm about 5'4", 115lbs, with shoulder-length, light brown hair and light green eyes. I'll wear a black leather jacket.

Pornfree: I'll wear a smile. See you at 8:00 pm.

Dana tilted back in her reclining desk chair and closed her eyes. She remembered it like it was yesterday. His story checked out, every word, so she headed down to the city, her stomach filled with butterflies. Arriving ten minutes late, thanks to Manhattan's typical evening traffic, she found him waiting patiently outside the restaurant, as unlikely a kinkster as she could have imagined. About 35 years old and 6 feet tall, with a beefy build, short, wavy, brown hair and a baby face. Big, milk chocolate brown eyes, framed by gold-rimmed glasses. Sporting a pinstriped blue Burberry jacket over khakis, a perfect cross between the preppy head of the chess club and the all-American quarterback of a Midwestern high school football team.

"PF?"

"Why so formal, Thissie? You can call me P."

She liked him instantly.

The waitress led them to a private table in the corner, where a bottle of white wine was chilling. "I hope you don't mind. I ordered a 1990 Château Rieussec Semillon Sauvignon Blanc."

"Okay. As long as it's from the northwest side of the vineyard. Otherwise, I'm outta here." She hoped her sarcasm masked the fact that she knew absolutely nothing about wine.

"I'm sure it will meet with your approval."

They sat for hours in that dark corner, sipping wine and dipping pieces of bread into different fondue pots of cheese, followed by assorted fruit that they pierced with long forks and submerged into ramekins of dark and milk chocolate. They laughed at their decadence and told each other their histories. Harrison was a well-known photographer. He often spent weeks at a time traveling the world, snapping pictures for various consumer and trade magazines. Kink was an interest of his, but he was a man of many interests. And he was tired of being alone.

"How'd you get into BDSM?" Dana asked.

"It's probably the same story most men give," he confessed. "I had a girlfriend in high school who asked me to tie her up and have my way with her. How could I say no? It was a rush, and I liked it. So I read magazines, books, found others with similar interests." He shrugged. "It was quite a bit harder before the Internet. You have it much easier than I did. Tell me what you've found out so far, what questions you still have."

Dana felt a great unburdening and an instant kinship. At last, someone to whom she could describe her fantasies, someone who might understand. And to his credit, he didn't come on to her at the restaurant, other than to playfully scratch his fondue fork against the back of her hand.

"You're so different than I expected," she said.

"What did you expect?"

"I don't know. I've never met anyone from the scene before. I guess I expected someone… more…sinister."

"Really?" He laughed. "Let me take you somewhere and show you exactly how sinister these folks are. What are you doing tomorrow night?"

They met again the next night around 7:00 pm, but this time outside the Empire Diner on 22nd Street down by 10th Avenue. Dana saw a table of eight against the far wall. As they walked closer, people waved to Harrison. It was a shocking sight, in terms of her preconceptions, anyway. There were a few plainly-dressed housewives in their 50's; a bookish-looking college kid; a male couple in their twenties—each sporting matching purple mohawks, but only one with a thin collar around his neck; a guy whose outfit shrieked advertising or Wall Street; a striking, red-headed woman who likely modeled; and last, a twenty-something woman in a peasant top, her hair adorned by multiple scarves. A few got up to shake Harrison's hand or kiss him on the cheek.

"Long time, PF. Where have you been? Avoiding us?"

"Not at all. But work's been crazy. Everyone, I've got someone here who wants to meet you. This is Thissie."

The girl with the peasant top stood up, and to Dana's surprise, hugged her tightly. "Thissie! I'm Auntie Maim. It's so nice to meet you at last. I love you on channel. You're hilarious." Others offered similar sentiments and invited them to sit down.

The group spent the next hour trading gossip:

"Did you hear that Glory Hole is playing with Chaste?"

"Mistress Gwendolyn broke up with Robert Recline?"

"Are you going to the ball at the Fetish Flea?"

And then the conversation turned to Dana:

"Why haven't we seen you at any play parties?"

"I have to admit, I've been wary. I was…scared… afraid someone would grab me by the elbow and pull me into some room to do God knows what."

"Thissie, the scene is about as regulated an environment as any you're going to find," said PainPal, the ad guy. "You think there are rules in society? In the BDSM world, it's protocol on steroids, very closely self-regulated. At a play party, Dungeon Masters oversee everything and guard everyone—think of them like overprotective fathers chaperoning their seventeen-year-old daughters on prom night. If anyone gets out of line, if anyone even touches someone without getting prior consent, the DMs show them the door."

"I never knew…"

"Most vanilla people don't," added Mistress Kate, the model. "They think S&M is one big, never-ending orgy with handcuffs and whips. There are some parties like that, sure—the good ones, ha, ha—but there are also close personal connections made, mentoring, friendly get-togethers, even classes where people educate each other on safety, different techniques, whatever."

Dana nodded, starting to comprehend. These people were nice, friendly, welcoming. What had she been so afraid of? Here was a group where she could finally fit in, belong—so different a feeling than on campus at club meetings and sorority gatherings. She leaned against Harrison who gave her a reassuring squeeze.

Around 9:00 pm, dinner broke up, and everyone embraced and demanded she join them at their next party. She promised it would go right into her calendar.

Harrison drew her close and walked her back to her

car. He faced her, ran his fingers through her hair, and then traced the side of her face with his index finger, stopping at her cheekbone. He left it there and put his thumb under her chin.

"Thissie, I'd like to see you again. Soon, while I'm still in town. I won't ask you to play until you're ready. And if you're not ready for a while, that's fine too. You're smart. And you're funny. And you're interesting and beautiful. And kink-curious. That's a package I don't encounter very often. What do you say?"

Dana found herself lost in his eyes, his deep voice, his gentle manner, the excitement of the evening.

"I'm ready now," she whispered.

Dana opened her eyes, back in the present, but with a longing to once again be that sweet, innocent twenty-year-old, embarking on life's first love. Why couldn't it have stayed that way? She banged her fist against the computer desk, and felt a throb that paled against the pain of her memories. At least she still had that wonderful group of friends, but why did Harrison have to go and ruin everything else?

CHAPTER 9

February 1st

WORD SPREAD QUICKLY WHEN THE owners of 42 Landsdowne Court returned from a month's vacation in Aruba to find the body of their real estate agent, Penelope Randolph-Purser, rotting in their basement. Correction. When Poochini found her. According to newspaper reports, as soon as the owners picked up their Bedlington Terrier from Camp Woof, his boarding kennel, the dog wouldn't stop sniffing and scratching at the basement door. When Mr. and Mrs. Goldstein went downstairs to investigate, they found Penelope tied to the hot water heater, where, ironically, she had died from dehydration. That was the coroner's determination, anyway. The local real estate agents knew better—they all agreed she had died from taking an overpriced listing, ensuring that no one would show the home in time to save her.

The Goldsteins also found a note pinned to Penelope's back, the letters in red, as if painted by a child. It read, "PAYBACK IS A BITCH!"

Again, as with Annika Henderson-Goldenblatt, the police visited the crime scene, watched the coroner cart away the body and then proceeded to ignore the entire affair. Deborah Lee Decker ranted and raved over the police's lackadaisical attitude toward what was now clearly the second in a series of real estate agent murders specifically targeting her firm.

Playing mother hen—not her usual persona—she gathered all of her agents into the conference room and as their self-appointed savior, loudly proclaimed that she alone would stand up for their welfare. Dana and her colleagues smirked in cynical amusement. Everyone knew that dead brokers meant less income for the agency, and that reality didn't jive with Decker's personal financials. She was still paying off the in-ground pool she'd installed last April, and she'd recently made a down payment on an upcoming summer cruise to Greece. Nevertheless, everyone watched as she dramatically dialed Captain Stuart Lasky of the Rock Canyon Police and put the call on speakerphone.

"This is Deborah Lee Decker, owner of Rock Canyon Realty. I demand an investigation of the murder of Penelope Randolph-Purser!"

"No can do," the voice on the other end of the call crackled for all to hear.

"What?!"

"No offense, Ma'am, but since Merriweather Stevens 'died', the Rock Canyon Police have recommitted to investigating *actual* suicides and *authentic* murders." The captain's voice dripped sarcasm.

"No, you don't understand. This one really *was* a murder," screamed Decker.

"Right. Knowing you, the woman kicked off and you used it as an opportunity to tie her to the water heater in another grandstand attempt for publicity. I'm sorry, but you're wasting your time. We're interested in law enforcement, not media hype. Good day." *Click.*

Decker stared at the phone in disbelief, shook her head, and warned her 'flock' to be more careful in the future. Then she locked herself in her office, presumably to make some recruiting calls to replace her two recently departed lead agents.

Dana signaled to Endicott, pointing to the conference room across the hall. He followed her and they shut the door behind them.

"So Endie, what do you think?"

"I think the boy cried wolf once too often."

"Thanks, Aesop, for that spot-on analysis. Are you saying we're screwed?"

"I'm saying I'm pretty sure the police aren't rushing to help. Maybe you should be more cautious, take a breather from playing sex games in those empty houses of yours."

"I don't think the killer wants to moralize; I think he wants revenge. Who do you think would want to kill a real estate broker?"

"Oh please. The question is, who wouldn't?"

"Heh, good point. I'm meeting with friends tonight in the city. Maybe they'll have some thoughts."

"The Kink Crew?"

"I wish you wouldn't call them that."

"What would you prefer I call them? The Libido Brigade? The Torture Troupe? Band of Bondage?"

"How about what they are, scene folk?"

"Or perhaps, lingering leftovers, the last vestiges of your days with Harrison. That pretty much on point?"

"Hey, they're the best thing that came out of that relationship. In any breakup, someone inherits the friends and in this case, that someone was me. They're a diverse group of smart, savvy people. I'm going to see what they have to say."

Later that evening, as Dana drove down to her group's monthly Friday munch, she split her thoughts between Endie's comments over her enduring attachment with Harrison's friends and her anxiety over the agent murders. Death won out.

Her concerns were multi-leveled. If the killer was targeting unethical agents who deserved payback, as the note suggested, she could be on the list. After all, there were a few real estate-related acts in her past that were…questionable. And those gaps in her memory that conveniently coincided with the time directly preceding the incidents—they gave her pause. She didn't truly think she was responsible but if the police ever investigated, what would they find?

The usual gang waved as she entered the diner. Perfunctory kisses all around. Introductions to a few newbies—a bald-headed and tattooed 40-something man nicknamed Bern who joked about fire play, and a butch older lady wearing mock fangs who called herself Vampira. Many of the group played in clubs around the tristate area, including her favorite, Quirts and Squirts, located in her college-town of Gresham, 40 minutes north of Rock Canyon, safe from the prying eyes of her family and clients.

"How are things with Dare?" Many had seen the two of them play at clubs and at private parties.

"Sadistic as always." She thought about showing them the faded bruises from her latest graduation scene but decided that in this case, silence was safer. *Why place myself with Dare at the time of the murders when he'd likely balk at providing me with an alibi?*

"You two are so much fun to watch—especially with

him wearing that eye mask all the time. Very mysterious, very Zorro," said Mistress Kate. "He should collar you."

Dana laughed. "Oh please. Dare isn't the collaring type and I'm definitely not interested in any commitments."

"One bad experience shouldn't taint your entire outlook," Mistress Kate countered.

"It hasn't. It's just… Everyone I've ever loved ends up dying. Or coming close. I'm going to do everybody a favor and stay single."

They all laughed except Auntie Maim, her trademark scarfs pink and red in honor of Valentine's Day, a few weeks away. Vanessa—her real name—knew Dana better than anyone there. They had often privately discussed Dare's notorious promiscuity. It was one thing to remain unattached and open, Vanessa had contended. It was quite another to have a 'boyfriend' who considered himself public property, America's Dom.

"Better glib than glum, I guess, Thiss," said Mistress Kate. "But at some point, we all need to connect."

"Speaking of glib *and* glum," Dana segued, "someone's killing off real estate brokers in Rock Canyon and the police don't give a damn."

"I read something about that," said Painpal. "I think it was a paragraph in the back of the Post. They called him the *Realtor Retaliator*. Scary stuff. I can't imagine who would kill real estate agents when there are still lawyers running around out there."

Everyone snickered.

"Any ideas who's behind it?" asked Auntie Maim.

"Well, that's where I was hoping you all could play a part. I figured an outsider's point of view might help."

The waitress appeared and voices at the table quieted until she finished serving their meals.

"There's someone who plays in your area that might

be able to help," said Vampira, between bites of Chicken a la King. "Do you know Cummings?"

"I've seen him, but we've never spoken."

'Seen' was an understatement. Dana clandestinely ogled Cummings whenever they happened to be in the same dungeon area at Quirts and Squirts. Tall, early thirties, jet-black hair, light blue eyes. Incredibly handsome. Rumored to have inherited his striking Irish looks from his mother and his Scottish surname from his dad. But there had never been an opportunity for her to introduce herself: he was always there with Bette Screams, a well-known Dominatrix, and she'd always been with Dare. Dana had caught Cummings watching some of her public scenes, but she had yet to see him play.

"I believe he's a detective," said Vampira. "It's kind of hush hush, but I've heard he used to be with the police, and then got kicked off the force. Now he does private work. Maybe you could talk to him at the club, at least ask his advice."

Others at the table murmured their agreement.

"I'll absolutely do that, thanks!" Dana was delighted to have an excuse to approach the delectable Cummings, even if it would have to wait a week until the club reopened for its next party.

After the usual dinner gossip, the group embraced and disbanded. Vanessa/Auntie Maim walked her to her car. "You should go for it with Cummings," she said. "He's hot."

Dana shook her head defiantly.

"Van, I'd love to. But he spends all his time with a Domina. My guess is he's a sub. Or, at best, a switch. I don't *do* subs or switches."

"Fuck that. Adjust."

"Not that easy. I can't kneel to a man who kneels to someone else. I like…I need fear. It gets me off. I'm not going to fear another sub. I need my partners to be unbreakable. Omnipotent. Otherwise, if I prevail, it's meaningless."

"Bullshit. You need a guy who doesn't loan his cock out like the latest library bestseller every time your back is turned."

"We never said we were exclus—"

"How many years, Thiss? Five? Six?"

"Umm, seven actually."

"Seven years. Isn't it kind of assumed that after that long, you're a couple? An exclusive couple? Hell, if you'd been living together for seven years, it would be considered a common law marriage in some places."

"But we're not living together. And there's more to it. But whatever. We're not having this argument again."

"Fine. But promise me you won't slam the door when it comes to Cummings."

They reached Dana's car and she groped in her purse for the keys.

"I tell you what. I'll leave it ajar. Happy?"

"Delirious."

Vanessa gave her a long, sisterly hug. "Love you. Stay safe, okay?"

"As safe as anyone can be while bound and gagged," Dana promised, wistfully picturing Cummings as her captor.

CHAPTER 10

Dungeon: March 12th

IT'S BEEN HOURS. I GLANCE over at the monitor, no motion. Disappointing. No limb wrenching. Not even gentle writhing. Gotta liven things up. Especially with this one.

Voice distorter in hand, I enter the room and again grab the bamboo cane. Stick with what works. I prod my guest's naked abdomen and am rewarded with a soft moan.

"Figured out what to atone for?"

"Please, I've been trying to concentrate but my throat is so dry. I can't think anymore. I need something to drink. Please. Maybe something to eat."

"What do you think this is, Lutece?"

"Okay, then could you let me pee? Please?"

"Fair enough. I have no desire to clean up your piss."

I untether my blindfolded captive from the table, but quickly handcuff wrists together and shackle ankles. Any thoughts of making a run for it, smashed to bits. We inch down the hallway to the toilet where I stand watch.

"Go on. You got a minute." I regret that I can't see the eyes; I know how gratifying a glimpse of humiliation can be.

Then we return slowly to what I lovingly refer to as my

Dungeon.

"Could I have some water? Please."

"Maybe. As long as you cooperate as I re-attach you."

I'm not sure if it was extreme thirst, weakness or resignation, but my guest complied without a struggle. Quite a letdown, but I know how to spice things up.

"Let me get you something wet," I say. Head lifts, lips smack in anticipation. I take my time, savoring the desperation before heading out to the faucet and back.

"Here's your water."

As the near-boiling liquid splashes across face and chest, my guest's shrieks of agony became deep, guttural moans that fill that aching gap in my afternoon. Nothing like searing pain and blistering skin to keep the party going.

"Think twice before making requests," I advise. "This is not the fucking Comfort Inn!"

CHAPTER 11

February 7th

DANA'S CELL PHONE RANG, JERKING her into consciousness and almost causing her to fall off a ladder she had no recollection of climbing. There was a light bulb in her hand; apparently she was productive enough during blackouts to make necessary repairs in her apartment. She carefully descended and put the bulb down on an end table before pulling her phone from the back pocket of her jeans.

The Caller ID read 'D.' She clicked 'Answer' and Dare launched into dialogue with nary a hello.

"Thiss, I can't make it to the club tomorrow night. We've—I've got a thing. And you know I can't make it on the 14th. So I thought if you could get your hands on an empty house…we could meet later today?"

Dana just shook her head, resisting her temptation to throw the cell phone against the wall.

"You do realize there's a lunatic out there killing real estate agents, right? Maybe we should reserve a hotel room?"

Even the hottest men could be so maddeningly dense. Locating discreet venues was essential, since meeting on home turf was out of the question, and playing publicly at the clubs was limited and therefore unsatisfying. Clearly a hotel room, while expensive, was really the only serial killer-free option for today.

"No, absolutely not. You thrive on fear. This should make it all the sweeter." Dare clearly had no interest in being denied. Dana quickly weighed the likely danger against the potential reward. As always, lust won out. She pulled up her calendar to see which of her listed homes would be free later that day.

That's where Dana's job as a real estate agent was invaluable—in fact, part of the reason she'd agreed to the job. She could access the keys to any empty house in town. Many were furnished, but overpriced, and therefore unsaleable. She'd simply pull up the online showing schedule and block out her 'appointment.' That would ensure no other agent would barge in and interrupt. It had worked out perfectly. So far, anyway.

"Got it," she told Dare, triumphantly. "98 Devendorf Drive. Perfect—a 1940's ranch that no one has previewed in months. What time?"

"Noon. Wear that purple and gold brocaded corset I bought you at the Fetish Flea last year."

"I'll consider it," she needled.

Click.

Despite her recently hatched plan to speak with Cummings, Dana still felt the usual tingles of anticipation that preceded any playdate with Dare. That last bit of insubordination—questioning the authority of her so-called Dom? Essential. Especially today, with him denying her the safety of a room at the local Best Western.

Compliance was about as foreign to Dana as admitting to be wrong—about anything. But Dare seemed to love to tame the untamable, and she was about as feral as they came. It was all playacting anyway; deep down, they both knew that she would ultimately give in to most of what he demanded, as long as he skirted her hard limits: playing with women, being shared with others, watersports, skat, canes, guns and knife play. He had always been very respectful of her boundaries—she had yet to use her safeword—it was her soft limits he loved to push, and that's what made their sex so scorching and addictive.

When Dana opened the door to the house on Devendorf, its musty smell overwhelmed her. That'll ward off any mass murderer, she thought. She immediately opened all of the windows to let in some air. The curtains, still drawn, waved flirtatiously in the breeze. All the unexpected housekeeping set her behind schedule, so when Dare rang the doorbell, she hadn't yet stripped down to her corset, nor assumed her required pose. He stood there, shaking his head in disapproval.

"Tut, tut, Thissie. First that utterly unnecessary crack about considering the corset and now this. Pity."

"I'm sorry. I try to obey, but honestly, sometimes it's just not that convenient."

Any hardcore Dom would have spanked her from there to New Jersey for a quip like that, but Dana knew her partner well. He'd use it as further justification for whatever torments he had planned for their encounter.

"I see. Luckily, I've brought the perfect cure for that attitude, Thiss."

It was then she noticed the shopping bag by his side. He reached down and pulled out a black executioner's hood, which he donned, masking everything but his eyes and mouth, and giving him a very ominous appearance.

"Sets the scene nicely, doesn't it? Why don't you take

out what's still in the bag, darling?"

She stepped forward, but he cleared his throat, and she froze.

"After you get into the proper attire, that is."

She rolled her eyes and *tsked*, but she did obey, unzipping her dress and unceremoniously dropping it to the floor. "You want to do it here? In the living room?"

"We'll need something sturdy. This coffee table will do fine."

He looked her up and down, approvingly. Dana had a small waist and C-cups and she was well aware of how her corset emphasized these assets.

"Okay. Now that you are properly dressed, time that you were redressed. Please take the package out of the bag and unwrap it so we can begin."

She walked past and bent over, giving him a close-up view of her heart-shaped ass. The bag was from a local toy store, the box inside innocuously gift-wrapped in puppies and kissy lips, and large enough to make her wonder exactly what he had in store for her that afternoon.

Curiosity getting the best of her, she tore away the wrap quickly, paper flying in all directions, revealing a Bingo set. Not any old set, but a deluxe version that included a big metal cage with a crank handle to mix the seventy-five wooden balls, a Master board (no pun intended), a stack of cards, and hundreds of little black plastic disks. She gazed back at him, amused.

"Did I miss something? Are we in church?"

"In a way, yes. You'd better pray you get five numbers in a row quickly, or you're going to be screaming for salvation."

Hmm. This sounds interesting.

Dare snapped his fingers twice. This was Dana's cue

to get on her knees and clasp her hands behind her back. He secured them with a pair of leather cuffs, no give.

"Stay."

He picked up the bag that once held the Bingo set and left the room to rummage around the kitchen and bathrooms. Dana heard the sounds of drawers pulled, closet doors creaking open and then slammed shut.

"Great house," he called out. "You did good...very good."

He returned and proudly produced the results of his treasure hunt, a "Poor Man's BDSM Kit" of everyday utensils that could produce the same pain or pleasure as the expensive specialty equipment sold at adult bookstores or online leather boutiques. He dramatically and gleefully unpacked the bag, revealing its contents: a plastic, two-headed slotted spatula that could also double as a pair of tongs; two giant chip clips; a bag of clothespins (ugh, how she hated clothespins); a dog collar and leash; a curtain pullback tie; some twine; a patriotic trio of candles in red, white and blue accompanied by a candelabra and some matches; packing tape; a feather duster; an egg timer; and a boar bristle hairbrush. A nice combination of torture and sensation toys.

"Okay, Thissie. To ensure it can never be said that I don't give you an equal say in these events, you get to pick. You've got 5 letters, B, I, N, G and O. And you have five implements to choose from: spatula, clothespins, candles, packing tape and the hairbrush. You get to match Column A with Column B. But I would strongly suggest—and I can't emphasize this enough—that you put the clothespins in the 'B' category."

Normally, she would have chosen the exact opposite, merely to spite him, but she decided to switch things up and cooperate, just this one time. She chose clothespins for 'B,' tape for 'I,' hairbrush for 'N,' the spatula/tongs for 'G,' and the candles for 'O'.

"Good girl."

He patted her on the head, and then buckled the dog choker around her neck. Dana despised wearing a collar and leash, though it did always shoot her right into subspace.

Dare spread the Bingo cards on the coffee table the way a casino croupier might display a pack of playing cards before starting a game of blackjack.

"Pick one. Anyone except for the top card," he encouraged. Like she had a choice.

"Ahem." She tilted her head toward her right shoulder to remind him that she didn't have the use of her hands.

"You're a smart girl. Figure it out."

Dana had never, ever backed down from one of Dare's challenges, not since Day One. It was a matter of pride to prove that she could beat him at his own game, forcing him to admit she'd won.

"Piece of cake."

"Excellent." He pulled out the kitchen timer. "You have one minute or I'll choose two cards for you. And believe me, you don't want me to choose two."

It was not the first time he'd used a timer— a sign that he meant business and not to screw around. But she was still confident that she could triumph. Once on her knees, the rule was that she was not allowed to stand up without permission, so instead, she tried to back up to the table and grab a card. Naturally, he'd positioned the pile so it was slightly out of reach. She sighed, shaking her head. *Tick, tick, tick.*

"Thirty seconds…I'd use that pretty little mouth if I were you."

Dana awkwardly turned herself back around, leaned

over, and tried to grab a card with her lips, but they were hard to separate. *Tick, tick, tick.* Undaunted, she stuck out her tongue to prod the top card from the rest of the stack. It refused to move. Desperate now, too competitive to let herself fail, she tried to push a few of the cards over with her chin. That worked. The top one tipped over, and she nudged it to the edge of the coffee table and proudly lifted it up with her teeth for all the world to see.

Bringgggggg went the timer and she spat out the card, which fell to his feet.

"Suck it! I win!"

"Thissie, Thissie, Thissie. That's a shame. A real shame." His voice dripped with pseudo-sympathy.

"What the hell do you mean? I won!"

"That's your biggest problem, darling. You don't follow directions. I thought we had dealt with this, but obviously you need a refresher course."

"I don't understand."

"What card did I tell you would be unacceptable?"

She thought for a moment, then shrank her shoulders, defeated.

"Did you say something? I didn't hear you. Which card?"

"The top card," she answered, almost imperceptibly.

"Two cards it is," he gloated. "Great for me. Not as good for you, I'm afraid. So here's the game, though being as smart as you are, you've probably already figured it out." He poured the Bingo balls into the metal cage. "You're going to spin the crank and mix the balls. As they come out, I will check to see if you have that number on…ahem…either of your cards."

Fuck him. He is enjoying this way too much.

"If it's there, I will cover that number with one of these

little black disks, and you will get a reward. If you don't have that number, oooh, painful."

"What will you do?"

"You chose it yourself. I will use the tool that you assigned to that column, and for the number of times, I will go by the number that you cranked out of the barrel. The game continues until you get one line covered in any direction…on both cards."

"You're kidding, right?"

"Not at all. And I know you can especially appreciate how everything has been in your power. The number of cards chosen, which implements are tied to which letters, which balls come out of the basket based on your spins. All your doing. Considering how much you like being in charge, this should suit you right down to the ground."

If I were still capable of love, this is the man I would choose. Forget his flaws, his infidelities. He alone understands what I need and how to push me there, turning my own damn pride and need for control against me.

"Ready?"

"I get the free spaces, right?" she asked, still halfway sure she could win this whole thing somehow. Eight numbers in a row. How hard could that be?

He covered each with a black disk. "Happy now?"

"Ecstatic, thanks."

"Good. Time to spin."

She started to inch over on her knees until Dare interrupted.

"Oh wait, I forgot something."

He picked up the curtain tie-back and blindfolded her. "Now you can spin."

"I'm doing this whole thing blindfolded?"

"That's right, my little adventuress."

"How will I know that you're telling me the truth about which numbers are on my cards?"

"Have faith."

"Not when clothespins are involved."

"I'm afraid you have no choice. Now spin. You have one minute to find the crank and turn it. Every time you miss a deadline, I'm afraid I have to take one disk off your card and throw the ball with the corresponding number back into the cage to be redrawn. And I work back from highest number down. Let's begin, shall we?"

Dana bit her lip, secretly thankful that Dare hadn't spun her around or moved the cage. He tugged on her leash to guide her. She edged forward, bit by bit on her knees, poking around with the top of her head until she hit the coffee table and heard the balls rattle. She used her lips to find and mouth the crank. But the process of maneuvering her head and upper body to get the cage to spin was strenuous. She was too dizzy to feel victorious as the first few balls popped out.

Dare theatrically cleared his throat.

"Here we go…oh wait, you know what we forgot? Chip clips. Can't have that, can we? Sit up straight, love."

Dana felt a tug on her leash as Dare pulled her a few feet from the cage and then upright. He gently freed each of her breasts from the constraints of the corset. Then she moaned at the familiar, yet agonizing pinch, as he affixed a chip clip to each nipple.

"Shhh, shhh…you can do this. You've gotten through it before."

She gritted her teeth, trying to adapt to the ache, not wanting to give him further satisfaction. He waited until she unclenched her jaw.

"Okay, *now* here we go. The first ball is I-17. Hmm,

lucky you, you've got it on Card #2. Which means not only will I cover up that square, but you get a little reward."

Dana felt the tickle of the feather duster flicking up and down her arms and across her chest. So far, so good.

Apparently, her first spin brought down more than one ball, so she had a short reprieve from returning to the crank.

"I-20. Oh no, Thissie. You don't have that one. Bad luck indeed. But at least you're going to save some money on electrolysis."

Dana heard him pull off a bit of packing tape. He rubbed it firmly over a small piece of her upper arm.

"Count to three, baby."

"Please don't do this—"

"That's not counting. That's pleading. And while it's pleasant to listen to, Thissie, it angers me when you don't do as I say. I really don't think you want to irritate me right now."

To illustrate his point, Dana felt Dare gently tug at the clip on her left breast.

"I know these clips hurt a little when I put them on but I think we both know the agony when I rip them off, don't we?"

"Yes," she answered weakly.

"Yes, what?"

"Yes, Sir."

"Good girl. So, how do we count, Thiss?"

"One. Two…"

He suddenly yanked off the tape, removing around two inches of arm hair along with it. She should have expected him to jump the gun; it was his usual M.O. Instead she shrieked in surprise and pain.

"Very nice, love the sound effects. Let's try that again

but this time, we'll count to ten."

It went on like that 19 more times, with him ripping a one- or two-inch piece of tape off some area of her arms or legs, Dana counting down from a higher and higher number, in constant fear of which one would initiate the pain. It took about ten minutes before Dare put I-20 to rest.

The next number was B-3. And it was not present on either card. Dare slowly massaged her body, trying to decide where to lovingly place each clothespin. He settled on a spot on her lower abdomen and then one on each underarm. The pain seared through her, merging with the pinch on her nipples to form one giant cacophony of ache that, after a minute or two, dulled into a constant reminder of how far she was from being in control.

"Oh, I'm out of balls, darling. You know what that means."

"You think you're out of balls now—wait until this is over and you uncuff me."

"Threats? Hmm…bad move. I-20 goes back into the cage."

"Oh come on."

"Wanna try for a third card?"

"No," she whispered, properly berated.

The sound of rattling Bingo balls filled the room.

"What are you doing?"

"Moving the barrel, sweetie. Now crank it up."

Dana heard the timer start ticking down the seconds. Panic set in because she really had no idea of where to turn. No matter which direction she chose, she came up short, exactly as she was sure he'd planned it. Except now, the chip clips that weighed down her nipples ensured that whichever way she moved, she'd experience additional discomfort.

Brrring! "Aww, good try, hon. There goes B-3, back in the cage."

He tugged on her leash until she again found the crank and repeated the awkward machinations of getting it to turn and release a few more balls.

"Mmm…jackpot! O-75. Now we're going to have some real fun. Hang out a minute, love, I need to find us a sheet."

After a few minutes, Dana heard some ruffling of fabric. Dare uncuffed her, removed her corset, and guided her now-naked body until she was lying face up with her arms overhead. She felt him bind her wrists together with twine and then attach them to what she assumed to be one of the legs of the coffee table.

"What's happening?" she whimpered, tugging futilely, unable to remember which implement she had assigned to 'O.'

"Shhh…time for a little art project. We're going to use your body as a canvas to create a beautiful wax painting."

"No, I've never done wax. I don't wa—"

"It's NOT on your hard limit list, is it?"

"No but—"

"Then you're going to give this a chance. Will you do that, please?"

She hesitated. She feared trying new things, especially when blindfolded, so utterly powerless. Then again, the fear is exactly what got her off.

"Okay. But I'm safewording the second I don't feel comfortable."

"Fair enough. Relax. With 75 drips, this is going to take a while."

Dana tried to calm herself, but every nerve ending was on high alert. When the first drop splattered against her ribcage, she jerked up the inch or two her bound wrists would permit. The wax cut like a knife for a split second, then the pain dissipated. When the next splash hit her abdomen, one inch north of the clothespin he'd left there, she convulsed again.

"Hold on, this is obviously not working," he said.

Dana heard some rummaging and then felt pressure on the chip clips that were still tormenting her nipples. Dare squeezed her cheeks, forcing her mouth open and placed a piece of twine inside. "Bite down," he ordered, and as she obliged, she felt the clips pull harder, causing her nipples to stretch.

"You need a task to concentrate on, something to distract you. I've strung some twine through the clip holes to make a little makeshift nipple clamp necklace for you. If you struggle, you're going to pull the clips off, and that's going to hurt like a motherfucker. If you talk or protest, you're going to drop the twine which will cause your breasts to drop, and that's going to be really painful too. So my advice is to lie very still and focus."

The dripping recommenced. With Dana unable to see, speak or move, the heat felt even more intense than before. And the longer and longer it continued, as the wax covered her breasts, her waist, her abdomen and her legs, the more excruciating the agony. Hotter and hotter, worse and worse until suddenly, the pain ceased. The dripping continued but there was nothing but a warm feeling spreading across her entire body that she didn't understand. She moaned with pleasure through gritted teeth.

"Welcome to Endorphin Land," Dare whispered.

Dana lay there, prone, enjoying an almost out-of-body experience. After he finished his paraffin painting, Dare left her to revel in her bliss for several minutes before commencing aftercare. First, he held each breast steady as he slowly released the chip clips, allowing her nipples to escape with minimal anguish. Then the clothespins. Last of all, she felt him cut the twine that had bound her wrists to the table leg. She spit the string from her mouth and whispered, "Thank you," truly grateful for this new experience and the accompanying euphoria.

"Lay still. This knife is very sharp," he cautioned as he began to painstakingly scrape the wax from her body.

It was in the middle of this tender aftercare that through the windows she'd left open earlier, she heard footsteps, the turn of a knob, a door squeak open, and some voices outside.

"I think you're really going to appreciate the mid-century appeal of this home," said a female voice Dana didn't recognize. Then, a very loud "Oh my God!"

Still blindfolded, she regretted that she couldn't watch this amusing reversal of plan. "It's quite the mess," she heard the woman say, "Let's go on to the next one, and I'll bring you back some other time when it's neater." Rapid footsteps led away from the home.

The pair both laughed, grateful that his executioner's mask and her blindfold had protected their identities. He finished removing the wax and stepped away but she lingered a moment longer, trying to savor every last second of the lingering endorphin rush. She felt a deeper bond with Dare than she had ever felt before and hoped he felt the same. Maybe they were meant to be together long term.

"Next time, I mark the house as temporarily off-market." She removed her mask, but her cheerfulness vanished as soon as she glanced over at Dare, who was smiling as he texted a communique, no doubt scheduling his next assignation.

If there is a next time. She made a mental note to definitely meet up with Cummings at Friday night's play party at Quirts and Squirts, the one that Dare had conveniently already indicated he would be unable to attend.

CHAPTER 12

February 8th

DANA TOOK GREAT PAINS TO 'tart' herself up for Friday night's play party; it would be her first time at the club unaccompanied and also the only occasion she'd ever visited with an agenda. She selected her favorite lime green corset from her fetish closet, the one with the bright yellow boa trim, darker green fishnets and yellow heels. She knew everyone would be decked out either in black or red for Valentine's Day (how *de rigueur*!) and the last thing she wanted was to blend in. As a final touch, she stuck a plastic green carnation comb in her hair and was ready to rock.

After 10:00 pm, the streets of the industrial section of Gresham were deserted. Dana's heels shattered the silence as they clicked against the pavement and echoed in the crisp winter air. The owners of Quirts and Squirts had wisely selected the most discreet of locations. The uninformed public passed by its nondescript façade daily without realizing what lay inside. Three knocks, a pause and two more knocks. Simeon, the red-headed assistant Dungeon Master, peered through the peephole, unbolted the door, and welcomed Dana inside.

"Whoa. Extra-hot outfit, Thiss. You on your own?"

"Just for tonight, Sim. I need to speak to Bette Screams, she around?"

"She came in earlier with Cummings. They're at their regular spot toward the back."

"Thanks. I owe you a drink."

"No need. As long as you promise to keep showing up dressed like that!"

Dana worked her way down two flights to the bowels of the building. Since the action usually didn't heat up until after midnight, it was still relatively uncrowded. She stopped by the snack bar to pick up a soda before heading over to speak with Cummings, but to her surprise, she discovered him sitting there, clad in black and checking his phone, waiting to be served. Her pulse quickened as she realized he was even better looking than she remembered, especially close up. Forget investigations. This guy should model for Samsung, she mused. Summoning her courage, she sidled up beside him, took the next stool over and called to the attendant, "Whatever he's having, put it on my tab. And bring me one as well!"

"Taking quite a chance, aren't you, Thissie? How do you know I didn't order Dom Perignon?" Cummings said without glancing up from his phone.

"What can I say? I live life on the edge."

"Clearly." His voice was the epitome of disinterest, though she found his slight Scottish brogue utterly endearing.

"Anyway, I'm not too concerned, considering it's a non-alcoholic bar and all," Dana pressed on, unperturbed. "Plus I passed Dom Perignon on the way over here, strapping his sub onto the spanking bench."

"Aye."

Could he be more apathetic?

"But I am impressed, how did you know my name?"

"Probably because I'm not brain-dead." He turned his head and took her in, top to bottom. "Everyone knows who you are. But I apologize. I hadn't realized it was Dress-Your-Sub-Up-Like-a-Lollipop Day. Where's your beau?"

"I'm flying solo tonight."

"Really!" Cummings finally registered some interest. "Trouble in paradise?"

"Yes, but not how you mean," she said, dismissing his sarcasm. "I actually came here tonight to talk to you. You know a woman named Vampira?"

"She hangs with a bunch of older women who play here sometimes. Why?"

"She came to our munch last week and suggested that you might be able to help me. You see, I'm a real estate agent. And I work at Rock Canyon Realty."

Cummings raised his eyebrow. "Heard something about that. Two down. What? Coupla thousand more to go?"

She felt the blood rush to her cheeks but she refused to lose her cool. "Vampira said you do some private investigation work. Is that true?"

"Sometimes."

Dana hadn't counted on Cummings being quite this unforthcoming. Doms usually went out of their way to charm her at the club, in case she ever decided to trade up. She decided that her suspicions had been correct; he was definitely a sub and therefore immune to her allure. Still, she was determined to get what she came for, no matter how cool his demeanor.

"Listen, the police are refusing to help and we are eager to get to the bottom of this before more lives are lost. Would you be willing to help us out or not? I'm sure the agency would gladly pay."

"You worried you're going to get knocked off, Thissie? Or are you merely coming forward as a concerned citizen?"

"Let's say I'm disturbed on multiple levels."

A supercilious grin spread across Cummings' face, causing Dana to clench her fists.

"What the hell is wrong with you? You've got some kind of problem with me?"

"It's just this is the first time I've ever seen you get flustered or desperate. I've watched you playacting with Dare, feigning all those *oohs* and *aahs*, those moans and groans as he works you over. Maybe your pun-infused anguish wows the crowds, but personally, I never bought in, never believed anything or anyone really gets to you or that you ever lose control. Those screams are as fake a mask as that ridiculous one your boyfriend wears over his eyes. But watching you here, now, exasperated…you actually seem real."

Who needs this shit? Dana pushed back from the bar and called to the attendant. "Cancel my order, please. My friend here will pay his own tab."

Cummings grabbed her arm and flashed a considerably warmer smile.

"*Keep the heid*, as my grandmother used to say. Which means calm down. I meant that as a compliment. You're cute when you're real."

Dana's eyes narrowed to crinkled slits, her head, a tinderbox about to explode. "I didn't come here looking for admirers. I came seeking your expertise. And as for psychoanalysis, I've got my own therapist, thank you very much." She shook his hand off her arm.

"$5,000."

"Forget it, we'll handle this on our own." She turned and started walking to the door.

"Okay, $6,000," he called after her.

She turned and glared.

"Better say yes before I raise it to $7,000."

"Good thing you're a detective because as a negotiator, you suck. You're supposed to go down, not up."

"I prefer to decide when I go down, thank you very much."

That broke the mood. A sucker for a clever turn of phrase, Dana couldn't hold back an appreciative laugh. "Okay, you win. You decide when you go down. But we're only going to pay $5,000. And you have to promise not to be such a jerk."

"Fair enough. $5,000 and a second chance, so I can prove to you that I'm *not* a jerk. Deal?"

Dana fought to ignore Cummings' striking resemblance to Orlando Bloom.

"Fine. But don't hurt yourself trying, okay?"

"I guess I deserved that. I'm going to need a few days to read up on the case, and I know some people at the precinct and the coroner's office who can fill me in on what they've got so far. Can I stop by your office, say Tuesday?"

"Sure, that should be fine. I'll clear it with the owner. Her name is Deborah Lee Decker."

Dana reached into her tiny green purse and handed him a business card. She thought about lingering a bit longer and flirting, but decided not to press her luck. This guy was as mercurial as Hudson Valley weather in March. "I've got to get going but here's the address. You can reach her at that main number."

He gazed down at the card and then back up again. "So

in real life, you're Dana Black, Realtor?" He extended his hand. "Pure dead brilliant. Aidan Cummings at your service."

CHAPTER 13

February 9th

Dana awoke with a start the next morning, more tempted to smash her cellphone against the bedroom wall than to answer it. The Caller ID flashed Vanessa-Maim which is the sole reason Dana decided to spare its life.

"This better be good. It's 7:00 am on a Saturday."

"So?"

"Van, I'm working on—" She squinted at her clock radio, "—about four hours' sleep. Be less cryptic, please."

"Four hours? Sounds like things went well with Cummings? Mr. Adorable?"

"No, four hours because my car wouldn't start and I had to call a tow service for a jump. Sorry to disappoint."

"Are you saying he wasn't cute?"

"Oh no, unbelievably so. But kind of a pain in the ass."

"Really?"

"He started psychoanalyzing me, telling me I was all fake when I played. I was like, what the fuck? He'd known me for exactly five minutes when he started going all Sigmund on me." Dana felt her temperature rising.

"Huh, it sounds like he didn't fall all over you at first sight. Like Harrison. Or Dare."

"Clearly a sub."

"Thiss, he doesn't sound very submissive to me. Sounds like you finally found a guy with a brain. And a backbone."

"Whatever. He's going to help investigate a series of murders. And that's all. I really don't want to have anything to do with him, other than to provide him with whatever he needs to get this thing solved."

"Uh huh. Sure."

"I mean it. This is not the beginning of a romance. I've got a Dom."

"Correction. You have a timeshare of a Dom. You get him once every six weeks or so, for an hour or two."

"Out of choice. I told you, I get what I need from Dare. I don't need any long-term attachments. It hurts too much when they're gone." Dana spoke with such conviction, she almost believed it herself.

"Everyone needs love, Thiss. Even you."

"Now you're sounding like Endie." *What are you two, a tag team in the nagging relays?* "For the last time, there will be no romance between myself and Cummings."

"You're saying he holds no appeal for you?"

"Zilch. Rien. Nada. Listen up. HE MEANS NOTHING TO ME."

"Then why are you yelling?"

"This call is over. I'll let you know when I have something meaningful to report."

"Sure. Get to the movies early, Thiss."

"What's that supposed to mean?"

"It means you don't want to miss the Cummings attraction. Bye." *Click.*

Between Vanessa's teasing, Cumming's accusation of her disingenuity, and her anger at Dare, Dana's brain had become Radio City Music Hall, and the Rockettes were practicing their big finale. No matter how hard she tried, she couldn't shake the pounding in her skull or will herself back to sleep. Was it true what Cummings had said? Was she an emotional imposter? Someone who never took things seriously or felt deeply, just played at power exchange without ever really handing over control? Possibly. But in a world of chaos and unpredictability, wasn't it safer to rely on logic?

Did she have to be Old Faithful, all waterworks on cue, to fit into his definition of a submissive? Hell, it's not like she even called herself a sub or purported to be one. She might not squeeze into his stupid narrow classification, but that didn't mean she didn't belong at Quirts and Squirts or in the scene. After years of emptiness, she'd found a kind of family, a place where she felt she belonged. Who the hell was he to destroy that for her?

In fact, who the hell was he, altogether? Vampira said something about him leaving the police. What was that all about?

Dana pushed back the covers, grabbed her robe, and headed over to her computer table. Research was her friend. It was how she was able to learn about stocks and afford to get the hell out of Centralia. It was how, with Endie's help, she'd finagled her way into buying her first house. And now that she had Cummings' whole name, it was how she intended to find out whom she was dealing with.

She typed "Aidan Cummings" into the Google search box and weeded her way through a page or two of unrelated findings—Facebook and Twitter accounts of kids with the same name, a PowerPoint demonstration on how to counterfeit money (hmm, could be interesting), some Irish hurler wiki. Dana went back and changed the criteria to *Aidan Cummings police.* Pay dirt. The first pertinent article was almost a decade old. It ran in the Middleville Times on July 17th, 2003 and was titled, "Fourth Generation Police Officer Joins Local Force."

Huh. He's based a few miles north of Gresham, not down in Manhattan. That's good. Convenient for his investigation and all.

She read on:

Aidan Cummings, the fourth generation of the Cummings family to serve and protect their local communities, is, at 21, also one of the youngest officers to join the Middleville police force.

Cummings, who was born in Scotland and immigrated to the United States with his family in 1997, was part of a group of ten officers sworn in this week. A graduate of the John Jay College of Criminal Justice, he is the first of his family to serve in North America. His father Baird, his grandfather Donnan, and his great grandfather Wallace, all served the Strathclyde Police Force outside of Glasgow with honor and distinction.

Impressive. She closed that article and scrolled down to the next one, dated June 15, 2012 which, though short, proved to be even more enlightening:

Middleville Police Officer Resigns After Suspension, Possible Ties to Prostitute

Officer Aidan Cummings, once considered the rising

star of the Middleville Police force, resigned today after being suspended from duty due to suspected ties to a local woman rumored to be a prostitute.

Police discovered Cummings with an alleged Dominatrix, who call herself Bette Screams, during a raid of Pain Street, a local S&M club with suspected mob connections. Both were questioned and released. No charges were filed.

"We had no choice but to suspend Officer Cummings without pay until the matter was fully investigated. It was Cummings' choice to resign," said Captain Alexander McLane.

Neither Officer Cummings nor Bette Screams were immediately available for comment.

Dana stared at the computer screen long after finishing the piece. She could imagine how his family had reacted to the suspension, considering their connection to the police force ran four generations deep. As her defenses dissolved, she felt less indignation toward Cummings, more a sense of solidarity. After all, who knew more about separation from family—emotionally or physically? She understood what that did to a person, the self-recrimination, the doubts, the emptiness and sense of loss. And at that moment, all she longed for was a chance to reach out and hug him and to let him know she'd been there too.

CHAPTER 14

February 12th

THANKS TO MR. BLABBERMOUTH, AKA Endie, no one at Rock Canyon Realty was particularly surprised when Deborah Lee Decker announced that she had taken it upon herself to hire a private eye to protect them all from the *Realtor Retaliator*. She conveniently omitted Dana's involvement in the enterprise, but Dana was secretly too excited about spending a wee bit more time with the handsome investigator to care about receiving the credit she deserved.

Despite the police's lack of cooperation—or even curiosity—the media's incessant coverage of the two murders had instigated a public outcry. After all, if unethical real estate brokers could be a target of a serial killer, then who was next? Used car salespersons? Lawyers? Politicians? A large segment of Rock Canyon's professional network suddenly felt vulnerable. Decker assured her agents that she would personally deliver them from evil, with the help of one Detective Aidan Cummings.

Price was no object, she assured them. And why would it be? She explained that $100 would be deducted from each of the agents' commission checks until the $5,000 was repaid.

Decker's office became Interrogation Central as Detective Cummings interviewed each of Penelope's colleagues, except for Melanie, who was apparently above suspicion since she'd been at Rock Canyon College, rehearsing for graduation, at the time Penelope was kidnapped. The others were called in, one by one, all competitive backstabbers—and therefore likely suspects—united by one common motive: greed. But only one agent lacked an alibi for the time of the murder, which was probably why Dana was called in last.

Initially, she had been both eager and trepidatious about her second encounter with Cummings, especially after her own investigation into his past. But the moment their eyes met, she sensed an unspoken détente. She bit her lip in a struggle to remain stone-faced until the suspect preceding her exited the room. Once they were safely alone, Aidan smiled and whispered, "Lock the door."

"I can't believe it, Thissie," he said in a hushed tone. "I thought the pervs were bad, but these folks? They're out for real blood. One actually asked how long I estimated until the next killing. She was working out her business plan and wanted to calculate her odds of getting future listings based on reduced competition."

"Yup, Cummings, you got me." She lowered her voice by several decibels to match his. "*We're* the killers. And I'm their ringleader. Wanna throw on the cuffs now or forcibly cross-examine me first?"

"Can't I do both?"

They both laughed quietly with an ease borne of shared secrets.

"Okay, we should get down to the matter at hand."

Aidan cleared his throat, obviously trying to regain some professional composure. "So, Ms. Black. Dana. Wow…where did 'Thissie' come from?"

"Well, when I started exploring the scene online—long before I had the guts to hit the clubs—I needed some kind of nick. The good ones, like 'Dead Horse' and 'Suffer,' were already taken. I wanted something punny, something that would make people laugh, so I chose 'This.' That way I could enter chatrooms asking, 'Does anyone want a piece of This?' and take credit when people typed, 'This is wonderful!' or 'This is the greatest thing since sliced bread.' Something to add a little spice to the scene's more mundane moments. But it seems to piss off a lot of the more serious players."

"Not many have a sense of humor online. Too busy posturing."

"I never thought the nickname 'Cummings' was your actual last name. I figured it was part of your evening plans."

"Not lately, unfortunately. Tell me, how is it that we've never spoken before?"

She tried, in vain, to ignore his inescapable charisma.

"Timing was never right, I guess." Which was true. Whenever their paths had crossed, they had each been attached to other partners.

Aidan cleared his throat and raised his voice to a normal level. "Okay, so what's the deal, Thissie? You were the one agent who wasn't at the ceremony. Please tell me you had a good reason."

Dana's heart started to race. It was at that moment, she realized she had no real alibi for either murder. Even if she could count on her mother to reliably account for her whereabouts around noon on the day Annika was poisoned, whatever had occurred earlier that day was a mystery. And the same was true for the day Penelope was snatched. That "opportunity" call reportedly came in before she arrived for her graduation rendezvous with Dare, though she was sure he could stretch the truth a bit for her, if she asked extra nicely.

She scrambled for a plausible retort.

"It slipped my mind, Cummings. As you intimated the other night, I have a particular dislike for authority, so when Decker told me I *had* to be at this graduation thing, I must have blocked it out. I was at my listing on Devendorf, sprucing it up for an upcoming open house. Ask the neighbors. I'm sure they saw my car in the driveway."

"And what about during the open house where Annika Henderson-Goldenblatt died?"

"I was probably touring homes like everyone else. I really can't remember."

"Did anyone see you, Thissie?"

"I can't think of anyone in particular, no. You know what a slippery character I can be." She winked, referencing an oil wrestling match at the club a few years back.

"Aye, I do know. And while I'm sure you had no part of this, if the police start nosing around, they're going to name you as a person of interest."

"Got it. Thanks for the heads up, Cummings."

"Would you please call me Aidan?"

"I'll consider it." She batted her eyelids coyly. When your back's up against the wall, the best recourse was to flirt and tease.

"Look, Thiss, if you happen to recall anyone—and I mean anyone—who can give you an alibi, get it for me, please. As soon as possible. This is serious."

"Deadly serious."

Aidan gave her a semi-scolding scowl. "Will I see you at the club one of these days?" he asked, almost whispering. "There's some sort of big party going on Friday night."

Dana's heart jumped but she tried to play it cool.

"I don't know. Maybe. You?"

"I was planning on it. I'll keep an eye out for you, okay?"

"Sounds like a plan."

"Oh, and Thiss?"

"Yes?"

"I know I d-don't have to say this," he stammered slightly, face blushing, "I'd prefer it if no one outside the club knows about my alter ego. Deal?"

Dana mimed locking her mouth shut and throwing away the key. He nodded. End of interview.

She stumbled out of the office a little dazed and smacked right into Deborah Lee, barreling back in to reclaim her office. She apologized and kept walking. Right to the storage closet.

Though she had tried to act nonchalant with Aidan, she was actually quite concerned over this "person of interest" moniker. Especially when one of her possible, though imperfect alibis, was so vindictive and unpredictable, she might accuse her own daughter of murder out of spite, and when the other, her married lover, had some very specific reasons for not coming forward. She was damned if her history of blackouts was going to land her in prison. She needed some inside info and quick.

Luckily, while rummaging for Wite-Out awhile back, she'd discovered that the storage closet strategically backed up against Deborah Lee's office. She slipped in without notice, and pressed her ear to the far wall. Even muffled, some insight was better than none.

"Who wanted to see two of your agents dead?" she heard Aidan ask Deborah Lee.

In her mind's eye, Dana could picture the petite blond manager half-listening to Aidan while rifling through stacks of files on her desk. "I've compiled a list of possible suspects for you to investigate."

"That's very helpful, thank you."

"What you've got to consider, Detective, is that the two deaths could be one giant coincidence. People don't realize what dangerous lives we lead, how exposed we are."

"Meaning…?"

"Think about it. Most agents are women, usually very attractive women. We post glamour shots on our signs and business cards and then list every possible way to reach us. Then, how's this for brilliant, we *advertise* that we're going to be alone in an empty house for hours on a Sunday afternoon. We have strangers join us in our cars, or we ride in theirs. We eat food at open houses supplied by God knows who. If we're not asking for trouble, then I don't know who is."

Aidan waited a beat or two to take it all in. "What about this Melanie Wright?"

He's asking about my sister. Interesting.

"What about her? She's our most successful agent—sells about 100 houses a year."

"I've asked around. I'm told she's very competitive and not well-liked."

"I suppose that's true. Very few highly successful people are well-liked in this or any other profession. What does that have to do with anything?" asked Deborah Lee.

"A few of the agents suggested that she might be

behind the murders, that she hired professional killers to take out her rivals. What do you think about that?"

"I think it's absurd. Why would she bother? She's slaughtering them in sales as it is, no pun intended."

"I thought so too. So I went to the Multiple Listing Service and asked for their statistics. It's true that at one time, Wright was handling around 60% of the business in town, but lately that number had fallen to 48%. Meanwhile, both Henderson-Goldenblatt and Randolph-Purser had their production shoot up. They were big competition for her and I hear she has a history of taking extreme measures to eliminate competition. Merriweather Stevens ring a bell?"

Wow, apparently everyone knew.

"I think you should pursue other avenues, Detective. If anyone was going to kill those two, it wouldn't have been Melanie. Hell, she's furious about the timing of this latest murder. It stole all the thunder from her newest advertising campaign. She's promoting herself as a doctor, and people are dying around her…not good for business."

No surprise that Deborah Lee would staunchly defend her biggest agent.

Dana could hear Aidan strumming his fingers on Decker's desk.

"Along with providing me with that list of disgruntled persons, could you tell me a little about Gayl Campbell? The woman who disappeared a few years back?"

Based on the silence that followed, Dana bet that at that moment, Deborah Lee's face went very, very pale.

"She disappeared. That's all I know. That's all any of us know." The well-rehearsed answer was identical to the response every agent at Rock Canyon Realty delivered concerning Gayl Campbell. No one had ever gone off script and Deborah Lee clearly had no intention of being the first.

"How did your agency happen to get involved with her?"

"She listed with us about 18 months ago, once the Merriweather Stevens nonsense started dying down. She was a problem client from day one."

"How so? All I've heard is that she was an eccentric millionaire who the locals nicknamed 'Noudeau Rich' because she sometimes forgot to dress before leaving home."

"She had a restored 1885 Romanesque Revival that she listed with several of our agents over the course of a year. No one could tolerate her daily harassment for longer than a few months. She'd demand constant marketing changes—this comma was unnecessary, that photo wasn't sharp enough. She knew that price adjustments attracted attention online, so she'd raise hers by a dollar one day and then lower it the next. She demanded newspaper advertising every week—like anyone searches in the paper anymore—and then four-hour open houses every Saturday *and* Sunday."

"She wanted special treatment…"

"And as a boutique agency, we are happy to provide that. When houses are saleable. This one wasn't. Gayl chain-smoked, so every tower and turret reeked less of charm than of stale tobacco. Even though the house was priced below market value, buyers couldn't get out of there fast enough."

"You couldn't explain this to Gayl?"

"We tried, but she thought she knew best. The one saving grace was the house's location on a busy street, offering lots of visibility for our signs. And because Campbell was such a curiosity herself, open houses were packed; everyone wanted a peek. Agents might not have sold Gayl's house to the buyers who visited, but they sold others."

"And then she disappeared," said Aidan.

"Yes. That's all we know."

"Wasn't that like a wish come true? Problem client goes *poof*?"

"It was quieter, that's for sure."

"Hmm..." Dana heard the click of a briefcase and the rustle of paper.

"The files state that she was gone, but her car was still in the garage. Her children, living in California and Louisiana, swore she'd never mentioned anything about leaving town. The administrators at the animal shelter where she volunteered were dumbfounded, since she'd said she'd be in the next morning."

"It was all pretty mystifying."

"What happened to the house?"

"After a year or so, Gayl was declared dead, and her children cleared it out, had it fumigated, and lowered the price. It sold right away."

"Who ended up making the commission?"

"The last agent who had it listed, a part-timer named Raven Devereux."

"Part-time. I assume that was a big commission for her?"

"Probably her largest ever."

"When the officers investigating the disappearance asked around, they learned that Deveraux's 'real' job was at Ashes to Ashes, the town crematorium."

"If you say so. I try to stay out of what my agents do during their off time."

"Naturally, it's a little suspicious, what with the main person benefitting from the disappearance being a real estate agent who happened to have a convenient way to dispose of the body."

"Are you making an accusation, Detective?"

"Not me, but Campbell's family was very vocal on this point, according to the report. Alleged that it was all part of an agency-wide conspiracy, started a petition to close you down. Consensus was that a real estate firm murdering its clients constituted really bad customer service." Aidan's cynicism oozed through the wall. *Hot.*

"There were rumors but nothing was ever proven. Of course, the silver lining for us was that no one ever again asked Raven to do an open house or change one word of copy."

"I was thinking that Campbell's family could be behind some of the killings," said Cummings. "They'd certainly have cause to hate the lot of you."

Good. Anything to take suspicion off my back.

"I suppose anything's possible. But then again, the people who really benefitted from Gayl's death were her kids, don't you think? They inherited 94% of the house proceeds. Not us with our measly 6%. And if your theory holds water, wouldn't they have murdered Raven first?"

"Good point."

Damn.

"If I were you, I'd go through some of the names on the list I gave you. That'll keep you plenty busy. We're real estate agents. Everyone hates us."

Dana heard a knock at Deborah Lee's door and a creak as it opened.

"Yes, Ms. Cooper, can we help you?"

In the three months since Annika's funeral, ambitious office admin Kerrianne had wormed her way into Melanie's good graces and into a position on the Wright

Team as personal assistant.

"I have something I think you should see, Detective," she said. "It came in today's mail. I opened it. Hope that's okay."

Dana heard rustling.

"Ordinary copier paper, standard inkjet printer used for both the letter and the envelope," said Aidan. "I doubt we are going to find any fingerprints, other than yours, Ms. Cooper. Still, we can try."

Dana could hear Deborah Lee's impatience through the wall. "All well and good, but what does it say, Detective Cummings? What does it say?"

Aidan cleared his throat. "*Melanie: Not next, but soon. Your turn is coming.*

CHAPTER 15

February 13th

DANA'S EYES SHOT OPEN, INSTANTLY realizing that she was lying on a strange bed in unfamiliar surroundings. She sat up slowly and tried not to panic, taking deep breaths to slow her racing pulse and pounding heart. The door to the bedroom was ajar, dim light streaming in from the hallway. She made out the shape of her purse on the nightstand and reached over, fumbling for her phone and its flashlight app. *Success!* She flickered the light around the room, silently searching for any clues to her location. Vases. A jewelry box. Finally, a photo on the dresser: Melanie, receiving an award from the mayor. Dana took a deep breath. *Thank God. I know where I am and it's somewhere safe.*

She tried to remember how she got from the storage closet to one of her sister's spare bedrooms. The last thing she remembered was Aidan reading the death threat. Despite the uncomfortable feelings her sessions with Dr. Lawrence had dredged up, it was clear she needed to continue therapy, especially now with the increased frequency of the blackouts. Luckily, she had an appointment later that day.

She sat up, a little shaky, and heard Melanie ranting in the breakfast room.

"This last week has been a disaster and now this? Can you believe it? Me? This lunatic thinks he can threaten me? And this pseudo-detective character—what's his name, Cummings? He's telling me to lay low? Like I'm going to shut my business down because some joker is playing games? No, I don't think so. He's dealing with the wrong person."

"Who?" Dana heard Melanie's husband ask.

"What?" she shot back.

"Who is dealing with the wrong person? Cummings or the lunatic?"

"Both of them. That goddamned assistant of mine—what's her name? Kerry something? She told everyone about that fucking note. Now the whole damn office knows. Half of them think I have a target on my back. And I know what's next. 'Oh, I can't list with you. So-and-so told me you're going to be dead soon. I want to list with someone who will be here for the long haul.' And the other half of the office thinks that I'm behind the murders, that I sent the note to myself to throw off suspicion. Well, I'm not backing down or backing off for anyone. It's going to be my best year ever. One hundred and nine listings. The damn doctor campaign's going strong; I spent about $4,000 on those billboards."

"Of course you did."

"Reid, are you mocking me?"

"Me? Never. I'm as concerned as you are." Dana imagined how much her brother-in-law was enjoying watching his normally unflappable wife come apart. Something to ease the boredom of his usual day, where he filled the trashcan with crumpled pieces of drivel masquerading as manuscript. "This is an abomination, a blight on the entire real estate community. And not just in Rock Canyon. Everywhere. I mean, if someone can threaten a Realtor, what real hope is there for the American way of life?"

"Excuse me. I don't need your snide remarks right now. It took me about a half-hour on the phone yesterday to convince that detective not to bother interviewing you or Mom as possible suspects. And now I've got to make sure I don't take a financial hit from all this nonsense. You should appreciate that. I mean, it's not like you've brought in a penny for the last two years."

"Nope. Not a one. Of course, you made my retirement possible. You and Merriweather Stevens."

Dana shook her head in sympathy. Prior to the hoax, Reid had been a leading investigative reporter with the Rock Canyon Gazette. But when Melanie spilled the beans, her husband was the sole writer she *hadn't* bothered to inform about Merriweather's non-existence. Despite 20 years of dedication, the paper unceremoniously ditched him, accusing Reid of withholding the truth to help his wife's brokerage. And let's face it—with the name Reid Wright, the man was pigeonholed into a career as either a teacher, writer, or a floppy disk. When no other paper would hire him, he dedicated his forced retirement to writing his first novel. In-between dusting, vacuuming and basting the turkey. Talk about ruthless. Not only had Melanie regained the lion's share of the county's residential business, but now she had a free manservant as well.

"You and I both know you could get a job doing something else if you wanted to. But no, you wanted to write your novel. So I said fine. And where is it? Where's one damn chapter? Show me!"

Melanie's cell phone rang and cut the argument

short. Dana listened to the click of her sister's heels as she walked out of earshot. Perfect time to make her entrance. She reached for her purse and headed toward the kitchen. Some tea would be nice.

"You okay? You were pretty out of it last night," said Reid.

Better known to her as Dare.

"I don't remember." She grabbed a mug and rummaged around in a ceramic canister for the Tetley's and some packets of stevia. "How did I get here?"

"You parked your car sideways across our lawn, banged and screamed for us to open the door, and then rambled on and on about having to protect Mel. You were so agitated, Lorelei came over and ran you a hot bath and then tucked you into bed. Are you on some sort of new medication?"

"Yes, something like that." She tried to sound casual as she waited for the Keurig to transform the tea bag into something warm, sweet, and caffeinated enough to help her survive this third degree.

"Are you feeling better now?"

She nodded. She wasn't used to Reid being so solicitous and it made her uncomfortable. It was awkward when her two worlds collided, which was one of the reasons she rarely visited Melanie's house. She never would have gotten involved with Reid had she known him as anything but Dare when they met. One of the few times she had counted on references instead of Google. It was years before the truth came out. One more example of collateral damage, thanks to Cassandra keeping her apart from her family for more than two decades.

But even if she hadn't been involved with Reid, she would have steered clear of this particular home. The tension was palpable.

"Nice pillow talk. Tell me again, why do the two of you stay together?"

"It's funny, I've fantasized about walking out a hundred times. But deep down? We have a connection."

Sure you do. A connection with the house, the Mercedes, the cabin cruiser, the beach bungalow in Costa Rica. All the things your workaholic wife owns but is too busy to appreciate.

"Did I ever tell you about how we got together?"

She always enjoyed the rare times when Reid would tell her anything about his personal life. In scene, as Dare, he was a man without a past.

"I've heard Melanie's side; I'd love to hear yours."

"I was right out of Northwestern, waiting tables at Le Bernardin while I tried to get a newspaper gig. She was in the city, entertaining some bigwigs at one of my tables, yakking about some big corporate park deal. I winked. She winked. She left me a big tip and her card, so I called. I mean, why not?"

"Why not, indeed?"

"We started seeing each other. She pulled some strings, got me an internship with one of her clients at the Rock Canyon Gazette. I gave up the waiter gig and instead, accompanied her on listing appointments. Apparently, some married women won't hire an unattached female broker, afraid she'll make a move on their husbands. Whatever, I figured, one hand washes the other. After three years, we decided to make things official."

"So you went from 'prop' to 'proper?'"

"Funny, Thiss, funny. Anyway, we had the wedding at the Plaza, and out of 300 guests, want to know how many were mine? Two. My parents. The rest were Melanie and Cassandra's clients. They called it the social event of the real estate season, but to me, it was one giant bore.

I spent about fifteen minutes trying to break into a few conversations and then gave up. Feigned a headache and went up to the Honeymoon Suite, along with a bottle of Jack Daniels and Helena, the maid of honor."

"You took Melanie's best friend upstairs to party? On your wedding night?"

"Not quite. According to Helena, all of the bridesmaids—including her—were extras, hired to play the part of Melanie's friends. Anyway, I fucked her twice and then told her to go downstairs and bring back a few of the others. I don't know if it was the event of the season for the brokers, but it worked out pretty well for me."

So much for commitment.

Dana already knew the rest of the story. Reid had never enjoyed sex with take-charge Melanie, even before the wedding, so he started advertising for companionship in some of the town's sleazier publications, using the nickname Dare. Whatever Melanie denied him, however small she made him feel, he'd take out his frustrations on the girls who answered his personals. He made them call him *Sir* and submit to his will, in private and in public.

His trademark was the mask worn over his eyes whenever he played at the clubs. A different color for each outfit he wore. Not only did it provide him with some anonymity, he thought it made him look, well, more daring. And when you've endured bullying your whole childhood over your parent's choice of a name, being seen as daring was definitely a step up. Over the next few years, he became quite adept at the Master gig, picking up new techniques from books and from the other Doms he met. His reputation grew, as did his stable of eager companions. He was never sure if

Melanie was oblivious to his wandering eye or simply too busy to care. In any case, he was discreet, and she never said a word.

And such was the case today—Melanie raced past the kitchen without glancing in. Emaciated as always, wearing a baggy Princeton tee-shirt over black leggings and Nike cross-trainers, her mahogany tresses pulled tight into a ponytail.

"I'm outta here. Don't forget to pick up the dry cleaning," she yelled, slamming the door behind her.

"Princeton? Did I miss something?"

"Princeton today." Reid poured himself another cup of coffee. "Yesterday it was Stanford. Last week? Columbia. Syracuse, Tufts, Skidmore. She's got about twenty of them—all different. A great conversation opener with prospective clients, or so she tells me." Reid cleared his throat. "Thiss, the house is empty, it's just you and me."

"For the moment, anyway."

Calling her by her nick was Reid's signal that he wanted to play. Dana was a little taken aback by his insensitivity, especially considering the setting and the circumstances. This seemed like an opportune time to switch topics and broach the subject of an alibi.

"While I'm here, I wanted to ask you someth—"

Reid's phone buzzed and he glanced down at a text message and chuckled.

"Excuse me, what?" He turned his attention grudgingly back to Dana.

"It can wait until you're less...buzzed. Maybe we can get together later. How about around 5:00 pm? Or tomorrow? It's Valentine's Day. At the house on Devendorf? There's something kind of important I have to talk to you about."

"I'd love to, Thiss, but I can't make it at five. I've got an appointment. And I already told you I'm tied up tomorrow as well. How is next week?"

Appointment? Reid doesn't work. Therefore, Reid doesn't have appointments.

Dana's mind flashed back to the last time they were at Quirts and Squirts playing and to Faith, a 19-year-old blond co-ed who whispered in passing how much she'd like to be "Double Dared."

Appointment my ass. The one fucking time I ask you for anything and you can't be there? "Okay, whatever." *You arrogant asshole.* She glanced at her watch. "Wow, I didn't realize it was already ten. I too have an appointment."

She abruptly headed for the door but as she wrenched her jacket from the coat stand, she accidently bumped into an accent table holding a dichroic glass vase she and Reid, as Dare, had snatched up at a flea market, years before. It shattered, scattering into hundreds of sharp, sparkling shards. Any other day, she would have offered to pick up the pieces. Today, she merely smirked at the irony, called out, "Don't forget to pick up the dry cleaning," and made a dash for her car.

CHAPTER 16

February 13th

"DING DONG. THE BLACKOUTS ARE back!" Dana chanted as soon as Dr. Lawrence opened the door to her office.

"Well, luckily you're here and not in Oz," she retorted, ushering her patient inside. "How long was the lapse between this one and the last time?"

Dana stretched out on the sofa.

"Awhile," she lied. "Maybe six months. I'm always having flashbacks and nightmares, but the blackouts—the ones I know about, anyway—are rarer, and so much more disorienting."

"What preceded this one? Can you recall?"

"A detective questioned me yesterday afternoon regarding the recent real estate murders and told me I could be a person of interest. And then Melanie received a threatening note, presumably from the killer. After that, everything went blank until I woke up in my sister's house this morning."

"That's definitely cause for anxiety. I certainly hope your sister is taking precautions?"

"Exactly the opposite. But then again, that's my sister.

Invincible. At least in her own mind."

"Why are you considered a person of interest?"

"Because I couldn't give the detective an alibi for where I was during the killings. But he knows me from…somewhere else. He knows I didn't do it."

"Why can't you give him an alibi?"

"Because I was with…my partner. Who is married. Who wouldn't want to come forward. I can't out him like that."

"If he's your partner, wouldn't he want to protect you? I'm sure the detective would keep his admission a secret."

"I'm working on it, hoping he'll come through for me. It's complicated. Can we talk about something else, please?"

Dr. Lawrence nodded and consulted her notes.

"Of course. Let's pick up where we stopped last time. You had just met Harrison, your first BDSM relationship…"

"And at that moment, everything changed. He introduced me to the scene, to a group of people who made me feel like I was somewhat normal, that I actually belonged."

"A new family."

"Yes, for a short time, anyway. Harrison was a travel photographer, which meant he was away more than he was in town. I threw myself into my studies during his absences but still found the whole situation frustrating. After a few months, I tried to break it off. He refused and instead, suggested I join him on the road. He wrangled me this great reporter job with *Travel Agent Trade Weekly*. So I left college and we spent the next several years traveling the world together."

"Sounds very romantic."

"It was. At first. Life was a whirlwind. We'd be away for two or three weeks at a stretch, coming home long enough to wash our clothes and file our stories and photos. Then we'd be off again."

"And your grandmother was okay with this? Leaving college and traipsing around the world with a man she hadn't met?"

"I didn't want to worry her so I found a workaround. I told her I was spending a semester in Paris. And then after, that I'd decided to stay there for good and write. Harrison had a friend there—Antoinette. She lived on the Left Bank and I hired her as my intermediary. I would write letters to my grandmother and send them to Antoinette along with part of my earnings, which I'd exchanged into traveler's checks. She'd swap out envelopes and mail them to my grandmother so the postmark would read Paris. And then she would forward the return letters back to me. It was a great arrangement."

"Apparently. Sounds like Harrison was your first real love?"

"He was probably the first person I ever really felt close to, other than my father or grandmother…or Endie."

"And your first actual experience with S&M?"

"That's another story. Harrison advertised himself as a Dom, but he really preferred other types of kink, particularly public play. The thrill of potentially getting caught. On our press trips, we had a secondary, surreptitious goal: to commit some outrageously inappropriate sexual act without risking our reputations and future invites. The more taboo, the better.

"I remember, there was this 'Don't Miss a Sec' exhibit in London—it was a public toilet, encased in a one-way mirrored cube, set right on the sidewalk across from the Tate Gallery. Whatever you did inside, it felt like every passerby was watching, so he particularly enjoyed having sex with me there. But we did it everywhere—the base of an inactive volcano in El Salvador, against Gaudi sculptures in Barcelona during a thunderstorm. He even rented out an entire gondola in Switzerland so we could screw as our cable car climbed to the top of the Shilthorn. Talk about hitting your sexual peak!"

"Wow!" Dr. Lawrence laughed. "That sounds like quite the introduction to the lifestyle. Did it adequately fulfill your curiosity?"

"It wasn't the BDSM of my fantasies but even so, those were glorious years. He was romantic, generous, smart and kinky. It was perfect. He changed my life." She paused, wistfully. "Until it ended."

The tears that Dana had been holding back broke through her defenses and she started howling uncontrollably.

"He had…changed…my life. He had…been my… world. And then…. he was gone… and so were…all of the dreams…I'd had…for a somewhat…normal… future." She grabbed at the tissue box and in-between sobs, dabbed angrily at her eyes and cheeks.

"What happened?"

"I…don't…want to…talk…about…it."

"I'm so sorry, Dana," said Dr. Lawrence once her crying jag subsided. "It's clearly yet another trauma you didn't need in your life. Between what you've told me about the death of your father and the loss of your first lover, we might have found a diagnosis. PTSD: Post-Traumatic Stress Disorder. You might recognize some of the symptoms—flashbacks, nightmares, even blackouts."

Dana grabbed a new tissue and blew her nose.

"Is there a cure?"

"No cure, per se, but there are many things that can help. Exercise, therapy, taking care of yourself. Volunteering and making a difference in people's lives, connecting with others."

"Connecting?"

"Yes, opening yourself up to new, perhaps healthier relationships. Not to preach, Dana, but a partner who you can't trust to give you an alibi perhaps isn't much of a partner."

"Dr. Lawrence, I'm happy to come here, exercise, all of that. And I do have new people coming into my life. But I won't risk another Harrison breakup. It's much easier to keep things light, maintain emotional distance. But falling in love? I can't deal with all that pain again."

Dana didn't know who she was trying to convince more, Dr. Lawrence or herself. She was making a really good argument for steering clear of Aidan. Her budding feelings for him were far more dangerous than all the edge-play she'd experienced with her kinky friend, Dare. And yet…

CHAPTER 17

February 15th

WITH A LONELY VALENTINE'S DAY behind her, and the long holiday weekend looming ahead, things were quieter than usual for a Friday. Dana's morning prospecting session? More like voicemail hell. Everyone was either screening their calls or vacationing down south. She hated the lull. As much as she tried to focus on business, especially in the wake of her revelations with Dr. Lawrence, her thoughts kept drifting back to Aidan and his invitation when they last spoke:

"Will I see you at the club one of these days? There's some sort of big party going on Friday night. I'll keep an eye out for you, okay?"

She kept trying to think of anything but Aidan: not his smile nor his dimples nor that hint of a well-developed chest and muscular arms lurking beneath his elegant, Hugo Boss button-down shirts. Even at the clubs, no clichéd fetish wear. Why weren't all the cute ones Tops, instead of subs and switches? What would he be like in scene if he ever turned forceful, Dom-like? She wished that perhaps once, she'd had the opportunity to watch him play.

And maybe this was her chance. He was, after all, inviting her to a play party. Well, kinda, anyway. Detective Cummings intrigued her. There was a little devil lurking underneath that unassuming exterior. What would it take to draw him out?

Dana closed her eyes and daydreamed about the possibilities. Wandering in, past the posers and the players, to the Dominatrix section, where Bette Screams, clad in red leather, usually conducted her scenes. And directly behind her, Cummings, Bette's constant companion, standing back and intently observing. Perhaps wondering about what life might be like as a Dominant. No doubt, looking as sexy as ever. Dana would walk into his line of vision and smile. Perhaps this was his one chance to find out. He'd turn to Bette, whisper something into her ear—permission to leave, perhaps?—and then wink, gesturing to the private rooms at the rear of the club.

She'd nervously walk back to the designated spot, and like a true gentleman, he'd open the door and lead her inside, her arm locked in his. Once the door closed behind them, he'd no longer be such a gentleman. Nor would she want him to be. He'd turn and push her back against the heavy knotted pine, grabbing her wrists with one hand and holding them high above her head, his body pressing against hers, hard and demanding. With the other hand, he'd grab her hair and force her head back until she'd be facing the ceiling, his lips at her neck. She'd feel her knees buckle under her, but his grasp would keep her upright. "Oh Aidan, I want you…" she'd start to say, but his lips would move from her neck to her mouth mid-sentence, clearly indicating that his desire for her kiss outweighed any need for conversation.

As his tongue explored her mouth, the hand clenching

her locks would release its grip and move south, caressing her torso, her hips and then, pulling her slightly from the door, her ass. Then they'd hear moans behind them. They were not alone in the room.

Aidan would release her and step back, revealing another couple in the corner—Dare and Faith—deep in play. He'd be wearing his signature mask, she'd be naked and writhing under the touch of his whip. As rapt and engaged as Dana had ever seen him, as if the past several years with her were just a pleasant distraction, an appetizer to hold him until the main entrée arrived. She'd open her mouth to call out, to tell Faith to get away and leave Dare alone, but all that would come out was… *Beep, beep, beep.*

Shaken, Dana opened her eyes and stared at her computer screen, where the alarm was alerting her to a new request to see one of her listings. At that moment, she made her decision. There would be no Quirts and Squirts Friday night party in her immediate future.

CHAPTER 18

February 16th

FRIDAY'S ROMANTIC REVELATIONS RESULTED IN a restless night of tossing and turning, only exacerbated by Lorelei's early morning call.

"We've been back a month, Dana, and you still haven't stopped by to see your mother."

Thanks for the pre-dawn guilt trip.

"She misses you, you know. It's so lonely for her, stuck here with just me for company."

Yeah, right. She misses me like Europeans miss the plague. Nice try. Thanks for playing. "How was Sarasota?"

"Warm, sunny. And the condo is so lovely. I do believe it's easier for Cassandra to be away over the holidays. Not reminded of the past, all those Thanksgivings and Christmases she spent with you kids when she was healthier and could do so much more."

Holidays? Together? How's the weather out there in your alternative universe?

"I'll try to stop by before noon, Lorelei." *Because that's just how I want to start my weekend. Click.*

On the drive over, after she'd unclenched her jaw, the

dutiful daughter wondered about the play party she'd missed and ruminated over her fantasies of Aidan's hard, insistent body. Those strong hands, holding her by the wrists, taut and vulnerable. That tongue, forcing her lips apart...

Reality check. Dana, you have a partner. A Bingo partner. Remember?

And then that relentless, annoying voice of doubt running amok in her noggin egged her into debate:

Why have you tolerated Dare's neglect for so long?

It's not neglect. It's an open relationship. We see each other plenty.

Do the math, sweetheart. Over the past seven years, you've played together an average of maybe once or twice a month?

We both abhor commitment.

Fair enough. So why are you upset when he sends out texts after your scenes? Or when you see him playing around with other girls in your daydreams?

I don't know.

Be honest, why do you stay with him? Really? Is it the ego boost of wearing the cuffs of the most in-demand Dom on the scene? The fact that he demands so little of you emotionally?

Yes, yes, all of that. But mostly, it's that he gets me. He pushes all the right buttons with those sadistic, addictive games of his. Otherwise, I would have kicked him to the curb ages ago.

"Not to preach, Dana, but a partner who you can't trust to give you an alibi perhaps isn't much of a partner."

What the hell? Dr. Lawrence slunk in here too? Three's a crowd. Toodles.

Dana put an end to this unwanted, cerebral tug-of-war just as she pulled into Cassandra's driveway. With a jolt, she realized that her thong was damp. Was it the thoughts of Aidan's undeniable charm or Dare's brutal ingenuity that had been—as they say in real estate lingo—the precipitating factor?

As usual, it took a few minutes until lumbering Lorelei answered the door. The caretaker welcomed her with the usual maternal embrace. "So glad to see you, dear, and I know your mom will be excited too." Then she turned and plodded back into the kitchen.

Dana trudged into the living room where Cassandra sat, propped up in an overstuffed easy chair, watching *Pokemon* reruns. She glanced at her daughter and harrumphed. "Who died?"

"No one died, Mom." She grimaced. "Well, that's not exactly true, but that's not why I'm here. I thought you might like a visit."

"Liar. I heard Lorelei call you."

"Fine. She called. But I came, didn't I? Doesn't that count for something?"

"Not much. Whaddaya mean, not exactly true? What's going on at the office?"

"Listings. Closings. People getting offed by a serial killer. You know, the usual."

The sarcasm was lost on Cassandra. "What the hell are you talking about?"

"You didn't read about it in the newspapers or watch the news on TV? About the two agents who were murdered?"

"Lorelei never puts on the news or gives me a paper. Says it will upset me, and nothing ever changes anyway. I suppose she's right in her way. Is Melanie okay?"

"Yes, the prodigal daughter is just nifty. So am I, by the way. It was Annika and Penelope."

"Hmm…don't remember them. Whatever. As long as

Melanie's okay. Any leads on the killer?"

Dana shrugged.

"They should check out Decker."

"Huh? Deborah Lee? Why?"

"That woman is nothing but trouble. Pure evil."

"Got anything to back that up?"

"Hired her as my assistant years back, when I first started out. Mediocre worker." She coughed.. "Cut corners. Cost me some commissions. I eventually—" She coughed again. "—fired her."

The memory of Deborah Lee Decker's incompetence threw Cassandra into a violent coughing fit. Lorelei rushed in to help, forced some liquid down her throat, rubbed her back, and then gently rocked her to and fro, like a mother comforting a small child.

"Maybe that's enough for now."

"Leave me alone, Lorelei. I'll—" She broke into more coughing. "—talk if I fucking want to."

"Fine. Your funeral."

The caretaker walked off, clenching her fists in frustration. Dana's eyes followed her in stunned silence. She'd never seen Lorelei lose her cool before. *Guess I'm not the only one grappling with relationship problems today.*

After about five minutes of sporadic hacking, Cassandra felt up to continuing.

"A few years after your dad died and I moved up here to Rock Canyon with your sister—" *Cough.* "—she tracked me down. The agency was advertising for managers, and by that time—" *Cough.* "—I was the biggest agent there. She warned me to recommend her for the job or she'd out me—" *Cough, cough, cough.* "—threatening to tell everyone in town that I'd driven my husband to suicide and had abandoned one of my daughters. Oh and that

I'd had two secret abortions and had embezzled funds at my old company, whatever lies she could—" *Cough.* "—concoct. Hell, that gossip would have killed me up here, especially with the religious right. I would have gone bankrupt. So I used my clout and got her hired. Later, she bought the agency from the original owners, and—" *Cough.* "—she's still there, heaven help us."

Until that moment, Dana hadn't realized that Deborah Lee might know her family tree, that she was Melanie's sister and Cassandra's daughter. They had all agreed to keep that little tidbit a secret when she'd arrived in Rock Canyon. Up to now, she'd assumed that no one outside the family knew. Except for Endie and his boyfriend, Grayson.

"That explains how she got the job. But not why she would want to kill any of the agents in the company."

"Maybe they got some dirt on her…something that would—" *Cough, cough.* "—threaten her position, knock her off her high horse. She'd do anything to keep that job, fucking power-hungry bitch…" Riddled with contempt, Cassandra fell back into her chair, exhausted.

Dana considered her mother's allegations.

It would be interesting for Aidan to hear them as well. And what a great excuse to text him. After all, it's been four days since we've spoken.

She reached for her phone, which, of course, was out of juice.

"Lorelei?"

Her mother's caretaker shuffled out of the kitchen, her black polyester pants and hair smudged with streaks of flour. *Less Spongebob, more Pepe Le Pew.*

"Taking out your frustrations on the cake batter?"

"We all do what we need to do. What's up?"

"Would it be okay if I borrowed your computer? I need

to send an email. I think it might be important."

"Of course. Always. Help yourself."

Lorelei's bedroom was across the hall from Cassandra's, everything in its place. *How can someone so disheveled keep their room so surprisingly neat?* Dana rooted around in her handbag for Aidan's card and grabbed the keyboard.

"Could you meet me later this afternoon? I might have some information that will help the case."

Since she was online anyway, and not particularly eager to head back into the fray, she checked both email accounts, business and personal, in case there was a note from Dare. Nothing. As usual.

Ding. A return note from Aidan. *Boy, that was fast.* Her stomach did a mini-somersault.

Can't tonight, but how about Poisson, Monday at 6:00 pm? My treat.

Poisson was Rock Canyon's newest, most romantic seafood restaurant. She felt flushed with anticipation.

Sounds about right, she wrote back. *Something's definitely fishy.*

CHAPTER 19

February 18th

SARDINE WOULD HAVE BEEN A more appropriate name for Poisson, even on a Monday night. Dana arrived twenty minutes early, wedged herself in at the bar, and nursed her Cosmo as she waited. The afternoon had literally crawled along, punctuated by one email from Dare, pushing back their yet-to-be-scheduled tryst by another week or two.

Wow, his "appointment" must have been hotter than he'd imagined. She hoped hers would be as well. The request for an alibi would have to wait.

At 5:57 pm, she saw Cummings pull up outside the restaurant and hand his keys to the valet. Black, pinstriped Canali suit, accentuating his broad shoulders and athletic physique. As he approached, she couldn't help but beam.

"Hey there *Detective*."

"Hey there yourself. You're looking fetching, as always."

"I don't do dog play, but nice try," she whispered, aware that their two worlds were colliding and unsure of where to draw the boundaries.

"I didn't mean that, and you know it." He lifted an eyebrow. "You done with that drink? I think our table's probably ready."

She felt a shot of adrenalin as Aidan's hand grazed her back. They followed the maître d' to a quiet corner of the restaurant. A little intimate for a business meeting, she noted with satisfaction.

"About that crack…please disregard. I don't usually hang with scene people outside of clubs and munches. Virgin territory for me."

"Are you planning to strip down to a corset and put on a blindfold?"

"Not before the main course, no."

"Then I think, as long as you behave, we'll be okay from here on in."

"You sound very knowledgeable about this double lifestyle. Do you bring all your subbies here?"

"Why? Does this restaurant put you in a submissive state of mind?"

"Well, perhaps, if I were subbing to MasterCard. I bet everyone gets screwed by the prices here."

"I wouldn't worry too much about that. It's my treat."

Their primary server, who introduced himself as Kelner, handed them each a menu. Then a second waiter poured water into their goblets and a third brought a basket of warm bread. When the throng had cleared, Dana half-glanced at the specials, but her curiosity over more urgent matters triumphed.

"So what's your story?" She stared Aidan straight in the eye.

"My story? I thought you wanted to meet me because you had some information about the case."

"I do."

"Show me yours, and I'll show you mine."

Kelner interrupted their repartee, quickly took their orders, and disappeared.

"I have reason to believe you should be investigating Deborah Lee Decker."

"What makes you think that?" Aidan smirked, obviously enjoying her attempt at playing Nancy Drew.

"I've been told she blackmailed her way into Rock Canyon Realty."

"Says who?"

"Someone important who used to work there."

"You have to give me more than that, Thiss. I can't move forward on hearsay."

"Why not? Haven't you ever heard of an anonymous tip?"

"Why can't you just give me a name?"

Dana fell silent, lost in the sudden realization that she'd been so hell-bent for an excuse to call Aidan, she really hadn't thought things through. But now everything was becoming frighteningly clear. If she told him the information came from Cassandra, he'd interview her. And learn that rich, successful Melanie, the agent with a target on her back, was Dana's sister. And that, despite his masked persona, her play partner Dare was Reid, Melanie's husband and beneficiary in her will. Also Dana's alibi for the second murder. Money, lust, reduced competition—in terms of motive, it was quite the damning trifecta.

"The person or persons asked to remain unnamed," she hedged. "I can't say that I blame them. If Decker is the murderer, no informant would want her to know they were the one who tipped off the police."

"Luckily, I'm not the police, remember? Anyway, Decker was at Melanie Wright's graduation ceremony. She has an alibi. Which, I might add, is more than can be said for you. Given any more thought to that?"

She donned her patented pout, buying time to think.

"Decker has plenty of people working for her. Any one of them could have done it. Or a different one each time…"

"And what would be her motive?"

"Maybe someone's blackmailing her into thinning the herd? Or else they'll reveal how she extorted her way to the top? I don't know. I'm not the detective, you are. Look into it, would you?"

"Okay Boss, I will."

"Don't I get a thank you?"

"You get the scallops you ordered. And if you're good, some tiramisu for dessert."

"Well, it's your turn."

"Hmm?" Aidan feigned innocence.

"Your story, Detective. What's your deal with Bette Screams?"

"Deal? Are you asking me if she's my Domme?"

"Yup."

"Why do you ask?"

He's enjoying this way too much, stringing me along, reeling me in. If he wasn't so goddamned delectable…

"Oh, because I want to know."

"Ah. I see."

"Well?"

"Well, she's not my Domme."

"But you're always together at Quirts and Squirts."

"Yes. That's because she's my sister."

"Your sister? You go to S&M clubs with your sister?"

"I go as her bodyguard. She's had some problems with subs before. They get possessive. I make sure they back off when she needs them to."

Aha! Dana thought back on the news clipping about

how he'd left the force. He hadn't been sleeping with a prostitute, after all. He'd been at the club, protecting his sister, at the time of the raid. Had Aidan resigned his job specifically so he wouldn't have to give away Bette's true identity? Good, respected Scottish family. That sort of news would have left them devastated.

"Oh. I guess that explains why I've never seen you play with her."

"You've never seen me play with anyone."

"Wow. That's right. Why not?"

"I'm surprised you noticed. You seem to be awfully busy when you're there. You two make quite the Dare-ing Duo."

She felt herself blush.

"Well, yes. I do play with him when I go."

Did play with him. Past tense. Especially with Dare being such a dick lately.

"Exclusively…it seems. At least for the last few years."

"I'm surprised that with all your bodyguarding, you noticed. But we were talking about you."

"Is he your steady Dom?"

"It's not written in stone or anything." No point in further explanation. After all, what's true for house hunters is doubly true for men: they always want what's already gone.

"Why him, Thissie? Between you and me, you could do better."

"How so?"

Aidan hesitated.

"Well?"

"Thissie, it's just that…I don't think it's as exclusive a situation for him as it is for you."

"Oh, that. I know that."

The muscles in his face tightened with surprise. "You

know he plays with others?"

"Yes. He's not into commitment."

"But…aren't you?"

"Cummings, this has worked for me up to now. I don't know about the future. I try not to focus that far ahead—long term planning leads to disappointment."

"Oh."

Does he sound crestfallen or is that just wishful thinking on my part?

"And I don't understand why this conversation has swung back to me," she continued. "I'm waiting to hear why I've never seen you play."

"It's because I don't play."

"Wait…you mean you don't play *in public*."

"No, I mean I don't play at all."

"But you go to the clubs. I know you're not there merely to protect your sister. I've seen you watch others play."

"I find the whole psychology behind it fascinating. The subculture, all its nuances. Sometimes amusing, at other times horrifying. But always riveting."

"People must come over, proposition you?"

"Constantly. No one can figure me out. Am I a Dom? A sub? A switch? I tell them I'm not allowed to discuss it, and glance up at Bette. They all figure I'm her sub, and they lay off."

"So you're…"

"Vanilla as they come. Sorry to disappoint you."

"It's not that I'm disappointed. Well, maybe I am, a little." She grabbed a piece of French bread from the basket and pulled it into two. "It's just that…it doesn't work for me."

"Vanilla?"

"Yeah. Could you please pass the butter?"

He obliged.

"Maybe you've never been with the right vanilla guy."

"I haven't done vanilla for a very long time." She plunged her knife into the butter and began to smear furiously. "There's no danger. There's no thrill. I know what's coming and it's all very mechanical. I need something a little more… stimulating."

"You *need* to be hit?"

"No. I need to not know what's coming. I get off on the fear. And on proving myself. The beatings, I tolerate, because I like to see how much I can take. And they're also a way to deepen the relationship with the Dom or Top, to show him what I'm willing to endure for his pleasure."

"There are other ways to deepen a relationship. Shared experiences, for example. Understanding each other. Building a history together. To me, albeit as an outsider, all this theatricality seems like an elaborate ploy to avoid real intimacy."

The waiter replenished their bread supply and Dana quickly pulled out another piece, this time pumpernickel, grateful for any excuse to pause the discourse. Not that she hadn't considered the issue before. Playing with Dare, with Harrison—had it ever been about more than fun and games?

Then she contemplated those sparkling eyes and broad shoulders and wondered for a moment if a vanilla relationship could possibly end in anything but a yawn. He *was* hot. She'd think on it.

"Let's talk about something else. How's the case going?"

"What's with it with the people up here?" Aidan sighed. "I've got a long list of possible suspects from Decker. But I'm having a difficult time getting anyone to speak with me."

"Ah, I'm not surprised. Rock Canyonites are an interesting breed. They like their own. It took me years of knocking on the same doors, over and over again, to get them to even peer through the peephole. A few months longer to get them to open up and invite me inside."

"And now?"

"Well, it's not exactly like taking candy from a baby, but at least these days, they'll give me a chance."

Aidan paused for a moment.

"Thissie, do you think if I brought you with me, I'd have better luck?"

"It's an interesting concept. The power of a familiar face?"

"Or that the very sight of a real estate agent at their door will rile them up enough to give themselves away. If they're guilty of something, that is. What do you say? Are you up for some detective work?"

"It feels more like I'm being dangled out as bait." She remembered a press trip she'd taken with Harrison to a safari park in South Africa. The tour companies would hang live goats from trees to attract hungry white lions, so onlookers could observe. It didn't work out so great for the goats, and now the lions were teetering on extinction as well.

"Maybe," she shrugged. "I'd be willing to give it a shot." *Anything to give me more time to tempt you over to the dark side.*

"Got time on Thursday?"

"I'm all yours." *In more ways than one.*

The conversation lulled as Kelner returned with their appetizers. Dana lost herself in her micro-sized portion of Coquilles St. Jacques. The scallops were so luscious, she almost became angry when Aidan interrupted her foodgasm with more shop talk.

"Tell me about real estate. Maybe some background will help me work this case. Why did *you* decide to become an agent?"

"Access to all the empty houses in town." She laughed. "I'm surprised you had to ask."

"I'm sure it was more than that."

"Let's see…I wanted to have control over my own schedule, be able to choose who I'd work with. I wanted to make decent money. *And* I wanted use of the empty houses. Plus, I suppose, there is a certain satisfaction in helping people move on with the next phase of their lives."

"So you enjoy the work?"

"It's frustrating. Buyers want a house in the best condition, in the ritziest neighborhood, at the lowest price. Sellers, on the other hand, want to pay the lowest commission for the most advertising and marketing. No matter which side you're working, you're screwed. Plus, when you make a presentation to sellers to get their listing, they either accuse you of lowballing the price to get a quick sale, or jacking up the value to increase your commission. You can never win."

"How do you handle that?"

"I specialize in expired listings."

"What are they?"

"Expired listings are properties that were on the market but never closed. Let's say there's a particular home I'd like to sell. I sit back and wait while one or two other agents advertise it—usually at the seller's price—which means it's probably listed too high for anyone to seriously consider. Six months goes by and the agency contract ends. Then, I go in as the third wife. By that time, the sellers are usually so beaten down by the market, they'll listen to reason. They end up listing the house for the amount I suggest, which was the right price to begin with. That's how I get my listings sold."

Aidan digested the information.

"Huh. So what I'm getting from this is that if someone is beaten enough, they'll finally listen to reason and be willing to try something more…moderate?" He winked.

"Why, yes, Mr. Cummings." She flirted back with a frisson of delight. "Maybe if you wait around long enough, you've got a chance after all."

CHAPTER 20

Dungeon: March 12th

I'VE *WAITED A LONG TIME for this one. The others were hors d'oeuvres. Delicious tidbits. This one is the main course.*

The Scandinavian bitch? So easy. Eager to accept the food I was supposedly catering. Never questioned the mask I wore over my nose and mouth so I wouldn't inhale the cyanide. Didn't think twice about eating the shrimp. Kosher, my foot. I yearned to stay long enough to watch her take that first, doomed bite, but I couldn't risk being seen. I missed the sweet, sweet terror of the realization that something was happening that she didn't understand and couldn't control—the rapid breathing, the seizure, the collapse, the cherry-red hue of the skin. We all have regrets in life, I guess. Missing that was mine.

The stuck-up whore, Penelope, was a more exquisite experience. So happy to show me her empty hovel. Willingly traipsed down the stairs to the basement of an empty house, even leading the way. Never saw the Taser coming. And that momentary paralysis was all I needed to put the chloroform on the cloth and induce a peaceful sleep. No struggle as I tied her to the water heater. Easy peasy.

The real payoff was when she awakened and I calmly explained the unbearable agony she was about to experience. Death by dehydration. The mental confusion as her brain cells shrank, pulled away from her skull and ruptured. How each of her organs would slowly fail and she would wither away. How no one would ever find her there, in that overpriced home, in the middle of nowhere. Her eyes grew big with realization that I was correct. I let her curse, scream, and beg, gorging on her distress like a starving man at a Las Vegas buffet. And then the best part. As I walked up the stairs to leave her to her tragic end, she begged for her mommy. That's always the pinnacle, the pièce de résistance. Ecstasy.

And that's what I hope for from this last one, lying helpless on my table. Still attempting the occasional struggle, slowly recognizing the final fate that awaits. I may let you live a few minutes longer if you'll grant me that one wish. Beg for Mommy. Let those be the last words that ever escape from your lips. The irony will have made it all worthwhile.

CHAPTER 21

February 19ᵗʰ

DANA PRACTICALLY SKIPPED OUT OF her house the next morning to head to her first appointment. *Just 48 hours until I see Aidan again. 2,880 minutes. 172,800 seconds.* This wasn't the usual excitement of meeting Dare for a scene, but instead, a fluttering of anticipation colored by something far more elusive, a sense of hope. She needed to deflate before she exploded—so she decided that after her appointment, she'd swing by the office and ask Endie to join her for lunch.

Rock Canyon Realty was housed in a grand Queen Anne Victorian of pastel pinks and purples, set back from the road with a fair-sized parking lot. But today, the entrance was blocked by two police cars flanking a school bus and a Cadillac, both slightly damaged. Barely a fender bender, no ambulances. About 20 schoolkids, all seemingly intact, were scattered on the sidewalk and lawn, shivering, chatting, checking their cell phones, waiting for a replacement bus. Curiously, Aisha Singhowitz (the new name was almost official now, the paperwork filed) was wandering around, snapping digital pictures of the crash.

Inside the brokerage, there was a flurry of activity. Every agent was on the phone, deep in conversation. She caught snippets here and there:

"No, it isn't safe…"

"There are districts where the drivers are better trained…"

"Better sell while you still can, while your kids are still in one piece."

Dana grabbed the receptionist as she walked by. "Judy, I saw the accident. It seemed like nothing. Was somebody hurt? Are the parents all calling, considering a move because of *this*?"

Judy gave her a blank stare. "No one called. As soon as that Caddie cut off the school bus, Decker called a meeting. Told everyone this was a perfect lead generation opportunity to call every parent in the Lilac Pines school district and urge them to move over to Marshall Woods."

Hmm, how convenient. We have a ton of unsold inventory over in Marshall Woods. Exactly which of Deborah Lee's relatives was driving the Caddie?

In disbelief, she headed back to the bullpen and saw Endie on the phone, putting the final touches to a listing agreement. She pointed to her watch and then to her open lips. "Too busy," he mouthed back. Her expression flashed with unrestrained disapproval.

He put his palm over the receiver and shrugged. "Hey, gotta get 'em while you can. Can you hang out for a few?"

And people wondered why the town was secretly applauding the recent broker body count.

About twenty minutes later, Dana and Endie were nestled in a little booth at Duprey's on Sunset. He loved the place, but she found it pretentious; arugula and goat cheese was to this chef what Spam was to Monty Python.

But she acquiesced because, well, because it was Endie.

"What's happening, what's the story, what's the gossip?" he started.

"What makes you think anything is up?"

"You don't ask me out unless there's something you want to dish about. And you're blushing, which confirms my theory. So spill it."

"Okay, okay, I kind of…had a date."

"Oooh, a real date? Or a Dare Me date?"

"Neither. A dinner date. Remember Detective Cummings?"

"OMG. He is sooo cute. If I'd even had an inkling he was available…"

"Uh huh. And if he were gay. And if you weren't taken. If, if, if."

"Well, you're kinda taken. Or have you finally wised up and dumped Reid-the-Writing-on–the-Wall?"

"I haven't dumped anyone. But I'm none too pleased with him these days. He's my alibi for the second murder, but I don't think he's going to risk coming forward to back me up."

"I don't blame you for worrying. But is that the only thing wrong in Shangri-La? I mean, he's not exactly Harrison."

"If you'll recall, Harrison ended up not really being Harrison either."

"Dana, he was good to you. And for you."

"Maybe. In the beginning. I admit, he was generous, even extravagant. But he made me dizzy. You weren't there when he'd blather on for hours, the photography books he was going to publish, the inventions he wanted to market, how life had no limits."

"No, I missed a lot of that. But I do remember a long argument we had once about Ayn Rand and why he was an atheist. How did he put it? As long as you accepted God as an ultimate power, it put a ceiling on what you, as man, could accomplish. Whether you believed it or not, it was certainly motivating."

"I'll admit that Harrison was a perfect, gentle introduction into kink. The one thing I've learned about the scene is that there are givers, there are takers, and there are lurkers. Harrison was definitely a giver. He wasn't a traditional Uber Dom; he was patient. Ideal for me at the time."

"Think this new man going to be as free with his cash? The theater tickets, the shopping sprees, the impromptu visits to Timbuktu or Fiji or wherever you used to go?"

"Doubtful. Not on a detective's salary. But you know, I got my fill of that with Harrison. I don't need that anymore."

"I remember how you were at the beginning, when you were trying to decide whether to move in with him or break it off. All those heart-to-hearts over hot cocoa and brownies. You were so scared of letting someone in, letting a man get close."

"Justifiably so. And notice how that all turned out. Let's change the subject, shall we?"

They'd been so wrapped up in conversation, they hadn't noticed that the waitress had already served their lunches: a grilled cheese for Dana, and the Arugula and Goat Cheese Special du Jour for Endie.

"Okay, tell me about the dick."

"Detective."

"Honey, one man's detective…"

She sighed and shook her head.

"Maybe this will be the big one."

"Big what?"

"The L word, Dana. L-O-V-E."

"Endie, stop being ridiculously premature. It's not going to happen for two really good reasons. First, he's vanilla. And second, I have no time for love. Love is about needing. And I've spent my life learning to never need anyone."

"Who cares about vanilla? Love comes in all shapes and sizes. And you can adapt. If you try to, that is. And besides that, love is *not* about needing. It's about wanting. Wanting to be with someone. Wanting to share. Wanting to help them be the best they can be because that's what you feel they've done for you."

"I don't see it that way. Other than you, anyone I've ever tried to love has left me, either through death or disaster. I don't want that attachment to anyone else, ever."

"Uh huh. Gotcha. So when was this big snoozefest of a dinner?"

"6:00 pm last night. Poisson."

"Fancy! And are you seeing him again?"

"Yes. Thursday. He's taking me out to help him with his investigation."

"Oooh, exciting! Dana?"

"Yes, Endie?"

"Tell me the truth. Do you like him?"

She felt herself blush. "I do. I like him. L-I-K-E."

"Then, can you do me one favor?"

"What's that?"

"Keep an open mind. Not every man is a pussycat sugar daddy like Harrison. Not every man is a sadistic narcissist like Reid. Maybe there is a happy medium."

"I don't know, Endie. What happens when you mix vanilla with rocky road?"

"I have no idea what they call it. But honey, it sounds absolutely delicious."

CHAPTER 22

February 21st

"COFFEE," DANA DEMANDED AS SHE stepped into Aidan's black Camry two mornings later. He probably looked as dashing as ever, but without her requisite caffeine, he could have been the love child of Brad Pitt and George Clooney and she wouldn't have noticed. It had been another long night of tossing and turning, most likely precipitated by her alibi issues and emotional confusion. But nothing that a quick pit stop at Starbucks couldn't cure. He grabbed a table. Dana stood, third in line, for her Venti Expresso Roast.

As she waited, her mind flickered back to the stack of mystery novels she'd check out of the Centralia Library every week, trying to escape the reality of her ramshackle, sulfur-scented adolescence. Then she glanced back at her handsome co-detective. *I'm going to enjoy the hell out of this adventure.*

She rejoined him, coffee in hand. "Who's up first, Cummings?"

"I'd like to think that you'd be up first, Thiss."

"Well, I am. Now." She lifted up her drink in a mock toast.

"That's not what I meant. Any more work on your alibi? I'd love to be able to clear your name before the police get involved."

"You can't believe I'm too, too guilty if you've asked me to help you investigate."

Aidan leaned in and lowered his voice.

"I don't. But unfortunately, soon, this won't be just about me. My contacts tipped me off that if there's another murder, the local police will have no choice but to intercede. They're getting pressure from the higher ups."

"Really? Because of a bunch of dead real estate agents? I thought they'd be cheering around a bonfire."

"They probably would, except the mayor has his license too."

"You're fucking kidding me."

"Apparently, he doesn't sell property, but he gives out referrals to other agents and gets some sort of payback in return."

"We don't call it 'payback,' Sherlock. We call it referral commissions. All completely legit. Though, in the mayor's case, I'm not sure if it's particularly ethical."

"I'm not judging ethics today." Aidan shrugged. "I'm trying to solve this thing and luckily, right now, I'm not constrained by precinct protocol to get the answers I need. Hence, you, here, now. Everyone in this xenophobic town seems reluctant to talk to me, but with you by my side, I've got an inside track. Plus, this gives me more opportunity to hone in and observe you, establish your guilt or innocence while you're at ease and unawares."

"I doubt you were supposed to give that last part away."

"Oops," he smiled. "I can't think straight when you're wearing outfits like that. Not that I mind, of course."

Now it was her turn to smile. She had purposely worn

her most Emma Peel outfit, tight-fitting black leggings and a fitted purple tunic top with a black stripe under each arm. Very catsuit. Another throwback to her youth, catching *Avengers* reruns on an antiquated, black-and-white Panasonic.

"I was disappointed I didn't see you at the club last Friday," he said.

"Something came up. I…I couldn't." She remembered the vision of Dare and Faith playing together and fumbled for a more legitimate excuse. "And maybe it's best that we're not seen together at a place like that while you're investigating this case."

Dana must have hit a nerve because Aidan cleared his throat and got back down to business.

"Our first visit is to a mortgage broker, one Anthony Caldaro. You know him?"

"Actually, I'm one of the few people at the agency he likes."

"Why is that?"

"You'll find out." She gulped the remainder of her Starbucks and they headed out.

Ten minutes later, they stood waiting in the deserted reception area at Reliant Mortgage.

"Hello?" Dana called out. Caldaro emerged and gave her a long hug and them invited them both to follow him past an empty bullpen of desks into his small, private office.

"How can I help you, Dana? What are you doing mixed up with this Cummings character?"

"He's a P.I. and I'm in training," she teased. With all of these vendors, she'd found that a smile and wink went a long way. Along with throwing them a ton of referrals. "You don't mind helping us out, do you?"

"For you, Dana, anything. You're the only decent one

of the lot. You never forgot me."

Aidan interjected. "There's no easy way to say this, Mr. Caldaro—"

"Call me Tony."

"Okay, Tony, there's no easy way to say this. We asked the people at Rock Canyon Realty who might be interested in taking them out, and, well, your name came up."

"Interested in taking them out?" Caldaro sniggered. "Dana can tell you, that's the understatement of the year. I'd like to find the guy who's knocking them off and shake his hand. That company can't go down the tubes fast enough for me. No offense, Dana."

"None taken."

"What makes you feel that way, Mr. Cald—umm—Tony?"

"I helped those bitches when they were starting out. They needed broker open houses catered, I provided lunch. For years. They needed public opens catered, I did that too."

"Wait," said Aidan. "I'm confused. I thought you were a mortgage broker. Why are you catering?"

"It's all part of the business. Many mortgage brokers supply food for agents' open houses in exchange for a presence there—either in person or by having our flyers distributed. It's a nonobtrusive way to drum up more business. Anyway, I spent a fortune on those lunches. And when the agents had buyers with credit issues? I fiddled with the numbers; I made the deals work. I went out on a limb so many times for those fucking broads, you'd have thought I was funding treehouses.

"What happens? They get big. They get independent. They don't need me anymore. So now I don't get any of their business. Except from you, Dana, thank you.

Which sucks, because I've got two kids in college. And Mrs. Caldaro? Or rather, the soon-to-be ex-Mrs. Caldaro? Not exactly a coupon cutter, that one. As far as I'm concerned, Rock Canyon Realty pretty much put my life in the crapper. I don't know how he's killing these agents but if you find him and he needs help? Tell him to give me a call."

Since further questioning revealed that Caldaro had been in divorce court at the time of one of the murders, and visiting his son at SUNY Cortland during the other, the sleuths moved on.

"What do you think?" Aidan asked as they headed back to his car.

"What do you mean? He's got an alibi. He's innocent."

"No, not about him. About the detective life. All you thought it would be, Ms. Marple?"

She gave him the once over, admiring his outfit, a dark grey cashmere sweater over a blue-and-white pinstriped shirt. "Well, the hours suck, but you can't beat the scenery."

Next stop was Elliott Beiner, owner of SureLock Homes Inspections, which he operated out of his residence. Dana knocked while Aidan stood off to the side so Beiner couldn't see him through the peephole. She hadn't worked with Elliott personally, but guessed he didn't have too many female visitors, based on the speed with which he yanked open the door.

Beiner appeared a lot older in person than Dana remembered from his cable ads. On television, he wore a hat and cloak, a pipe in his mouth and a magnifying glass in his hand, examining appliances, fuse boxes and roofs.

"Can I help you, Miss?"

"Hi. I'm here assisting Detective Aidan Cummings

with his investigation of the fallen real estate brokers. No loss, if you ask me, but he's still insisting on asking questions. Would you be willing to speak to us?"

Maybe it was her calculated turn of phrase, but he did let them in. Turned out Beiner was as thrilled as Caldaro about hard times falling upon the agents at Rock Canyon Realty, but not quite as brazen about offering to help out the killer.

"Evidently, I was *too* thorough for Decker and her crew." He pulled some corroborating folders from his file cabinet and then flung them across the desk. "As you can see from these reports, I was honest about what was wrong in the houses they were trying to sell. I guess I killed too many of their deals. Word spread and soon my business was kaput."

"So you're not doing inspections any longer?" Dana asked.

"I'm enhancing my services." He pointed to a new sign he had propped up against the far wall of the living room. It read, "SureLock Homes Inspections and Security."

"Nanny cams are all the rage these days," he continued. "They can be disguised as pictures hanging on the walls, books in shelves, sometimes as a clock radio or a child's toy. Let's see how the agents who killed my business like it when home owners eavesdrop on their showings, hear what their beloved brokers are really saying to the buyers."

This was disconcerting. Dana made a mental note to learn more about how to recognize a nanny cam; she had no desire to have what *she* did in empty houses become front page news.

"He's a possibility." Aidan scribbled in his notebook as they climbed back into the car. "No alibi for either murder. Sounds like someone else I know."

"That's because he's spent months closeted off in his house, depressed, trying to diversify his business. I don't think he's your killer."

"On what basis?"

"Broker intuition. That skinny, nerdy guy isn't capable of masterminding anything. He gets off uncovering everyone else's mistakes."

En route to their last appointment, a call came in, and Aidan put it on speaker. She knew it was probably a safety precaution but she also noted with satisfaction that he felt comfortable enough in her presence to discuss an active case on an open line.

"It's a no-go on Randolph-Purser's cell phone, Cummings," said a female voice.

"That's Detective Cummings to you."

"Hmm. Tell you what. Solve the case. *Then* I'll call you Detective."

"Can't find it?"

"Either someone shut off the phone or it's run out of juice. We can't seem to trace it via the GPS."

"Subpoena the phone records?"

"No, I was busy getting a pedicure."

"What?"

"Of course I subpoenaed the phone records, you gom. But on the down low, so no one catches on."

"And?"

"And you're not gonna like it. Whoever called Randolph-Purser and lured her to that house called her via Skype from the Keystrokes Café. It's that Internet coffee house over on Briggs. I cashed in a favor and sent Hastings and Vannoy over. It's a dead end. They located the computer through its IP address, but the place only accepts cash. So no credit card receipts to identify users. None of the baristas or cashiers working that day remember anyone unusual using the computers or talking over Skype."

"Don't they have a group of regulars there?"

"We followed up that angle too. Everyone who works there or patronizes the joint is from the college. Different students every day, visiting whenever they have openings in their class schedule. No one's there often enough or cares enough to really pay attention to the clientele."

"So we have…"

"Nada."

"Terrific. Keep up the good work."

"You betcha. What's on your plate this afternoon?"

"Some background work." Aidan glanced over at Dana and winked. "I'll talk to you tomorrow."

"Cummings, solve this, okay? It'll make your parents proud, and maybe it will convince you to come back to us on the force. We miss you."

"Hey, O'Brien, thanks for the pep talk. Keep trying to trace that phone, okay? You never know when it might get recharged or found."

"Will do. Bye."

"You two sounded cozy," Dana remarked as Aidan disconnected the call.

"Jealous?"

"No, just terribly observant. That's why I'm here, aren't I?"

"Nah, you're here because your face gets doors opened, and because if someone else gets knocked off, at least you'll have one alibi. That, if you must know, was Shanahan O'Brien, my former partner when I was with the Middleville Police. We used to work the streets together. She's still willing to do some research for me, even if this is outside of her precinct."

"Aww, how sweet. Why is she sending other people out instead of investigating it herself?"

"A few years back, we were involved in a shoot-out. Neither of us was physically hurt, but it left her pretty badly shaken. Now, she's on desk duty."

Dana felt compassion for his ex-partner, but was secretly pleased she wouldn't be underfoot. This was *their* investigation.

The last and most interesting stop of the day was a small house on Carnaby Street, owned by an unmarried librarian named Gwendolyn Havens.

"A librarian? What's she going to do, shush the next Realtor to death?" quipped Dana as they headed up the front walk.

"According to Deborah Lee, this particular librarian has made a career of writing weekly to your brokerage, complaining and threatening everyone who works there. The most recent letters include confessions to the murders. Deborah Lee doesn't really take her too seriously, but you never know."

They knocked, and after a few moments, a bespeckled, suggestively dressed woman in her forties answered, opening the door about three inches. "Yes?" she asked, giving Aidan the once over, while completely ignoring Dana.

"Ms. Havens? I'm Detective Aidan Cummings and this is…my associate. I called earlier about the murders over at Rock Canyon Realty?"

"Yes, Detective, come in. Carefully, please." She opened the door barely wide enough for him to squeeze through. Dana forced her way in behind him. Once inside, she could understand why Havens had been so guarded. There were about 50 cats milling about the living room and entrance foyer. The stench of urine assailed their nostrils.

Havens invited Aidan to sit on a Louis XIV antique chair in the parlor. After sidestepping several feline obstacles, she positioned herself seductively on the sofa across from him. Dana stood in the corner, unwilling to negotiate the mounds of dust and hair adorning every surface.

"You may have come to arrest me, but you'll never get a conviction, you know. I'm the pride of the county. I've done what everyone wanted to do but couldn't."

Havens crossed her legs, her mini-skirt rising up higher than appropriate, revealing thighs thick with cellulite. Two Siamese cats sprang onto the sofa to her left, three tabbies to her right, and a large Maine Coon leapt right onto her lap. Aidan started wheezing from the dander, and by the way he was clearing his throat, it was obvious the ammonia was already causing his bronchial tubes to swell.

"Ms. Havens, I want—"

"Call me Gwennie. All my friends do." She batted her lashes awkwardly, as if trying to dislodge something in her eye.

Aidan fidgeted uncomfortably.

"I'm afraid it's an official call so I must stay formal, Ms. Havens. I wanted to ask you about your issues with the agents at Rock Canyon Realty. I'm told you've written hundreds of letters of complaint, and still write them, even though they've sold the property in question."

Flirtations unreciprocated, Gwendolyn Havens eyes turned cold. "Yes, Melanie Wright sold my mother's estate on Paradise Court. And now I want her fired. And then dead. But until then, I plan to kill every other agent there."

"But she sold the home, didn't she?"

"Yes. But I didn't like the way she did it."

Two cats jumped up onto Aidan's lap and a third pawed at his shoulder from the top of his chairback. He politely tried to push them off but froze after seeing the reproachful expression on Gwendolyn's face. Clearly, he had no desire to be sued for animal abuse.

"About half of these cats belonged to my mother, God rest her soul. When she died, I needed to sell her place so I could afford a bigger house where we could all live together. Raising a blended family is never easy, I gotta tell you, but that's a topic for another day."

"I can imagine," said Aidan. "Was that when Ms. Wright became involved?"

"Exactly. I invited Melanie over to give me her so-called expert opinion of what to charge, but she wouldn't shut up about how the house stunk of cat piss and how it would never sell until I had it fumigated. Can you imagine?"

Dana could very well imagine, but said nothing.

"I told her if she didn't like it, she could get out. And she did. She filed a lawsuit against me, claiming I exposed her to hazardous waste. Cat urine, hazardous? Please. Said she'd lost time at work and potential income because she'd developed some little respiratory infection. What rubbish. So I don't use litter boxes. Now that's a criminal offense?"

"She didn't get the listing?" Dana couldn't resist fueling the fire, despite a reprimanding glance from Aidan.

"Not initially. But since I'd let our homeowner's insurance expire, and I wasn't going to waste time and money hiring a lawyer, Melanie won her stupid suit. The court slapped a $10,000 lien onto the property—$10,000! Can you imagine? That, on top of the back taxes I already owed."

"A cat-astrophe," Dana murmured as earnestly as she could muster. Havens nodded, completely oblivious to the pun, grateful for the sympathy. Aidan turned to Dana, raised an eyebrow and shook his head.

"What happened next?" Dana was dying to discover precisely how low her sister would stoop to earn a buck.

"Melanie came back, threatening to call the Department of Health and have the house condemned if I didn't list with her. So what choice did I have?"

"But in the end, she did get it sold." To his credit, Aidan was staying focused on the facts and not buying into the drama.

"Yes. The problem was the price she wanted to charge: a measly $200,000. I told her I needed $300,000 to buy a house big enough for all of us to move into."

"Was the home worth $300,000?" Aidan sounded dubious.

"That's hardly the point, Detective. It's what I needed."

"Purr-posterous," Dana injected.

Havens nodded again, appreciative that someone, anyone, understood. Aidan just rolled his eyes.

"What could I do? After paying off the fees, the taxes, the liens and the cost of the hazmat crew, I walked away with almost nothing. We had to all squeeze back into this place because I couldn't afford to buy anything bigger. I figure Rock Canyon Realty owes me another $100,000. I'll take it out in flesh."

It was a lot to take in. If this woman didn't have a valid motive, Dana decided, then no one did. And this seemed to be an opportune moment to play bad cop to Aidan's good cop.

"So how did you kill them?" she asked matter-of-factly, aware that while the real estate community knew all the gory details, the local newspapers had remained purposely vague, specifically to hinder false confessions.

"Huh? I killed them. That's all."

"But *how* did you do it?"

They watched Gwendolyn stammer and lose control.

"I don't know what that has to do with anything. You know they were murdered. You know how they died. What can I add to that?" She balled up her fists and waved them up and down, her eyes brimming with tears of frustration. "The point is that now it can all come out, what lying cows those women were. How they mistreated their clients. How they bottom-fed on our misfortune. Home sellers will notice me, appreciate that I stood up for them. I doubt the lawyers will even charge to represent me. The papers will carry my story. Maybe I'll even write a book."

Aidan had evidently heard quite enough. He got up, rubbing his thighs, trying to smooth the cat hair off, and signaled to Dana, gesturing with his head toward the door. "Ms. Havens, I'm sorry for your loss. Truly, I am. And when you're ready to write out a full confession, detailing how you killed those women, I'll be happy to have the police come back and arrest you, so you can call your lawyers and publicists. But until then, could you hold off on mailing any more letters? I know the tree huggers *and* the post office would appreciate that. We'll show ourselves out. Have a good day."

CHAPTER 23

February 24th

FOUR OR FIVE NIGHTMARE-FREE HOURS of sleep were a luxury Dana resented losing any morning, but especially on a Sunday, when she wasn't bound by social convention to join her fellow Rock Canyonites at church, the gym, or even the dog park. Instead, she preferred lounging languidly on her 400-count Egyptian cotton sheets, followed by an extended bubble bath, and perhaps a Marshall Karp mystery. But Endie's 8:00 am call put an end to all that.

"Are you watching? Can you believe this?" he asked, unable to contain his excitement.

"The only thing I was watching was the inside of my eyelids, thank you very much. What is so important that—?"

"Turn on Channel 4. Now."

She reached for the remote and pointed it at the 37" Mitsubishi.

Kerrianne Cooper's face was splashed across the screen. Then a shot of a brown, rundown Cape Cod, with paramedics wheeling out a gurney carrying a body bag. Dana turned up the volume.

"Ms. Cooper had recently left her position as personal assistant to local celebrity Realtor Melanie Wright and had opened her own real estate practice. We will return to this breaking story after these messages."

Having no interest in a promo for the next episode of *Judge Judy*, Dana returned her attention to the phone. "What the hell, Endie? What's going on?"

"They've been talking about it all morning. The station even filmed my comments. I was on TV!"

"A shame I missed that, but—"

"Oh, don't worry. I recorded it."

"Glad to hear it. Endie, calm down. Tell me, what exactly is going on?"

"Kerrianne was apparently already a broker when she took the assistant position with Melanie. She faked the admin part so she could infiltrate our agency, get a gander at the Wright book of business…"

"No, no, no. I don't care how she was able to open up her own agency. The body bag. What's up with that?"

"Well, excuuuse me. Okay, so get this. She'd taken her first solo listing, an expired over on Justin Circle that used to be Melanie's. Ring a bell?"

"The one with all garbage inside? The hoarder house?"

"Exactly. The very one."

"Who would want to market that place, anyway?"

"Um, excuse me Ms. Mega Not. Don't you remember when you started out? Didn't you take a listing on a mobile home?"

"Point taken. So she takes the listing and…?"

"She invited a bunch of us to come and join her for an all-night Declutter Party, remember? Lysol and Lager? Martinis and Mr. Clean?"

"I vaguely remember seeing something about that on the Internet. Didn't she try to recruit the entire town, get everyone involved like it was some sort of non-profit event?"

"Right. I guess she got there early to set up. When a few of us arrived at midnight to help, we found her in the living room, crushed to death under some large boxes."

"Oh my God, that's awful!"

"Not pretty, hon. Not pretty."

"Pulled the wrong box out at the wrong time, I guess. Bet she stunk at Jenga."

"Very funny, Dana. Do you whistle in graveyards too?"

"Only in the presence of black cats as I walk under ladders. On a positive note, it sounds like an accident. Not this serial killer again."

"I wouldn't be so sure about that, Dana. The boxes that fell on her?"

"What about them?"

"There were words written on them."

"Like *linens*, *books*, that kind of thing?"

"No, some kind of message. The press thinks this was the work of the *Realtor Retaliator*. And so do I."

Wonderful. And me without an alibi, once again.

At least there was still a bright side. All Rock Canyon Realty agents and brokers were asked to cancel their Sunday open houses and instead report to the office to meet again with Detective Cummings. Dana was pleased at the prospect of some impromptu flirting. But unfortunately, according to Deborah Lee Decker, this time around, Mayor Margolin had intervened, and ordered Captain Stuart Lasky of the Rock Canyon Police to conduct the interviews. They had kept Aidan on as consultant, since he had already laid the groundwork of the investigation.

Agents were milling about everywhere—the

conference room, the kitchen, the bullpen—nervously trying to find something to do until their names were called. Dana and Endie sequestered themselves in the storage closet and were chatting when they heard Melanie emerge from questioning, only to be cornered by a few of her less-friendly competitors in the hallway, including Lori Wrobbel, queen of condo sales.

"Hey Mel, this kinda worked out for you, didn't it?"

"What the hell does that mean?"

"Let me spell it out. Kerrianne worked for you, knew all your secrets, started stealing your clients and, oops, suddenly she's dead like every other agent you've seen as a threat."

"Well if that's true, Lori, I guess you'd better start watching your back. With Annika and Penelope out of the way, aren't you second in line—after me, of course— for Agent of the Year? Now if you'll excuse me, I've got to go and take a listing. And then shoot a few practice rounds with my AK-47. Ta."

Melanie stormed out of the building just as, "Dana Black, please join us in Ms. Decker's office," boomed over the loudspeaker.

Captain Lasky sat behind Deborah Lee's desk and to his right, a very formal Detective Cummings. He was still sexy as hell, but there was no smile curling around the edges of his mouth like last time around.

Dana introduced herself and shook each of their hands, giving Aidan's a tiny extra squeeze before sitting down opposite them. "How can I be of help here?"

"Ms. Black, how well did you know Kerrianne Cooper?"

"Call me Dana, please. Not well at all. I think the first time we met was at Annika's funeral."

"And your impressions?"

"Only that she seemed very ambitious. I haven't really seen her since. I don't work in the office all that much."

"Any enemies you can think of?"

"We're Realtors, Captain. Every agent here stands between every other agent and their next commission."

Aidan glared, obviously not a fan of her frank and flippant response.

"And you? Did you dislike Kerrianne?"

"As much or as little as anyone else, I guess. As I said, I barely knew her."

"Where were you last night around 10:00 pm?"

"In bed, asleep."

"Do you have anyone who can confirm that?" asked Aidan.

"No, Detective. Unfortunately, not." Subtle as a falling piano. "Should I assume that this was more than an accident? Am I being accused of something?"

"No accusations, Ms. Black. But Detective Cummings tells me you've already proven very helpful, offered him great insight with this case. We have a bit of a riddle on our hands, and we were hoping you might be able to help us solve it."

Dana smiled at Aidan. "Sure. Shoot."

"The boxes that fell on Ms. Cooper. There was a different word or set of words on each one. *Oppression. Blow. Cute Boy. Orange.* We think it's some kind of code. Any ideas?"

Lasky pushed a piece of paper across the desk bearing the list of clues scribbled in red ink.

"I certainly appreciate the compliment and vote of confidence." Dana folded the list and stuck it in her purse. "Can I think about it and get back to you?"

"Absolutely, we would be grateful for any help."

"Am I free to go?" Dana hoped against hope that Aidan

would find some excuse to extend the interview, sneak in a suggestive comment or meaningful glance.

"Yes, Ms. Black, of course. Have a nice day."

Oppression, Blow, Cute Boy, Orange.

Dana kept repeating the words throughout the day. Wrote them down on snippets of paper and mixed up the order. Rearranged the individual letters, searching for anagrams. Nothing.

Around 11:00 pm, as she was watching more of the non-stop Kerrianne coverage (Who knew she wore chartreuse underwear?), it came to her. Thank goodness for the power of the unconscious mind. She raced to the phone and dialed Aidan, happy for the opportunity to speak with him without a supervising eye. He answered after one ring.

"Aidan Cummings."

"Yes, Sir, Detective Sir. I believe I've solved your riddle."

"I had a feeling if anyone could, it would be you. What are you thinking?"

"It's a play on words, all involving *crush*. You crush oppression. You get a crush on a cute boy. You drink Orange Crush. And you can land a crushing blow."

"Nice work. So you don't think it's a code. You think someone's just jerking us around?"

"Something like that. Or a warning to Kerrianne that she was about to get crushed. Anyway, hope this helped." *Ask me out, ask me out, ask me out.*

"Thanks again, Ms. Black. I appreciate your help. Good night." *Click.*

Dana stared at her cell phone, taken aback by Aidan's curt, cold response.

Who the hell was that? Aloof Cummings, Aidan's alien

twin?

Sunday ended exactly as it started, with an upsetting phone call. And in between, a disturbing revelation. *Someone's setting up Dana Black, consummate punster, for a murder rap.*

CHAPTER 24

February 24th – Aidan

"TOLD YOU SHE'D FIGURE IT out," said Aidan as he hung up the phone, wishing he could have been less stiff, friendlier.

Captain Lasky puckered his brow, clearly skeptical.

"She's the one without the alibi?"

"Yes, but she's working on it."

"Or so she says. You were one of the brightest on the Middleville force. What does your gut say?"

"It says she's innocent—she has no real motive. Melanie Wright? Now there's someone with a motive. Top agent, nervous about the competition. We already know she'd do anything to win. She leaked the whole Merriweather Stevens story to the press. Not that they were in the right, duping the public, but she threw them all under the bus so she could regain her market share. And the way she treated that Gwendolyn Havens character? Threatening to turn her into the Department of Health and get her evicted, just to get a listing? Even her colleagues suspect her, say there's no depths she wouldn't stoop to in order to get ahead."

"Well, calling them *colleagues* is a bit of a stretch,"

said Lasky. "They're her rivals and they'd love to get her out of the picture. We have to take anything they say with a grain of salt."

"Fair enough."

"This is why I'm thinking Black. Many killers are competitive, trying to get one up on the police. Playing cat and mouse, almost taunting us with clues to their identity. Here she leaves a pun on the boxes…and then when we ask her to solve it, she miraculously comes up with the answer, our brilliant savior, proving how smart she is. Almost like she's using us to validate her own intelligence and wit."

"I don't think that's how Dana operates, Captain. She had no way of knowing we'd ever ask her to solve the clue."

"Say, Cummings, since we're short on manpower and you two have seemingly struck up a friendship, why not get a little cozier? Hang out, get her to lower her defenses, find out what you can? At least until she presents us with an alibi that holds water. She's a looker, shouldn't be too much of a sacrifice."

"I'm not sure I'd want to lead her on."

"You wouldn't be. You'd be a close friend, a confidant. I promise you, if you help us solve this thing, I'll find a top spot for you on the Rock Canyon police force. You can put that whole Bette Screams/Middleville suspension behind you. Make a decent living, guarantee yourself a pension. I mean, you can't be making much with this P.I. gig."

Aidan considered Lasky's offer. It would be wonderful to spend a bit more time with Dana. He liked so much about her—her beauty, her sass, and her obvious intelligence. He suspected that she'd reciprocate his affection, if she could just get over the vanilla thing and ditch her good-for-nothing, cheating Dom. He'd seen Dare without Dana at the clubs over the years, playing with so many other subs, it made his head spin. *Why couldn't she demand better?*

Dana's lack of alibi troubled him as well. *If she had been with Dare, why not simply say so? What was she hiding? What made this girl tick?*

Getting back onto the force was also an enticing prospect. He still remembered his father's obvious disgust, his mother's stoic attempt to hide her shame, when the scandal broke and spread like the plague through their small town. Even after the press reluctantly reported that Bette Screams wasn't actually a prostitute, it did little to sway public opinion. No more of his mother's goose at Christmastime, no more Easter egg hunts with his younger cousins. Hell, he couldn't even come home for Sunday dinner without feeling their scorn and disdain.

He didn't second-guess his decision, no matter how personally painful the result. Better to quit the force than endure the investigation necessary to lift the suspension. He was strong and could endure the forced exile. But had he outed his baby sister to save his own skin? If word had gotten out that Bette Screams, who secretly moonlighted as a Dominatrix to make ends meet, was really Laura Cummings, the apple of Baird and Moira Cummings' eye? He didn't even want to speculate how Laura or their parents could have handled the humiliation.

The real question was, as much as he'd love to get in good with Lasky, could he bring himself to follow the captain's suggestion and romance Dana, simply to gain her confidence? He was no user—winning Dana over had its own rewards. But even if he was that calculating and mercenary, she seemed far too guarded to ever lay back, relax and confess all, no matter how much he turned on the charm. Perhaps the first line of attack should be to poke around her past and find out what he could, piece the story together without her knowledge.

"I'll see what I can do, Captain. Leave it with me."

"Good man!" Lasky scribbled a note onto the file on his desk. "But keep it clean, okay? Stay out of those clubs. We don't want a repeat incident, do we?"

No indeed, thought Aidan. That's why he insisted that Bette now play at Quirts and Squirts, where there were no mob connections, where the Dungeon Master greeted every visitor, and where, if the police ever were to arrive for some reason, Simeon could hit a secret alarm that would alert everyone to hide in the sub-basement.

"No Captain Lasky, Sir. No more clubs. You can count on me."

CHAPTER 25

February 25th

MUCH TO DANA'S RELIEF, THE rest of the night and following day passed without further incident. She knew that, like her fellow agents—all possible murder targets—she should have been scared for her life. But she was more concerned about her relationship with Aidan. Every hour she went without speaking to him, the more baffled she became over the tenor of their last conversation. Was he mad because he'd been displaced, that she had involved him in an investigation he no longer controlled? Or that she'd been the one to figure out the 'punny' box riddle they couldn't solve? Or, more distressing, had he decided he'd prefer a vanilla girlfriend, one who would be less of a handful? Without a follow-up conversation, she was without answers, and true to her personality, she was too damn proud to call.

As she drove over to Dr. Lawrence's office, she realized that her upcoming session also had her anxious. While it was easier to return to therapy with a tentative diagnosis under her belt, she also knew that if they were to continue their chronological tour of her past, she was going to have to start holding back. There were some things she could never divulge to anyone under any circumstances, both for her sake and the sake of others.

"I heard about Kerrianne Cooper. How have things been going? Are you okay?" Dr. Lawrence asked, topping off her candy bowls as Dana plunked herself down on the sofa.

"Confusing. I'm torn between a lot of decisions right now, but I'm grateful that I haven't woken up in any strange beds or been crushed by any heavy boxes lately."

"Do you want to discuss what's puzzling you?"

"I'm not ready for that yet. But happy to talk about other things."

"Understood. When we stopped last time, you were telling me about Harrison. You intimated that there was an upsetting split but didn't want to elaborate, so let's fast forward. How long did it take you to get back on your feet after the breakup?"

"Do you mean, emotionally? Workwise? What?"

"Well, emotionally to start with."

"I don't know that I ever have, to be honest. It was a very difficult period."

Dana grew silent and sat for a moment with her thoughts. She took a deep breath, trying to summon the strength to continue.

"Shortly after I left Harrison, I got news that my grandmother Gloria had died. Lung cancer, thanks to the sulfur in the air. Another Centralia casualty. Antoinette received a letter from my sister and in turn, emailed me, but by the time I heard, they'd already buried her. I was devastated. I drove out to pay my respects…and I swore…" Dana felt her face swell and grow hot with fury.

"You swore what?"

"I swore…I swore…I'd never forgive myself or my

family for not being there when she needed us most."

"You had no way of knowing—" started Dr. Lawrence but Dana shook her head violently, angry that she had almost said too much, almost broken her promise to herself.

"Enough about that. Enough. Let's just say that after losing both Gloria and Harrison within a month of each other, I swore to keep things light, non-committal. So far, so good."

"Including the current partner who's holding back on that alibi?"

Dana ignored the question.

"Workwise, after the breakup, I left the travel magazine. I didn't want to end up with assignments where Harrison and I might run into each other. Too many memories, too awkward."

"So you totally uprooted?"

"Not a lot of choice. I loved living in Manhattan, but without his lion's share of the rent, I couldn't even afford a fleabag hotel. And our friends from the scene? They were more interested in getting us back together than taking me in as a roommate. So I called Endicott."

"Your college friend."

"It definitely wasn't an easy call to make. We hadn't spoken for several years, other than an occasional postcard. Somehow, when I'd left college, it seemed easier to make a clean break from my old life than have a foot in both worlds. But now, I didn't have a foot in either."

"How did that go?"

"Endie is such a gem. No animosity. No reproach. We picked up as if I'd never left. The only difference being, he'd gotten his real estate license in my absence."

"And he helped you find a place?"

"Eventually. When I first got back into town, I had no income, almost no money left. He let me stay with him for a while until I found work, rebuilt my savings. All he asked for in return was a New York City care package—David's bagels, Magnolia's cupcakes, a vintage Chardonnay..."

"Sounds like a great stopgap solution."

"Almost. Except that his boyfriend, an IT guy named Grayson who had moved in during my absence, was none too thrilled with me suddenly being underfoot. I don't know if he saw me as a threat to their relationship or what, but he was so nasty. Accusing me of slumming, of using Endie for his friendship and generosity."

"So how did you mend those fences?"

"I cooked and cleaned for them every day—which showed Grayson that my intentions were honest—and called the marketing department of every business in town, asking if they needed any freelance corporate communications work—brochures, newsletters, that kind of thing. Grayson was satisfied that I was working hard to get myself out of their hair, and he calmed down."

Dana reached over and grabbed a Krackel mini.

"After a few months, with some cash in my pocket, I started calling around Gresham for rentals. I couldn't find anything I liked, or anyone I wanted to room with. That's when I started to research real estate loopholes so I could actually buy a home of my own."

"I didn't realize there were many loopholes."

"Oh, back then? Yeah, you'd be surprised. And for me, it was simple, having a friend in the business and all. I asked Endie to search for any listings that were basically unsaleable, and he came up with 41 Pine Valley Court, a property so dilapidated and overpriced, no one had shown it in months. Apparently the absentee owners,

Jay and Amy Ladinsky, were either too unrealistic or too busy to care."

"Does that happen a lot?"

"Unfortunately, yes. Anyway, on a Monday, I wrote a letter and mailed it to myself at the house's address. On Wednesday, I went to the home, suitcase in hand, along with a duplicate key Endie had 'mistakenly' slipped into my purse. Once inside, I called the phone company and had the service transferred into my name, claiming I had rented the home from the Ladinskys."

"And they did it, just like that?"

"Yes. It's amazing that no one at utility companies ever thinks to double-check the leases. I guess that's the beauty of bureaucracy; no one wants to take responsibility or initiative. Anyway, next I called the local locksmith and had him swap out all the cylinders. He never even asked if I owned the place."

"Unbelievable."

"I know. People were far more trusting back then. Even when I hired a local painter to coat the entire interior of the house in the most vulgar of colors—fuchsia in the living room, dark brown and yellow in the dining room, and black in the bedrooms."

"Didn't he think it was odd?"

"Oh yes, but when he started to ask questions, I told him I'd pay him double if he just forgot his curiosity. And forgotten it was."

"Fascinating. I never knew any of this was possible."

"It's not as easy now, since they've clamped down some, but back then? Anything was possible as long as you understood the way the law was written. Once I had lived in the house for thirty days, paid for any renovations, had utilities turned on in my name and arranged for mail to be delivered to Dana Black—all without anyone protesting—it was essentially my home. Squatter's Rights and all. Anyone who wanted it back would have to file for eviction. Turned out it was a year before anyone noticed. By that point, the Ladinskys had declared bankruptcy, losing the home to First United."

"Didn't the bank force you out?"

"Luckily, it's not that black and white. New York State protects its tenants. When they discovered I was living there, they filed for eviction. I ignored the notices. Rather than harass me and risk having me destroy the place, they came up with a compromise. The bank manager offered to let me stay on for free as long as I maintained the property and allowed agents to show it. Evidently, that was less costly than paying the legal fees to evict me, and then assuming the utility and winterizing costs. So I agreed."

"And it sold?"

"Uhh, no. But I'd laid the groundwork from the start. Turns out buyers couldn't see past bright pink, dark brown, and black walls. After a few years, when the bank lowered the price of the house to what I considered rock bottom, I purchased it myself, with the provision that no one would ever mention my squatting history."

"Wow. That's an amazing story."

"Thank you." Dana stood up and took a little bow before grabbing a Mounds and plopping back into the recliner.

"Sounds like you had your career on track and your real estate needs filled. How about your love life? Is that when you met Mr. Alibi?"

Dana had skated around the topic of Dare for the past three sessions but now, on this warm February afternoon, the ice was starting to crack under her feet. She pursed her lips and checked her watch.

"That story will have to wait for a different day, I'm afraid. I have a listing appointment across town. We'll pick this up next time, okay?"

But she knew that based on the direction the conversation was headed, next time would never come.

CHAPTER 26

February 25th

AIDAN DIDN'T HAVE A LOT to go on, but decided to start with Vampira, the munch newbie who originally directed Dana his way. His sister Laura, a.k.a. Bette Screams, connected him with Vampira, who in turn, pointed Aidan to someone who could help.

Auntie Maim, known outside the scene as Vanessa, initially refused to speak with Aidan, reluctant to discuss her close friend behind her back. But when the detective expressed concern for Dana's safety, Vanessa agreed to meet him for lunch at D'Alliance, a hip bistro on Gresham's west side.

Vanessa was practically incognito when she entered the restaurant, her signature 'scene' outfit of peasant garb and multi-scarf hairdo replaced by the conservative corporate attire befitting her role as bank executive.

"What's up, Cummings?" She smoothed her gunmetal grey suit and sat down, immediately reaching for the menu. which she started to scan. "How can I help the cause?"

Aidan put his finger on top of her menu and pushed it downward so they could look eye to eye. "Up to now, the murderer has only targeted agents from Rock Canyon Realty so it's fair to assume that's where he'll strike next. I am checking into each agent's background to see if there's any common thread between the deceased agents and the ones that might be next on his list." A plausible story, he had decided, one he was rather proud of. "Anything you can share about Thissie's private life, her early days?"

"She's okay with this?"

"I didn't want to disturb any of the agents, raise anxiety levels higher than they already are. So I'm conducting research on the sly. I'm hoping you'll keep this between us. There's no need for you to share anything you believe Thiss would consider confidential. Can I count on your cooperation?"

Vanessa peered over the top of the menu and nodded. "Sure. As long as you'll permit me to study this thing so I can order."

After selecting the cassoulet, she gave Aidan her full attention. "What do you want to know? I'll tell you what I can."

"Start at the beginning. Anything unusual about her past?"

"I know she grew up dirt poor. Lived with her grandmother in some hell hole of a coal mining town in Pennsylvania that's always on fire…Central something. Apparently, it got so bad the government paid everyone off and evicted them, and she came up here to Gresham for college. In either her sophomore or junior year—I can't remember which—she got chatted up online by a guy who was part of our munch group—this rich travel photographer from Manhattan."

She picked up her water glass, admired the crystal, and took a few sips.

"That's when she and I met. He brought her to some of our get-togethers. Soon afterward, she moved in with him and he got her a job at some magazine. Toured the world for years, him shooting pictures, her writing the articles. We all thought it was a great match. Well, at first, anyway."

Aidan's stomach twisted as he thought of Dana with another man, especially one rich enough to offer her all the niceties that he couldn't afford. Certainly not on a private investigator's salary, anyway.

"What was his name?"

"His nickname was Pornfree. His real name? I think it was Harold or Harry or something like that. We don't do the 'real name thing' much around here, as you well know."

"You said it was a great match *at first*. What did you mean?"

"PF—that's what we called him—swept Thiss off her feet. Expensive dinners, theater, jewelry, you name it. He made her the center of his world. It would have dazzled any woman but Thiss, growing up a pauper, her grandmother working all the time? All that attention was extra exciting. Her first love. She fell hard. I kept checking the mailbox for a wedding invitation. But after a few years, whenever I'd hear from her, she sounded troubled, anxious. I got concerned, so the next time she was in the city, I insisted we meet for dinner."

The waiter interrupted, serving them a cassoulet and a roasted codfish dish called *cabillaud r*ôti. Thank goodness for expense accounts.

"So what was the deal?" asked Cummings, in-between forkfuls of fish.

"Thiss was an emotional wreck. PF changed moods faster than he changed his designer suits. When they were in New York, in-between trips, he became bored, like a caged animal, desperate for stimulation. He'd get angry and depressed, close down. She said he took risks she couldn't abide. Some days, he went on shopping sprees and maxed out his credit cards. Or shoplifted. Other days, he went skydiving. She was at a loss; she didn't know what to do."

Aidan felt an ache in his chest, contemplating Dana in emotional pain. "Bipolar?"

"That's what our munch group figured. We see it sometimes in the scene. From what I've read, people suffering from bipolar syndrome tend to be adrenaline junkies with a need for high stim activities. And the sex games *we* play can definitely be high stim. But that's not to say everyone in the scene has mental issues…"

"No, of course not."

"But in this case, that was clearly the situation. I begged Thiss to leave him, return to school or to her grandmother. But she felt this deep loyalty toward PF. He had done so much for her. So she ignored my advice. A few months later, her world caved in."

The waiter came back to fill their water glasses but Aidan shooed him away.

"Don't stop there. What happened?"

"They were back home in Manhattan. He told her he was going out. No explanation of where. She asked him to stay, to help her edit an article. He ranted on and on about how she didn't own him, that he was in charge of his world and he could do anything. He believed it too, that the world was limitless. I'd heard him give those kind of speeches myself. So she let him go, scared to spar with him when he was in that kind of mood. Turned out he'd gone to the racetrack."

"Horseracing?"

"No, drag racing. Some professional track. Apparently, he'd been going for some time. Without her knowing, obviously. Borrowing some friend's car."

Aidan put down his silverware. He has lost his appetite.

"He was gone all day. Not answering his cell phone. Thiss was worried sick. Around 9:00 pm, there was a knock on the door. Three guys she'd never seen before, two representatives of the racetrack along with a police officer. They told her there had been a terrible accident. She assured them they had the wrong address, no one there raced. But I think, deep down, she knew she was wrong. Yet another crazy, death-defying stunt.

"They came in and sat her down. Told me how PF's car caught fire during a run at about three-quarter track. At that point, he lost control, and the car went airborne. He struck a retaining wall, and the fuel cell exploded. He was trapped inside the car upside down."

"Oh my God. Was he okay?"

"They almost didn't get him out in time, but he lived. He had a concussion, and they kept him in the hospital for observation, but amazingly, he was otherwise unhurt. I wish I could say the same for Thiss. She was the one left shell-shocked. A few days after he came home, she walked out."

Aidan stared down at his plate, feeling useless, overcome by a desire to wrap his arms around Dana and make it all better. He could scarcely imagine what she had endured—the sorrow of losing her soul mate, the anger over the demons that made him take stupid risks. The realization that their love life hadn't been enough to satisfy him. Now he understood a little better why she tolerated her non-committal relationship with Dare, why she avoided the disappointments that came with long-term planning.

"Has this been helpful at all?" asked Vanessa, finishing off the last of her stew.

"Extremely, thank you."

"Good because…" Vanessa's voice trailed off.

"Because?"

That tiny nudge was all Vanessa needed.

"Because he still calls her. Wants her back. She won't pick up the phone but I know he leaves messages on her voicemail. Cummings, please, please, please don't tell her I told you this, but he's a loose cannon. I worry what he's capable of when he doesn't get his way." She gave him an imploring look.

"I promise not to say a word."

"And it's not like Dare is going to protect her," she added, her lips puckering at the mention of name as if she'd just sucked on a lemon. "Him being *married* and all."

Click. Click. Click.

Aidan had never considered that the killer might have a personal, non-real estate-related vendetta against a single person. Could this PF character be out to destroy Dana's life as payback for deserting him? Killing her fellow agents and then setting her up to take the fall? It was a possibility. But there was something else. He'd never realized that Dare had a wife. It made him even more of a bad choice for Dana but it also explained why she was reluctant to use him as an alibi. And in the plus column: Vanessa was patently hinting at a potential opening in Dana's love life. Good. He needed someone in his corner.

"Don't worry, Auntie Maim. I'm going to do everything in my power to keep Thiss safe." And he meant it in more ways than one.

CHAPTER 27

February 25-26th

AFTER LEAVING D'ALLIANCE, AIDAN DUCKED into the nearby Gresham Library and started researching towns in Pennsylvania starting with the letter C. It didn't take long to find Centralia and read about its long, slow demise. How the fire had started just before Memorial Day in May of 1962, when the town council hired the volunteer fire department to clean up the smelly town landfill, located next to the town cemetery where the mourners would soon congregate. They set it ablaze but, unlike in previous years, they failed to fully extinguish it. The flames spread, unnoticed, through an unsealed opening in the landfill pit to the maze of abandoned coal mines that lay beneath the town.

By 1981, the steam caused by the fire started causing sinkholes. The first one measured four feet wide by 150 feet deep and nearly swallowed up little 12-year-old Todd Domboski, who had been playing in his own backyard. Had his older cousin Eric not been there to pull him out, he would have surely perished. The town analyzed the steam billowing from the hole and found it contained lethal levels of carbon monoxide—a sure sign to abandon ship.

Aidan shook his head in disbelief as he continued reading. Even with poisonous gas permeating the ground, the local residents failed to act, many arguing that the fire didn't pose a direct threat to the town. Time proved them wrong. In 1984, Congress stepped in, offering more than $42 million to help the townspeople relocate, but many stayed on. In 1992, the governor invoked eminent domain, condemning all properties in the area, and yet some hangers-on remained, even past 2002, when the U.S. Postal service revoked Centralia's zip code.

So that's where Dana gets her stubborn streak. He decided to make the trek to Centralia to see what else he could uncover about Dana and her grandmother.

Bright and early the next morning, Aidan stopped by the bakery, picked up breakfast in the form of a half-dozen black-and-white cookies, and then embarked on the three-hour, sometimes scenic journey, from the Hudson Valley to Pennsylvania.

He arrived in Centralia a few minutes after noon, startled to find the eerily silent, deserted streets totally devoid of snow. Instead, intermittent patches of brown-gray grass dotted the landscape, from which occasional fumes of smoke escaped into the air. On what must have been the ghost town's main thoroughfare, a few remaining ramshackle houses remained, perilously unsteady and mournfully isolated. To Aidan's surprise, on the corner he spotted a young man with curly red hair, perhaps twenty or so, clad in a heavy parka and painting a glorified shack. He headed over.

"Hey, you got a minute?" he called from his car window.

"All I've got is time." The man set down his brush

and headed over to Aidan's car, arm extended. "Name's Jedidiah Valentine. But everyone calls me Jeddy."

"Everyone? I didn't know anyone still lived here." Aidan shook the man's hand.

"You with the government?"

"Me? No, I'm out exploring. I've been thinking about filming a movie about the area. A documentary about towns that have fallen on hard times."

Jeddy's interest suddenly piqued. "There's a few of us still here. Me, I got nowhere to go. This is my folks' home, paid for free and clear. I'm not going nowhere until they force me out with a shotgun and maybe not even then. Happy to talk 'bout that on camera or 'bout whatever you wanna know."

Aidan tried to dodge the spittle that flew from Jeddy's mouth as he became more animated, but it was a lost cause. He dug around in his jacket pocket for some tissue.

"Can you tell me if anyone is still around from maybe, thirty years back?"

"The one old person still here is Emma Mae. She said she'd never leave and hell if it didn't turn out to be true! Law came and tried to force her out but she got her kid, lawyer out in Ashland, and he brought the news folks from Channel 12 and yelled on and on about age discrimination, racism, whatever he could come up with. Finally, they let her be."

"Good for her. Where can I find Miss Emma Mae?" Aidan dotted his face with the tissue, trying to be inconspicuous. He had no desire to offend such a willing source of information.

"Sure you're not with the government? 'Cause it's against the law if you say you ain't and you really are. Lawyer told me that too."

Aidan held up three fingers. "Scout's honor."

"See that house on the other side of the street?" Jeddy pointed at the solitary structure across the way.

"Couldn't miss it if I tried."

"You'll find her there. Should still be awake. Don't take her afternoon nap till 3:00 pm."

Aidan gave him a smile. "Thanks for your trouble. You need anything—anything I can get you from the next town over?"

Jeddy studied the car, tried to peek through the side door window. "Got any Elton John records in there?"

"Nah, all out. Got a black-and-white though." Aidan reached into his stash, pulled out his last cookie, and handed it over.

"Hey, much obliged. Say hi to Emma Mae for me. And don't forget to come back with your movie camera!"

Aidan drove down the street and walked up to Emma Mae's front door, giving it three loud raps. After a minute, a frail, African American woman appeared, wearing a pale pink housecoat and her silver hair in a bun.

"Can I help you?"

"I'm sorry to disturb you, Miss Emma Mae. Jeddy from down the street said you might be able to help me. I'm a detective and I'm trying to find out some information about someone who used to live around here. A Miss Dana Black?"

Emma Mae's eyes lit up.

"Dana? That's Gloria's granddaughter. Is she okay?"

"I hope so. She might be in a tight spot, and I'm trying to find out as much as I can about her past so I can help her. Would you mind answering a few questions?"

"Oh, oh. Yes, of course. Dana was such a lovely girl. And oh, how Dana adored Gloria. The two were inseparable. I don't want anything else to go wrong for her. Come in. Please."

Emma Mae led Aidan into her small sitting room, decorated in early flea market, with a variety of furniture styles and knickknacks, and asked him to sit down. She offered him tea but he declined, eager to get to the point.

"Miss Emma Mae, you said you didn't want anything *else* to go wrong for Dana. What did you mean?"

"She had a hard life, is all. Gloria lost her husband during World War II. He left right after Cassandra—that's Dana's mother—was born and he never came back. She scrambled to make ends meet, taking in boarders, doing whatever it took to raise that child alone. Then, after all that, when Cassie turned 16, she ran off to New York City to be a big star. That pretty much killed Gloria. She didn't hear from Cassie for years."

"*'It's a sair ficht for half a loaf,'* as my grandmother would say. Life's hard and you only get out of it about half of what you wanted."

Emma Mae nodded and continued. "Next thing she knows, it's the early 1980's. Cassie's living in Drysdale, raising two kids, selling real estate when her husband dies. So she comes back and leaves six-year-old Dana, her youngest, on Gloria's lap. Tells Gloria to change Dana's last name back to Black so no one gets suspicious about her living here. Then takes off again."

Aidan's eyes grew wide. "What happened to the father?"

"Never said. Gloria didn't ask. Cassie started over. Moved to Rock Canyon, sold lots of homes, and showed up every few months to take Dana out, leave a few bucks."

"By that point, wasn't the underground fire making it difficult for them to remain here?"

"Oh yes, but Gloria conveniently overlooked all that. I think she was so grateful to have Dana living here, she closed her eyes to a lot of things. A second chance to enjoy a child. Something she could never do when she was working herself to the bone to raise Cassie."

Emma Mae shook her head, remembering.

"She had the cough bad but she got Dana away from the fumes as much as she could. She took cleaning jobs in Ashland, even talked one of her clients into letting her use their address so Dana could go to school there. Poor kid. Spent half her day commuting, always wondering when her mother was coming back to take her home for good. Always asking why her sister never called or wrote. But we never saw her cry. Not once. Thank goodness that money showed up when it did."

"You mean the money from the government? So they could move out of town?" asked Aidan, remembering Vanessa's story.

Emma Mae cocked her head to the side and eyed Aidan curiously.

"The government never gave Gloria any money. She damn well refused to give up her home. She lived here until the vapors got her."

"But…I thought…where did the money come from to help Dana pay for college?"

"Another good question. We never knew. Gloria thought it came from Cassie but Cassie said no. Anyway, Gloria never let Dana know she hadn't left town. She'd write to her at college, using a P.O. box as a return address. Whenever Dana came to visit, Gloria claimed her new place was too small and messy to entertain. Always met her out at some diner. Then Dana went off to Paris to study and it wasn't an issue anymore. Gloria kept that secret till her dying day."

"When did she pass?"

"Must have been what, seven, eight years ago? You have to forgive me, dates get hazy for me these days. In any case, Dana never came to the funeral. I was surprised, but guess maybe being in Paris and all, word got to her too late. Last time anyone ever saw her around here was a few months later."

"She came to pay her respects?"

"In a way, I suppose. I didn't see her myself but Jeddy did. He happened to be walking by the cemetery when he heard her raising up a hell of a ruckus. She was standing over Gloria's grave, throwing stones and screaming something like, "I'll get you for this. You had the money but you let her die anyway. I'll get you. I'll get you all." We never saw her around here again after that."

Aidan sat, silently taking it all in. Vanessa had mentioned that Dana had lost her grandmother and PF around the same time. But there was so much she'd omitted—if she even knew. A dead father. Abandoned by her mother and sister. Living in this toxic town, every breath of air a potential death sentence. What does that do to a person? He had to find out.

"Emma Mae, one other thing…"

"Yes?"

"You said Dana changed her name back to Black. What did she change it back from?"

"Beckett. She was Dana Beckett."

"Thank you, Emma Mae. You've been more help than you'll ever know." He shook her hand and ran out, determined to hightail it to Drysdale before its library closed for the day.

CHAPTER 28

February 26th

AIDAN, DRIVING AT BREAKNECK PACE, ran a few red lights and stop signs on the deserted, one-lane Pennsylvania roads heading to Drysdale, and managed to make it to the library by 3:45 pm. The librarian was very accommodating and led him right to the Reference Room. She explained apologetically that they were years behind larger cities like Rock Canyon and Gresham when it came to scanning past issues of their newspaper onto the Internet so he'd likely have to search microfiche for what he needed. He started with January 1980 but it was close to 5:00 pm until he found what he was seeking on the front page of the issue dated March 14, 1983:

Husband of Top Realtor Dead: Found by Teenage Daughter

Brent Beckett, 45, former stock market speculator and husband of top area real estate agent Cassandra Beckett, was found dead yesterday afternoon in the living room of his home at 72 Cavalry Court, in the Sandusky section of Drysdale. Police report that Beckett was found with a revolver in his right hand and a bullet lodged in his skull. The body was discovered by daughter Melanie, a high school junior, upon her return home from class. At the scene, police found Melanie's sister, Dana, beside the body, covered in blood and cake frosting, wearing a party hat and mumbling incoherently. Yesterday was her sixth birthday.

Neighbors and friends report that they were not surprised by Beckett's death, which is being characterized by investigators as a clear case of suicide. They described the deceased as being "low in spirits" due to prolonged unemployment.

"What do you expect?" said his father William, speaking from his home in Dublin, Ireland. "He was Irish, and we are proud people. He was not happy being supported by that wife of his." Others remarked that they hadn't seen Beckett socially in years.

Wife Cassandra Beckett of Foremost Realty could not be reached for comment. Services are yet to be scheduled.

It's gaein be awricht ance the pain has gane awa, thought Aidan. Even the worst of times turn good again. But after this glimpse into Dana's dismal past, it was clear his grandmother's favorite expression didn't always apply. Bad enough that her father was gone, but she saw him commit suicide? How would a six-year-old react? With grief? Or with guilt that it was her fault, or maybe that she could have stopped him? It was a miracle she wasn't a basket case. A trauma like that—it had to leave a person with major issues. Precisely how deep did that damage go?

Something else was bothering him. The sister. Named Melanie. He put the microfiche away and walked into the main reference area.

"We're closing in 15 minutes," warned the librarian.

"I won't need that long." Aidan grabbed a spot in front of a computer. He pulled up Google and entered 'Melanie Beckett' into the search box. Bingo!

Front page of the social section of the Rock Canyon Gazette, dated September 2, 1990:

Rising Gazette Journalist Weds Local Realtor

Reid Wright, Northwestern graduate and rising star reporter for our very own Rock Canyon Gazette, today wed real estate broker Melanie Beckett, daughter of realty magnate Cassandra Beckett. The ceremony and reception for 300 was held at Manhattan's Plaza Hotel. The couple plans to reside in Rock Canyon within the Beckett family compound.

Aidan stared at the photo of the happy couple. Melanie looked considerably younger and less haggard than when they'd spoken at the office following the hoarder box debacle. But Reid…there was something so familiar about him. He couldn't put his finger on where he'd met him but he knew that eventually, it would come to him. He realized he had about five more minutes until the library closed. He quickly googled 'Cassandra Beckett,' just for the heck of it. A series of entries popped up but he clicked on the one that came up first, dated December 2nd, 2007 and again appearing in the Rock Canyon Gazette:

Local Realtor Cassandra Beckett Suspected in Rental Scandal

On December 1ˢᵗ, a long line of moving vans, U-Hauls and overladen SUVs jammed the streets and driveways of seven Rock Canyon homes. Reportedly, each property had been rented out to seven separate individuals and couples, all allegedly represented by the same individual, local real estate broker Cassandra Beckett...

Aidan blinked. The story went on to describe renters screaming, crying, demanding their money back. Their lawyers insisted on free housing for a year to cover their clients' inconvenience, plus compensation for their embarrassment at being made to look foolish in front of the entire world. Cassandra Bekett, of course, could not be reached for comment.

He remembered seeing another entry of interest and scrolled back to bring it up onto the screen. It was dated the following day, December 3ʳᵈ. He only had time to read the first line before the librarian started turning the lights on and off, his signal to skedaddle:

Cassandra Beckett, who stands accused of embezzling hundreds of thousands of dollars from unsuspecting renters, today was rushed to Good Samaritan Hospital, reportedly suffering from a stroke..."

On the drive back home, Aidan's head was spinning as he reviewed all he had learned over the past two days. Dana, seemingly innocent Dana, had emerged from a childhood more hellish than most could imagine. She'd watched her father commit suicide. Then, her mother abandoned her in a town that was practically an allegory for death itself. Years later, when she found out her beloved grandmother had died, she blamed both herself and her family of neglect and swore vengeance.

Then, a few years later, this real estate scandal. The anxiety over which, no doubt, caused her mother to have a stroke. It made no sense to think Cassandra was behind the scheme. She was a real estate mega-agent from everything he'd read. Why would she risk her license and reputation on some scam?

And why had Dana conveniently neglected to mention that she was related to Melanie, the lead agent at the firm, the one with the target on her back? He decided to keep what he'd learned to himself, not let on that he knew her secrets. But why hadn't she confided in him? Could she actually be the one behind the murders? After all, she had reason to hold a grudge—a well-deserved one—against real estate agents, especially two of the most successful ones in the area. What really brought her back to Rock Canyon and to her sister's firm? Considering her lack of alibis, could she be the guilty one, after all?

"Yer bum's oot the windae," he said aloud, something his father always warned him about whenever Aidan would jump to conclusions and start spewing nonsense. This was Dana he was talking about. He'd watched her for years. *Maybe it was time to watch her a tad closer.*

CHAPTER 29

March 1st

DANA STARED AT THE PHONE and willed it to ring. It was Friday and she still hadn't heard from Dare to reschedule their date, an opportunity to secure her alibi. At first, she hadn't really believed she'd need one. Aidan would find the killer soon enough and deep down, she knew he didn't believe she could be involved. But now that the police had stepped in, the alibi was vital. And more importantly, she needed to know that she hadn't wasted the last seven years playing with someone who wouldn't willingly sacrifice his anonymity to protect her.

It had also been several days since she had heard from Aidan. Their last conversation still made her heart ache, but she hadn't managed to come up with an excuse to call. And damn it, why did she even care? Why had Aidan hit a nerve no one else had touched in a very long time?

She spent the afternoon vacuuming and dusting, anything to distract her from her thoughts. But when 4:00 pm came around, she knew she had to make a decision. There was another big party at Quirts and

Squirts starting in a few hours.

Chances were, both men would be there. Aidan, she knew, would be protecting Bette Screams, but would Dare be alone or in the company of another sub? She envisioned her lover choosing from a long line of eager partners, and then settling on the young, nymph-like Faith. In an uncharacteristic display of emotion, Dana grabbed the can of Endust she'd left on the sideboard and hurled it across the room, leaving a grey smudge on the dining room wall.

Don't be irrational, she admonished herself. You've got everything you ever wanted. A non-committal Dom/ Top who services upon request. No rights, no claims— on either side. Perfect, yes? But if so, why doesn't this feel right anymore?

And who's to say that even if Dare were there with someone else, that once he saw her, he wouldn't make an excuse to leave his *sub du jour* and join her? They had been the "it" couple for years, drawing a crowd whenever they played. She wasn't sure if it was the prowess of his technique, or that people really liked to watch smart-ass Thissie get her comeuppance for all those bad puns, but they definitely attracted spectators on a regular basis.

The more she thought about it, the more certain she became that everything would be fine, that she had nothing to fear. To hell with Dr. Lawrence's warnings. Maybe opening up to new relationships would be good for her mental health, but did she really want to settle for vanilla? She needed her encounters charged, theatrical, with a smidgen of fear. Aidan was adorable, that much was true. And she had to believe that watching others play wasn't only fascinating for him, but arousing as well. He must be curious. But after investing nearly a decade into her relationship with Dare, she decided she wasn't going down without a fight.

She hit the kink closet and searched for something provocative to wear under her camelhair winter coat—something designed to stop Dare in mid-stroke. And there it was: a black brocade-patterned corset with a matching ruffled tutu-like skirt, black garters, hose, and 5" spiked heels. Little black sheer gloves that tied at the wrists. Her temperature rose, just picturing herself in the ensemble.

With teased hair, heavy blush and mascara, slut-red lipstick and a spritz of her signature scent, Design by Paul Sebastian, Thissie was ready to rumble.

During the 40-minute trek up to Gresham, she reviewed several possible scenarios and scripts. How she would forgive Dare for playing with others. How she would excuse his hesitance over monogamy, but suggest that perhaps, it was finally time to make their relationship a little more exclusive.

As usual, when Dana knocked on the club's heavy wooden door, Simeon opened it without hesitation and ushered her inside.

"Much of a crowd downstairs?"

"More than usual. Someone's doing a cupping demo. That usually draws 'em in."

"Is Dare doing it?" she asked, her stomach dropping.

"Nah, I think Davo's got center stage tonight."

"Davo? Isn't he that really tall guy who nailed a rubber chicken to a pole at some party and called it cock torture? That Davo?"

"He's a man of many talents."

"Apparently."

She climbed down both flights to find that Simeon hadn't been exaggerating. The place was packed. Dana joined the throng of spectators, all crowded into the demo room where a bearded Davo, clad in a plaid flannel shirt and overalls, stood over his naked and appreciative partner, Subtle, who was lying face down on a table. Using a suction device to pull rounds of skin into small glass cups, Davo had already started to turn Subtle's back and ass into an abstract masterpiece of red raised circles.

"Why is he dressed as a farmer?" Dana asked Willow, a sub from her munch group.

"He came in carrying about ten crops. A few of them had dollar bills attached. He called them his cash crops. Classic Davo."

Dana felt a competitive pang of punnery, but swallowed it.

Across the room, she saw two other observers: Bette Screams and Cummings. Both seemed mesmerized by the demo. Her heart jumped a beat, but she kept her cool, splitting her attention between Davo's scene and Cummings who, dressed in khakis and a preppy white button-down shirt with faded pink stripes—the first three buttons open—looked hotter than any other perv at the party. Maybe absence did make the heart grow fonder after all.

Damn it, that's not why you're here! She tried to turn her attention back to her three goals for the evening: 1. Wow Dare. 2. Get him to commit and 3. Get an alibi. She now added a fourth: Watch the cupping, not the cutie!

Though she'd never been cupped herself, as Dana watched Subtle writhe under Davo's touch, she felt herself drawn in, noting the scene's undeniable sensuality. How can anyone witness this and not understand that vanilla could never compare? Aidan must have sensed her presence and her thoughts. She glanced up and saw him lift his head in greeting. She smiled and returned the nod.

The demo ended and the crowd dispersed. Dana wandered over to the mocktail bar and ordered a cranberry juice and soda. Aidan joined her a few moments later, squeezing in immediately to her right. They stood there, facing forward, pressed hip to hip, for what seemed like an eternity, neither saying a word. A silent game of chicken. She finally turned and saw him suppressing the same grin she'd been fighting for the past few minutes. They both let out a laugh, and the tension eased.

He turned to face her, the tip of his finger grazing her cheek before pushing back a few strands of hair from her face. Time froze as they stood there, gazes locked, the only two people in a crowded room. His hand moved down her back and explored the brocaded texture of her corset. He pushed even closer and whispered into her ear, "I was wondering if you were going to show tonight, Thiss. I was hoping I'd see you."

"I knew I couldn't dodge the law forever." She nuzzled his collar, hoping humor would temper the intensity of the moment. "But I thought maybe you were angry with me."

"Angry? What made you think that?"

"The way you were short with me when I called to tell you about the words on the boxes."

"Oh no, nothing like that. I was in the station working late when you called, and the captain was right there beside me."

"Oh." She suddenly felt very foolish. "Hmm. Any leads?"

He ignored the question. Instead he reached over and selected a lock of hair from the back of her head, and slowly twirled it around his finger. She stood breathless, waiting to see what would happen next. He experimented, studying her reaction as he pulled ever so slightly, one tiny tug, then another. She bit her lip to keep herself from gasping.

His lips were at her ear again. "Want to get out of here and go somewhere quieter where we can discuss it?"

"Yes, please."

"You stay here. I'll go and tell Bette she's on her own tonight."

As Aidan walked away, Dana realized she was drenched in sweat. *I need to clean up a little before we go anyplace,* she told herself. "Tell Cummings I'll be right back," she called to Carlos, the bartender, and then headed toward the bathrooms at the rear of the club.

And that's when she saw them. Not in one of the exhibition areas, with her on a cross or a wheel, and him wielding a crop or whip. That she could have understood. That she could have dealt with. No, there they were—Dare and Faith—secluded in a dark corner, curled up together on a love seat—and even that, she could have forgiven. But they were kissing…and everyone knew that Dare never kissed. Not on the lips. Not in the ten years he'd been going to that club. He'd always told everyone that personal feelings and play don't mix. Play was the stuff of fantasy, not real life.

Except apparently with Faith. With her, it looked like it was very real. And it hit Dana like a sledgehammer to the gut. She stiffened, taking it all in. The room began to blur, and a reflux as bitter as castor oil sprang up and assaulted her taste buds. *I can't risk a blackout, not here, not now.* She ran for the door, desperate to escape before Dare could see her, before she lost control, before she did something she might not remember tomorrow.

The next thing she remembered, she was trying to hail a cab in the freezing cold, wearing only a black corset and crinoline tutu, now speckled white from the lightly falling snow. Then the warmth of her coat as Aidan caught up and wrapped it around her.

"What was that all about?" he half-asked, half-accused, as he tried to catch his breath.

"I'm sorry—Aidan, I'm so sorry—I can't do this now. I...I..."

"You saw them."

"Yes."

"I tried to tell you, but you said you knew."

"I knew there were others, but...I didn't know *that*. I thought the others were like me. Not...not..." The floodgates opened. She couldn't catch her breath between the sobs.

He stood there in the snow, cuddling her, letting her cry into his shoulder. She realized he must be freezing.

"Where's your coat?"

"I was in such a rush to catch up to you, I forgot it inside. Never mind, Bette will get it to me. Why don't you and I find someplace dry, where we can warm up over a cup of hot cocoa?"

She looked up at him and wondered if the usual allure of her puppy-dog eyes was enhanced or marred by the mascara she felt running down her cheeks. "With whipped cream and marshmallows?"

"With anything you want, little girl. Let's get you back to your flippant, punny, frustratingly stubborn self."

CHAPTER 30

March 1st-2nd

THE FIRE CRACKLED AND SPLUTTERED as Aidan and Dana snuggled together on a leather couch under a plaid, mohair blanket at Java, Gresham's all-night coffeehouse. It was deserted, but for a few hipster wannabe writers typing away on their laptops, in-between sips of their mocha lattes. Much to Dana's relief, no one seemed to take much notice of her fetish garb. She didn't want to inadvertently out her detective's double life to the world.

It took two cups of spicy Mexican hot chocolate before he broached the topic of the evening's events. "You up to talking?"

She nodded and licked the cinnamon-laced whipped cream from her lips.

"Thiss, tell me, how did you even get involved with a guy like that?"

"You really want to know?"

"I really do."

She took a deep breath.

"Fine. You have to understand. I'd gone through a rough patch, a real string of losers. First, there was Peter, who decided to pull out Little Peter during dinner on our first date. He even had the gall to ask for critique. So I told him, "Your parents must be very proud," excused myself, and left the restaurant."

Aidan sucked back a chuckle and signaled her to continue. As usual, using humor to both deflect pain and self-medicate was helping her feel a whole lot better.

"Then there was this guy who went by the nickname 'Oster.' Like the mixer? He liked to beat people while they baked. An hour in, I discovered that he was far less interested in sexual stimulation than in eating a fresh batch of Toll House cookies."

"Two for two."

"You got it. But the real winner was Portnoy. At first, I thought the name was merely a witty take on the Phillip Roth character. But no. Portnoy brought me home and handed me a script, containing a litany of emasculating insults which he requested I perform in my best Yiddish accent. When he decided my tone wasn't degrading enough, he smeared pâté onto his penis and went into the other room to fuck a blow up doll. I was torn between yelling out, 'What am I? Not chopped liver?' and reminding him that he never called or wrote. Instead, I took the high road and quietly slipped out the door."

"Funny, Thiss, very funny. Now that we've finished your stand-up routine, can we get around to discussing Dare?"

"Hey, Mr. Spoilsport, I needed to set the scene first, so you'll understand why he stood out and struck my fancy…and eventually a whole lot more."

"Fair enough."

"It was years ago. I'd decided to try a new club called Cane Mutiny. While I hate canes, I can always appreciate a good pun. There had been talk on EPain.com about a

Dom who played there, someone very skilled, fascinating to watch. Since my recent encounters had clearly been somewhat less than fascinating, I decided to check it out.

"I remember the loud, hard-banging beat of Depeche Mode's *Master and Servant* greeting me as I entered the pitch-black foyer, finding my way to the main playroom, thanks only to some tracer lights along the floor. At the back, past the spanking benches, the bondage wheel, and the St. Andrew's cross, there was a wall covered in chain-link mesh and moveable carabiners. This allowed Doms and Tops to easily position their bottoms' wrist and ankle cuffs at any desired angle. There were three spotlights pointing to the wall but a huge crowd surrounded the middle one. And that's where I first saw him. Sure you want me to go on?"

"Absolutely."

She signaled to the waitress to bring her another cup of cocoa, and then continued.

"Dare turned out to be the first person I'd ever met who put any thought or imagination into his play. He was very nondescript, dressed like all of the other Tops and Doms in the club, bare-chested, sporting a pair of comfortable-fitting dungarees. But what set him apart was his brightly colored eye mask, which made him resemble a Mardi Gras refugee. It wasn't his disguise or curiosity about his real identity that had generated the huge audience. It was technique, pure and simple.

"Being shy and demure, as you know me to be, I pushed my way through the horde to get a better view. He was pure, epitomized artistry—an athlete with a suede purple flogger, inflicting a steady, rhythmic series of strokes. The naked girl facing him whimpered, her arms stretched upwards, ankles spread almost uncomfortably apart. With each blow, there was a satisfying thud, but

I could tell that that wasn't what was causing her to moan. It was either shame over whatever crime she'd committed, or the embarrassment over the public display of her punishment that was upsetting her.

"Dare knew it too. He maintained eye contact throughout the scene, and every five strokes or so, he massaged the points of impact and whispered comforting words into her ear. 'You can do this; you can get through this. I'm proud of you for enduring this for me, good, brave girl.' Sweet nothings, but I could see they weren't nothing to her. She nodded, her tacit consent that the scene could continue. I instantly sensed the connection between the two of them. He held that emotional bond with her through the whole scene, alternating between strikes and murmurings, keeping her in a state of thrall.

"When he was done, she slumped against her bonds, thankful that she had made it through, while Dare stood back to admire his handiwork. The sub had red marks painted across the entire front of her body, now limp with relief. He caressed every welt, rubbing each one gently with Aloe Vera. Then he unhooked her from the chain mail as the crowd clapped appreciatively at his finesse. He grabbed a robe that was hanging on a nearby hook, wrapped it around her, and led her to a bench. Then he brought her a cup of cold water and put his arm around her as she rehydrated."

The waitress handed Dana her third cocoa and she took a long sip before setting the mug down on the coffee table that lay between the couch and the fireplace. She stared, mesmerized by the flames, as she resumed her narration.

"I tried to pay attention to the other scenes going on around me but my eyes kept darting back to Dare, and the aftercare he was devoting to his sub. I watched in surprise as another Dom came over and led the sub away. Dare caught me staring and waved."

She turned to face Aidan.

"Still want me to continue?"

"Aye. Tell me everything. I can take it."

"Okey dokey, you asked for it. I blushed and wanted to run, but his gaze was so damn powerful, even with the mask. He walked toward me and asked me my name. I told him "Thissie" and he seemed to recognize it, so I suppose he'd seen my nick online. Then he asked, 'Like what you saw?' in a tone that sounded less cocky than inquisitive. I shrugged, not wanting to seem like some overeager newbie.

"He explained that Randi—the girl he'd been working over—belonged to someone else, and had committed missteps she had to atone for. Her Dom had asked Dare to handle it for him. I told him he sounded like some sadistic gun for hire. He introduced himself and asked if I was in the market for guns."

"Smooth. A regular James Bond. "

"You said you wanted to hear this."

"I did. I'm sorry. Go on."

"I told him no, I'd been home, bored, so I decided to come out and window shop. And he said, 'No one comes to an S&M club just because they're bored.' He wouldn't accept any of my excuses and I liked that. Finally, someone who took charge. He asked me to meet him the next day in town, so he could hear all of my hopes, dreams and confessions. I was intrigued, so I went."

"And you played."

"You know, if all we'd done was play, I probably would have never gotten involved. We shared lunch, discussed our BDSM philosophies and both agreed we didn't want any heavy involvement. He gave me no name other than his nickname and no contact information other than his cell number. But he did offer me reassurance in the form of about a dozen names of subs who he promised would eagerly attest to his safe and responsible play. Which was crucial because, as I assume even you know, Mr. Vanilla, smart players never get involved with anyone without references. One negative review or the hint of dangerous play is all it takes to put a player out to pasture. With good references, however, the world is your oyster."

"I do know a little something about references, yes. Protecting my Domme sister and all."

Dana ignored his snide comment and went on.

"What sealed the deal came after we finished lunch. He walked me over to the bar, handed me a pad, a pen, and a sealed envelope, and requested that I write down every drink order I overheard. 'I'll be back in twenty minutes,' he said, 'and if I've found you've written down fewer than ten orders or you've opened that envelope, you'll never see me again.'

"'What happens if fewer than ten people order drinks?' I asked.

"'You seem resourceful, Thissie. Figure something out,' he said.

"This was different than anything I'd ever been asked to do before, and I was intrigued. When he returned, he scanned my list. Twenty orders in total: five gin and tonics, two vodka martinis, four beers, five glasses of wine, and four more exotic drinks. Then he told me to open the envelope and read what was inside:

Vodka-based Drinks—Whip
Gin-based Drinks—Crop
Rum-based Drinks—Quirt

Wine—Clothespins
Beer—Minutes Wearing Nipple Clamps
Other—Dom's Choice

Your Reward = Utensil corresponding to Drink Type x Number of Orders

"That's when I started to grasp and appreciate the depth of his imagination."

Aidan fidgeted in his seat. Dana decided to press on, to help him to really understand what got her off.

"I have to admit, it became addictive, wondering what new depravity he'd invent each time we met. Every game ultimately linked my fate to my abilities or lack of them. We'd play Verbal Bondage, where he'd start a discussion, but forbid me to use the word "the" or any words starting with *B*. It left me so self-conscious, I'd lose track of the train of the conversation. And when I did, ten whacks.

"Or he'd give me ten dollars and tell me to buy a fancy outfit for the evening. When I surprised him in a lovely gown I'd picked up at a yard sale, he asked to see the matching purse. Since there hadn't been any money left for accessories, another ten whacks.

"He anticipated every loophole I'd try to dangle as an excuse, every way I'd attempt to sidestep his demands in my endearing PITA way. They all received an appropriate, albeit painful, response.

"Dare and I became a *thing*, which didn't particularly endear me to any of the subs at the club, but the truth was, I really didn't care about what enemies I might be making. At last, I was learning about real BDSM, exploring my fantasies and enjoying the ride. It was a creative, exciting time…in Picasso speak, my 'Black and Blue' period. And it remained that way for years."

"Fascinating story, Thiss." Aidan's blatantly sarcastic tone underscored his jealousy, much to Dana's satisfaction. "But something obviously changed or you wouldn't have shot out of that club tonight."

She shrugged, took another sip of hot chocolate, and tried not to be entranced by Aidan's dancing blue eyes. "It's not fair of me to hate Dare for being Dare. He never promised me anything. Nothing is different now than it was yesterday or last week or last year—except tonight, for some reason, I care."

"Maybe you're not the same person you used to be."

"Maybe not. Anyway, that relationship is over, and it's not polite to speak ill of the dead. Let's talk about you. How's the case going?"

"Exasperating at best. There's no one in this town who has anything but contempt for agents. Everyone seems to have a motive. And when I tried to work the personal angle, talk to Melanie Wright's family? She kept blocking me, making excuses. Would you have any idea why?"

Aidan looked Dana square in the eye.

"None." She glanced down into her mug.

"She said not to bother, which seems insane. Why would the town's richest broker, the one with an unemployed, reportedly philandering husband, ignore the fact that he's the person with the most to gain from her demise? Unless of course, she's the one killing off her competition and then trying to throw others off her scent by mailing herself that note. After she destroyed her entire agency's reputation by uncovering the Merriweather Stevens deception, it's clear she'd do anything to stay at number one."

Dana nodded, but inside, a knot was tightening in her

stomach. She was pretty sure Melanie had better things to do than knock off her competitors. But Dare? Could he be the one behind all this? True, he'd been with her when they'd heard about the deaths, but who knew how much earlier in the day those murders had been committed? Where had he been during that time? She had been so crazed, worrying about her own whereabouts, she had never taken the time to consider his.

Now was the perfect time to tell Aidan everything, she realized. Come clean about her alibi, Dare's identity, her blackouts, anything that could help him with his investigation. But how likely was it that either she or her play partner really had it in them to execute anyone? Dare was doing fine financially with Melanie alive. Would he really risk killing the goose laying his golden egg? And as for herself…she was no killer. At least, she hoped not. Did she really want to create that kind of doubt about her character in Aidan's mind?

"I'm really tired." She pulled off the blanket. "Would you mind walking me to my car?"

"Not at all, Thiss. As long as you promise me two things."

"And what might those be?"

"First, that you're not too tired or upset to drive. And second, that I'll get to see you again soon. Under less upsetting circumstances."

"I give you my solemn oath, Detective. On both scores." She smiled, happy with her decision not to stir the cauldron with wild, unfounded accusations. Especially now, when things between them were looking much more promising.

CHAPTER 31

Dungeon: March 13th

IT'S TEN MINUTES PAST MIDNIGHT, and I'm already tingling with anticipation over the day that looms ahead. D-Day. So-called because, for my esteemed guest, the 'D' stands for the Big D. Death. The end of the road. And, not coincidently, the culmination of a plan, years in the making. I check the monitor but there's no movement. I turn on the mic. Time to poke the embers a little, reignite some terror.

"Good morning, Sunshine. It's after 12:00 am, which means today's the day! Any progress on your confession?"

I witness valiant attempts to speak, but no words emerge. Can't have that. Can't have my friend die of thirst before I've had my fun. I head inside the makeshift dungeon with a glass of water and a straw, which I poke through parched lips. My guest draws long and hard, sucking life back into a failing body.

"I want to help. I do," the voice rasps after finishing the last drop and spitting out the straw. "I know that I must have done something somewhere, somehow that's

upset you. I apologize. Please tell me what it was."

"It's simple. Very, very simple. I had a future. You messed it up."

"Wait. What? This has nothing to do with real estate?"

"In some ways, yes. In some ways, no."

"So, you didn't kill the other agents?"

"Oh, I absolutely did. Kind of the frosting on the cake, covering my steps."

I can't hide the pride in my voice. All the work, all the planning. But the reward is going to be so sweet.

"I don't understand."

"Couldn't have 'em figuring out it was you I was gunning for, sweetheart. Agents, non-agents. Over the years, I've managed to get rid of everyone who's ever gotten in my way."

"Sir? Miss? I don't know who you are or what you want, but I'm coming up empty. I can't help you without knowing more."

I'm no moron. Someone here thinks that if they keep me gabbing, I'll give them the ammunition they need to talk me out of my plan. Salespeople. They're all alike. Always trying to uncover motivation.

"Keep thinking. Not like you've got much else to keep you busy, what without access to your precious clients and listings. Think back on the things that were once important to you, places you left, people you lost. Then you'll figure out who I am. Better be quick though. My hospitality is wearing thin, and it's almost check-out time."

CHAPTER 32

March 2nd

AFTER AIDAN WALKED DANA TO her car and wished her goodnight, sadly with only a brotherly peck on the cheek, she drove straight home and jumped into bed. But she couldn't relax, her feelings still a jumble. She'd accepted that her relationship with Dare was over, but she still needed to see him, at least one more time. She deserved some form of allegiance from him, at least in the form of an alibi. Otherwise, it could be her face on a Most Wanted poster hanging in the Rock Canyon post office.

Then her mind floated back to Aidan and how she wouldn't mind being Most Wanted in that particular circumstance. She wondered if she could lure him to the dark side, hand him a pair of nipple clamps or a crop and convince him to experiment.

Ah the irony. I am as bad as my buyers. They demand the impossible trifecta—best location, lowest price and great condition. Kind of like me, wanting Dare's imaginative kink, but with the deeper relationship and emotional intimacy Aidan could provide.

Dana realized that somewhere along the line, she was

going to have to make a choice.

But something obviously changed...

His earlier analysis bounced off the sides of her brain like a Crazy Ball in an empty elevator. How much easier life would have been had she broken things off with Dare as soon as she'd discovered he was Reid. If ending that addiction could have only been that simple...

She remembered the day everything changed. She was in shock, having seen the news reports about her mother's stroke on television. She asked Endie and Grayson if they thought she should go to the hospital. "They think you're in Europe," her co-conspirators reminded her. "You think they're going to believe Cassandra's stroke is being broadcast in Paris? Then again, they're so full of themselves..."

"It's not like you're going to add much—when was the last time you spoke to them? Think they even remember what you look like?" Grayson added.

That logic was irrefutable. She hadn't seen her sister since she was six, her mother since she was fifteen. All she had been to them since that time was a series of correspondence relayed to her grandmother via Antoinette. Her sudden reappearance would not only have been jarring and unexplainable to her family, but also born out of guilt, not concern.

She shot off an email to Antoinette: *If you get some sort of urgent communication from my family, call me immediately at 845-555-2010.* Better to tie up loose ends before they unravel. She couldn't risk her family finding out about her lies and then connecting her to fraud.

The rental scheme had all been part of a multi-year plot to avenge the death of Gloria. And they had pulled it off masterfully.

It had come to her as she was driving home from

her grandmother's gravesite. The best way to make Cassandra pay was to hurt her where she lived—her career. The real estate deals that had always taken precedence over parenting Dana or providing healthcare for Gloria. She drove right to Endie's house, laid out her scheme, solicited his assistance. No fan of mega-agents who demeaned less prolific colleagues—such as himself—at every turn, he was eager to get on board.

Their first step was to have Endie leave his real estate firm in Gresham and apply for a job down at Rock Canyon Realty, where he could act as her man on the inside. Bigger cities meant higher commissions. An ambitious go-getter, he gladly endured the forty-minute commute in each direction to claim his share of the pie.

After a few years, when Endie was no longer 'the new guy' and therefore above suspicion, he and Dana enlisted Grayson's help to break into the Beckett files. As an IT professional who hacked on the side, it was a no-brainer for him to provide them with the fodder they needed: the names and contact information of Cassandra's snowbird clients, the ones who rented out their homes each winter while they vacationed south in Florida or the Carolinas.

Since Endie was a recognizable local agent, they disguised Grayson as Cassandra's assistant, and had him approach seven of these snowbirds in April to list their rentals, five months earlier than was customary. That ensured that the homeowners never called Cassandra in September as they had in previous years; in their minds, everything had already been handled. And as per Dana's theory, her mother found more important things to do than chase after owners to see if they were still planning to rent out their homes over the winter. Again, Cassandra's neglect was about to bite her in the butt.

Right after Labor Day, the trio stuck Cassandra's "For

Rent" signs on those owners' lawns. Since the homes were on the fringes of town, Cassandra never really noticed, not that she necessarily would have anyway. When you are a 'super' agent with 50 or 60 listings at a time, you start losing track.

The trio never advertised the rentals on the Multiple Listing Service, but instead used Craigslist, where interested renters could contact them via an anonymous email address. They priced the homes slightly under market value at around $2,000 a month and didn't make a big deal about restricting pets or requiring high credit scores to qualify.

As they expected, demand for these low-priced rentals was overwhelming. Over the course of September and October, with the homeowners already out of town, Dana, Endie and Grayson cherry-picked seven applications for each one. They chose to work with the most inexperienced of renters—real estate neophytes who didn't really understand the process, and were so happy to be considered that they didn't ask to meet the owner or confer with a lawyer. They blindly signed on the dotted line. Each renter received a one-year lease in exchange for an upfront payment of three month's rent—first month, one-month security, one-month real estate agent's fee. In total, Dana and her fellow schemers collected just under $300,000, which she split into $20,000 increments, converted into money orders, wrapped in Cassandra's letterhead with a request for anonymity, and donated to various Rock Canyon charities.

Then they stood back and waited until move-in day—Dana's moment of revenge—when they knew the shit would hit the fan. But, as glorious as it was to watch the media coverage, it soon proved to be a Pyrrhic victory.

The following day, as they tuned into the nightly news to see if any of the charities had admitted to having received a $20,000 'anonymous' donation, they were shocked to learn of Cassandra's stroke.

Over the next few days, Endie called the hospital every few hours and kept Dana apprised of her mother's progress. No one found this suspicious; every agent in town was watching closely to figure out the best time to swoop in and steal her clients.

"Your mom's doing better," he'd reported. "The doctors believe there's no permanent neurological damage, and she'll be transferred to rehab soon. But Melanie is going nuts. Between hiring a P.R. firm for damage control, going on listing appointments, showing homes and visiting Cassandra, she's a bitch to be around, total horror show. Rumor is they're liquidating some of Cassandra's stock portfolio to pay back all the defrauded parties. And guess who gets to find all those people authentic rentals, at no finder's fee, of course? That's right, yours truly."

"I'm sorry, Endie…I never realized all this would cause you extra work."

"Ah, it's okay, sweetie. Most of them are pretty understanding, happy anyone's willing to help. I guess if they like me, they'll use me if they ever buy something later. The bigger problem is Grayson. He's complaining about all the late nights I'm out showing homes."

"He'll come around."

"I hope so, but he's also a pill to be around right now."

"Are they going to press charges against Cassandra? Are they taking away her license?"

"From what I hear, no. Melanie and Deborah Lee made a pretty convincing argument that if Cassandra wanted to defraud people, she wouldn't use her own signs and operate under her own agency's name. Being as prominent as she is, the authorities seem to agree that she's an easy target. And since we never deposited any of that money into her account, there's really nothing to tie her to the crimes. Plus, there's no real motive."

"Isn't money a motive?" Dana asked.

"Hon, she was never exactly short on funds; she's richer than dirt. I don't think they're going to press charges. Probably not what you want to hear, but really, Dana? You probably achieved your goal even if she doesn't go to jail. I don't think Cassandra Beckett is ever going to sell real estate again in this lifetime."

"It seems like such a shame that we went through all that work for nothing—oh wait, Endie, hold on. I've got a call on the other line."

Dana didn't recognize the number on the Caller ID bearing an international exchange. "Hello...?"

"Thissie?"

"Dare? Is that you? Where are you calling me from?"

"I thought I recognized this number. Thissie, I'm calling from Paris. From the home of a lady named Antoinette Nombidonne. Sound familiar? Because she had your number to call if anyone contacted her about Dana Black or her family. Wanna explain that?"

What the hell? Was he with the police, investigating the fraud?

"I don't understand. Why would you have anything to do with that?"

"Let's see. My mother-in-law just had a stroke, and lucky me. My workaholic bitch wife sent me out on a wild goose chase to find her baby sister, Dana, who allegedly lived at this address. I'm supposed to bring her back home from Paris so she can take care of her sick mother."

His wife? Melanie is his wife? Dare is Reid Wright? Fuck. Fuck, fuck, fuck, fuck.

She sensed it was a lost cause, but she tried to salvage what she could.

"And what would any of that have to do with me?"

"From the pile of correspondence and emails Antoinette has shown me, it turns out that you *are* her sister. But of course, you already knew that. Might have been nice if I'd known it too."

"Right. Because you're always handing out your business card, which reads, 'Melanie Wright's Husband.' and you spend hours talking to me in bed about your *wife*. Really? Do you think if I'd known who you were, if I'd suspected you were married to Melanie, I would have fucked you?"

"I have no idea. I don't know who you are or what kind of game you're trying to pull. Wanna tell me why your family thinks you're in Paris when you're living a few towns over?"

Dana sighed. They were both the butt of some giant cosmic joke, and of course, as usual, Cassandra was at the core of it.

"It's a long story. Please don't tell them where I am. Not yet. Come home. I'll tell you all about it. And we can figure out where we go from here."

Once the shock had worn off, Dana had fantasized a bit about how the meeting with her Dom/brother-in-law would go. How he might punish her for withholding the truth that was as much of a surprise to her as it was to him. What game would he devise to reprimand her? A perverted *To Tell the Truth* or *What's My Line*, perhaps? She'd squeezed her thighs together, just thinking about it.

The actual meeting took place the afternoon following

their discussion. He drove directly from JFK Airport up to Gresham. She'd invited him to her house, figuring all bets were off anyway since he now knew her identity.

She answered the doorbell. He pushed his way past her, without any greeting.

"What the fuck, Thissie?"

"You act like I knew."

"How do I know that you didn't? This is my *life* we're talking about here."

Your life? Not my life, but exclusively yours? More like your meal ticket is at risk.

"What the fuck yourself, *Reid*. I haven't spoken to my sister since I was six, when my mother unceremoniously dumped me on my grandmother's doorstep. The reason I even knew that Melanie got married was because my grandmother mentioned it in one of her letters. No photos. I never knew your name or what the fuck you looked like. Plus, I might add, you never even told me you were married."

"You're telling me you never even researched the wedding pictures in the newspaper?"

Dana glared at him in anger.

"Why? What was the point? I cut myself off from that family when I was fifteen. Maybe it was my survival instincts kicking in, but I stopped following Melanie's life a long time ago because it hurt way too much. So no, I never saw your picture or knew your name. Even though it's not as if you *told* me your real name, even after all this time."

Dare, scratch that, Reid, sighed and shook his head. "What do we do now? I've been commissioned to bring you back to Rock Canyon from the bohemian Parisian lifestyle your family is convinced you've been living."

"Why now? Because Cassandra had a stroke?"

"You knew?"

"You mentioned it on the phone so I googled it." *What difference would one more lie make?*

"Melanie doesn't have time for playing nursemaid. She says it was about time you contributed to the family."

Dana felt her cheeks flush and her head practically explode.

"Time *I* contributed? I haven't been part of that family since 1983. It's fucking 2007. Let me do the goddamned math for you—that's twenty-four years that I haven't been part of anything except my grandmother's pain. That woman breathed in cancerous fumes year after year, working herself to the bone to raise me. Where's *their* contribution?"

"That's not the way they see it. They think you've been gallivanting through Europe, writing stories and having the time of your life." He looked around the living room, suddenly aware of his surroundings. "What *have* you been doing, anyway? These are pretty sweet digs for someone as destitute as you claim to be."

"I'm not destitute. My grandmother was. And I sent her money every month until she died. I do write, but not fiction. Corporate stuff. Brochures, press releases, web content. And this place was a foreclosure of sorts. It came cheap."

"Sell it. You're coming back to Rock Canyon."

"Really? Well, I'm not going." To emphasize her point, she hit her fist against the nearest wall in anger, a pretty stupid gesture because it felt like she might have broken a bone or two in the process.

Reid chuckled, probably reveling in the irony of her hurting herself for a change.

"You okay?"

"I'll live."

"In Rock Canyon." He smiled.

He could be so fucking charming; it was hard for her to stay mad at him. And really, she wasn't as mad at *him* as she was at Melanie and this entire ridiculous situation. Not to mention at herself for actually instigating it. Karma was a bitch.

"Remember, Thissie, *I'm* in Rock Canyon. How bad can that be? We can see each other more often." He winked.

"Right, what was I thinking? We can fuck right on my mother's sickbed while she's sleeping."

"Well, I wouldn't go that far, but there are ways to make this work." He laughed, and she could see his brain churning away. "I'm an investigative reporter. Which means I know locations of condemned buildings, apartments that are cordoned off as crime scenes, that sort of thing. We can get some privacy. And what with you being a neglected child? I bet I can concoct a Cinderella/Prince Charming scene that will make your toes curl."

He walked over and hugged her from behind. She leaned into him out of habit. Then he grabbed her throat and squeezed tighter and tighter, permitting only an occasional gasp of air. Breath play always sent her immediately into subspace, and he knew it.

"You're coming, aren't you, *Thissie*?" he threatened into her ear.

She shook her head, unable to speak. She hated herself for being so weak, for feeling guilty about her mom, for enjoying his touch as much as she did, even now that she knew he was her sister's husband.

One more squeeze, and he let her go. "You've got exactly ten minutes to pack a bag or I'm going to spank you like there's no tomorrow. Get moving."

Later that afternoon, Reid loaded her two suitcases into his BMW and drove them directly from Gresham to her mother's house in Rock Canyon. Make that the Beckett-Wright compound. There were two houses: a mini-mansion, Tudor-style, which was Cassandra's abode, and then a large colonial behind it, where Melanie and Reid lived. She sneered bitterly at both homes as they pulled into the long driveway, remembering the house where Gloria had raised her. A boarding house, renting out rooms to out-of-work miners and the clean-up crews hired to douse the underground flames. The smallest one-bedroom apartment, she'd kept for herself. Gloria had used two bookcases to divide the living room in half, and Dana slept at the far end on a tiny mattress.

The prodigal daughter was overwhelmed with a mélange of conflicting emotions—rage, fear, guilt, apprehension—as she followed Reid down the path to her mother's arched and oversized mahogany front door. Much to her surprise, he rang the bell, unleashing a peal of chimes that would have put a midsize church to shame.

"You don't have a key?"

"Your mother likes her privacy. It's a long story."

A middle-aged woman answered the door, who Dana assumed was the maid until she threw open her arms and yelled, "Dana, my baby sister! Welcome home!"

Melanie pulled her into the foyer and enveloped her in an impassioned hug reminiscent of the day Gloria sent her off to college.

She was startled by this unexpected display of affection and when she pulled back, she was even more stunned by Melanie's severe and haggard appearance. So different from how Dana remembered her. With her hair pulled back, nothing hid the wrinkles more appropriate for a woman ten years her senior, or the dark under-eye circles of someone who, at best, slept three to four hours a night. Real estate was obviously a demanding mistress.

Dana had no idea of what to say or how to react, and peered over Melanie's shoulder to Reid for support. He wasn't even watching; he'd poured himself a double scotch and skulked off into a corner. Not so 'Dare-ing' at home, she thought to herself.

"I'm sorry about Mom." A halfway decent opening comment, and one that was at least partially true. She was sorry to have been the one to cause the stroke, and she regretted having been dragged home to act as caretaker.

"It's been crazy around here. Let me take you into the den so you can see her. We're keeping her on this floor because there's no way she could possibly tackle the stairs. Then we can have some tea and you can tell me all about what you've been up to. I'm so excited to see you!"

Melanie led her down a long, dark hallway to the last door on the left. It creaked as she opened it. The room was also dimly lit, shades drawn. In its center was a hospital bed, with a lift alongside.

From what Dana could see, which wasn't much, her mother appeared brittle and drawn, not at all the dynamo she had recalled in her nightmares, screaming into her cell phone and sending back some disappointing part of her meal, be it a steak that wasn't rare enough or a knife with a finger smudge. Beside her was a heavyset woman with long, reddish hair, wearing Cheapmart's finest.

"She can't get herself out of bed yet, but we're hopeful," whispered Melanie.

The woman beside Cassandra came over and, like

Melanie earlier, shocked her with a unexpected embrace. "I finally got her off to sleep. You must be Dana. I've heard so much about you. I'm Lorelei. Don't you worry about your mom. I'm here and I'll make sure she gets the best of care."

"Thank you," she murmured, still dumbfounded by such an effusive greeting from a total stranger. She watched Lorelei return to her mother's side and dab her brow with a cold compress.

"Who *was* that? And why was it so dark in there?" she asked, once outside the shrine.

"That's Lorelei. Mom's assistant from the office. That's the good news. Originally I thought you'd have to move home to pitch in, but it turns out Lorelei used to be a nurse. She came by yesterday and asked to swap her administrative duties for nursing detail. I guess she must really need the money. Anyway, it felt right, especially since they know each other, and so far, it's working out fine. She says she's keeping it dark because it puts less pressure on Mom's eyes."

Great. So they didn't need her after all.

"You can chat with Mom later. She's already started to say a few words. Phone. House. Sell. Not a lot, but at least it's a start. I'm sure she'll be excited to see you."

"I'm sure."

Melanie led her back down the hall to a much brighter kitchen with a sunny breakfast nook and started feverishly searching through her cabinets.

"What kind of tea would you like? I've got Orange Pekoe, Darjeeling, Irish Breakfast, and Chamomile. Oh, and these adorable little pastries I picked up yesterday." Melanie fluttered about nervously, like a teenager on a first date. "Now where did I put those?"

"Melanie, it's fine. You don't need to go to any bother."

"No, I want to. It's been sooo long."

She decided on Irish Breakfast tea and set down some macarons, a delicacy Dana hadn't enjoyed since a press trip she'd taken to Lyon, years back. The shops in Gresham certainly didn't carry them, but then again, Rock Canyon was a mecca of sophistication in comparison.

"Tell me all about Paris. And your writing. I've dreamed about you and how thrilling your life must be."

This was not the Melanie she had been expecting, the Melanie who everyone said would just as soon stab a competitor in the back as shake their hand. She wasn't complaining, just utterly flabbergasted.

"Unfortunately, the fiction didn't take off so I've been translating French copy into English for multi-national corporations." It was a story she'd fabricated on the drive down, and it wasn't as much a lie as another half-truth. She had been a writer. "And Paris is…Paris. Another big city. Hot in the summer. But very romantic." She and Harrison had been there once or twice, but she decided to stay vague, to avoid making any possible blunders.

"I bet."

Dana set down her teacup and glanced around the kitchen, noting its marble floors and high-end appliances.

"You seem to be pretty well-off. Surely you've been?"

"You know where I go? To the office. And then back. I've dreamt of globetrotting, but there's no time. Always a buyer who's in the middle of a home search. Always a deal that has to close. I wish I could live abroad like you have, but I can't afford to. I have to support my family."

Melanie—rich, successful Melanie—jealous of her?

"But, Melanie, you have so much."

"Perhaps. But I think I'll always be that little girl from Drysdale, scared of losing the roof over my head with every stock market downturn. Maybe you don't remember all the arguments over money, all the trips to the pawn broker, but I sure do. Rich one day. Poor the next. I swore to myself that I'd never live that way again."

"Don't you have someone at the office who can cover for you?"

"Again, I wish. My clients are demanding. They require the best. More than the best. One mistake and you're dead. Like what happened to Mom. Reid must have told you on the flight back from Paris. Someone pulled some kind of stupid scam and now her reputation is shot. I've managed to salvage some of those relationships, but they won't work with *her*, only me. The police said it looks like a set-up, but of course the moving van pile-up made front page news. The truth? That Mom wasn't even involved? Buried on page 14, a week later."

Dana decided to bypass the entire fraud discussion and instead began munching on her third macaron.

"Do you think she'll ever work again?"

"I doubt it. Doctors think she might talk again. And walk again. But not any time soon. It's going to take a lot of rehab."

"Aside from Mom, it seems like all is copacetic in your world?"

"Workwise, yes. Knock on wood. It's not like I have much else." She leaned in close, conspiratorially and whispered, "It's not exactly a carousel of fun at home, you know?"

"You. Reid. Not good?"

"It was never a match made in heaven." She shrugged. "Best thing I got was the name. Wright. The Wright Agent for the Wright Place at the Wright Time."

"You married him for his surname?"

"I married him because I needed to be married. It is what it is. I've got my work to keep me occupied. He's got…whoever he's got. Keeps him busy, out of my hair."

A dumbstruck Dana almost choked on her pastry. Not only was Melanie aware of Reid's carousing, but she seemed utterly oblivious to precisely how creative a player he was. She hoped her sister didn't have any idea of exactly who was keeping Reid engaged.

"You don't care?"

"Not really. As long as he's discreet and it doesn't go public, it's kind of a blessing. I don't have to worry about getting home on time, making small talk, all that garbage. He's got his life and I've got mine."

"So, is there someone else in *your* life?"

Melanie winked and said nothing.

Dana switched topics. "How long do you think you'll need me to stay, now that you've got this woman from the office to help out?"

"You just got here. And it's so nice to have another woman to talk to. It's not like I ever have time to make friends. You absolutely have to stick around for a while. There are years and years we have to catch up on. I don't know what's gone on in your life. You never answered any of my letters."

"Letters? What letters?"

"I used to write them every week. Why didn't you ever write back?"

"I never got them."

"You're kidding."

"No, I figured you all wanted nothing to do with me. When Mom visited, she always said you were too busy to come along, that she didn't want to disrupt your life."

"Wow. She told me the same thing. I always wanted to tag along on her jaunts to Centralia, but she said it would upset you too much."

They gaped at each other, slack-jawed with amazement. Kept apart for years with no idea why. Maybe Cassandra had decided it would have been too much bother to deal with both of them at the same time.

"We're going to make up for lost time now, little sister. How much money do you make writing?"

"Not a lot. Enough to get by, I guess."

"Well, that's all going to change. The housing market is booming. You're going to get your real estate license and you're going to start making some big bucks."

Dana wanted to protest. Considering the lines on Melanie's face and the circles under her eyes, she knew real estate would be taxing. Perhaps even more so than the survival-mode scavenging of her youth. Then she considered her sister's majestic house and its trappings… the Limoges tea set, the crystal chandelier. She pictured the designer suits Endie had been wearing since joining Rock Canyon Realty. And then she visualized having access to the keys of all the empty houses in town. All those potential playdate venues with Dare, who obviously wasn't being missed at home. But the clincher? The realization that this was her chance to actually belong to a family—*her* family. "Okay," she said, surprising herself as much as Melanie. "Maybe I'll give it a shot."

"You? Real estate? Are you going to take the home of every owner you don't like and paint the interior black?"

Two days later, she and Endie were sitting at the Gresham Café, sharing afternoon tea, as he expressed incredulity over her newly chosen career. She doused her scone with an unhealthy helping of strawberry jam and clotted cream, burying fears of leaving Gresham, her adopted hometown, in an avalanche of sugar.

"Oh please, Endie. You could be a little more supportive."

"Oh, I love it. You and me, working side by side. Knocking each other out of deals. Bludgeoning each other's reputation. It's a terrific idea!"

"I don't plan to be that kind of real estate agent."

"No one does. It evolves naturally. Like apes into humans. Only in reverse."

"I can do this. I know I can. And still look myself in the mirror in the morning."

"Uh huh. Whose mirror will that be? The one in the house you'll be sleeping in with your sister's husband?"

"I knew I shouldn't have told you about that. Endie, no one's going to be hurt by my 'borrowing' their overpriced home. Especially if I'm pricing it according to *their* demands. And hey, I can't exactly have him come to my house, can I? Especially now that we'll be living in the same town. He's known, after all."

"Where are you moving to, anyway? In with Sis? Or Mommy dearest?"

"No way. Melanie asked, but I think that would be an awful idea. Reid would freak. No, I found a small studio over on Grant. Very simple. Cheap."

"And what about the Gresham house? You adore that place."

"I'm going to rent it out. I know how much you *love* that daily commute. Maybe I should get a two-bedroom in Rock Canyon instead. Then you could move in with me."

"Grayson would just love that. You're not exactly number one on his hit parade these days, you know."

"I don't understand why he dislikes me so."

"He's very possessive. You're in my life and he doesn't like sharing. The fact that you came first doesn't seem to make a difference. Now that Project Destroy Cassandra is over, he has no more use for you."

Endie reached over and tugged on her hair. "But you'll always be my little Daney Waney Subby Sub."

She rolled her eyes and swatted him off.

"I hate when you call me that."

"I know. Especially when you're the least submissive person I know. That's why I'll say it twice today."

She mock-punched him in the shoulder.

"I think we can make this happen. Working together could be fun."

"I know you think that. Your naivety is adorable. Really. Have you thought about the elephant in the room?"

"What's that?"

"You. Your face, your picture, Little Ms. Whips and Trips, going up on signs all around town. Won't your pervy friends out you to the world?"

"Oh, I wouldn't worry about that. Scene people keep to themselves. They respect each other's privacy. After all, if they outed someone, wouldn't they be outing themselves in the process? No, I'm more worried about you and all these other agents screwing me out of potential deals. Would you really do that?"

"Every chance I get, baby, but don't worry. I may throw you a bone or two while you're starting out."

"Gee, thanks"

"*De nada*, girl. This is Darwin Country. Survival of the fittest. Watch your back, never mention details of a deal to anyone, and never take anything at face value. Remember, buyers are liars and sellers are storytellers."

"But I don't get it. I'm there to help them, aren't I? How can I do that when they're lying to me?"

"They mostly want to help themselves. They don't

really believe they need you. They think they know everything, and you know nothing. They'll try to screw you at every turn so they don't have to pay you a penny more than necessary."

"Lovely. Sheesh, you make it sound like working in real estate would be like swimming in the Amazon with a school of piranha."

"You'd be lucky if they were only piranhas. Selling real estate in Rock Canyon is much more like swimming with the candiru."

"The what?" Endie, the trivia buff, never missed an opportunity to remind her about how much minutiae he knew.

"The candiru. They're tiny Amazon parasitic catfish that either swim into the gills of other fish and eat them from the inside out, or swim up the urethra or anus of humans, who later die from the infection caused by the fish rotting inside them."

"I'll show you, Endicott Coxwell. I'll prove I can swim in the Amazon *and* avoid the piranhas and candiru."

"If anyone can do it, Dana, my money's on you. But while you're in the water, watch out for the pacu. They'll go after your balls and judging by the size of yours, it'll be like Thanksgiving at the Waltons'."

Later that afternoon, Melanie and Lorelei decided Cassandra was strong enough to spend some quality time with her second-born. They ushered Dana in, expecting some sort of momentous reunion. Cassandra opened one eye and groaned. That was it. Welcome home, baby girl!

"Not today," Lorelei sighed. "Don't worry, honey, we'll try again next week."

Dana was not exactly unhappy to get out of that

bedroom and away from the anemic, shriveled version of the cyclone that had once been her mother.

The next month consisted of classes over at the Rock Canyon Board of Realtors. Most of the other students were bored housewives or socialites trying to fill up their afternoons in-between massages and charity work. Rather than fraternize with the likes of Binky, Bumpy and Boo, Dana spent the majority of her time trying to absorb as much as she could.

She never mentioned her connection to Rock Canyon real estate royalty to anyone. After consulting with Cassandra (as best one could, considering her condition), Melanie decided it would be best if people didn't associate the three of them as relatives. "You wouldn't want any of your real estate victories to be discounted as nepotism, would you?" she had asked. While her comments stung, especially since such "discounting" hadn't exactly hurt *Melanie's* success, the truth was that Dana didn't mind distancing herself as much as possible from Cassandra's underhanded brand of real estate. Luckily, since her mother's last name was Beckett, Melanie's married name was Wright, and her grandmother had legally changed Dana's name back to Black, no one would likely connect the three.

The day after she received her license, Deborah Lee Decker called her into the conference room.

"Congratulations, Dana. I'm proud of you."

"Thanks so much."

"I want you to do me a favor. Do you have any clothes that are a little less…tailored?"

She gulped hard. "What do you mean?"

"Something…frankly, something trashy. Hot pants, halter, that sort of thing."

"Um, I guess so. Maybe something from an old

costume party," she faltered, knowing full well that she had a closet full of slut-wear, exclusively for role play.

"Great. On Sunday, I want you to drive over to 20 Augustine Place, dressed in your most provocative outfit. The owner will leave a lounger and a boom box out on the front lawn. All you need to do is sit in the chair, play some loud music, and drink a beer or two, which he will also supply. We'll pay you $100 for two hours of sitting on your ass in the sun."

"I'm not sure I understand. What does that have to do with real estate?"

"Everything, that's what. Melanie Wright, our leading agent, has a home for sale around the corner from Augustine, over at 14 Moseder Drive." Decker handed Dana a listing sheet. "The owners at 30 Augustine are having an open house on Sunday and so is Melanie. We want ours to sell."

"How is sunning myself on a lawn chair going to sell Melanie's listing?"

"No one wants to live next to some cheap skank who drinks beer on her lawn and blasts heavy metal on a Sunday afternoon. At least no one who can afford $430,000 for a home. So we've paid the owner at 20 Augustine good money to let you sit there, turn off potential buyers, and then drive the traffic around the corner to us. Are you with us, or do you want to carry your license over to Milligan Homes where they'll pay you 20% less of a split?"

Dana didn't know why she was so surprised. All that coursework about fiduciary responsibility, just so she could use scare tactics to sully the competition's listings.

"Does Melanie know about this?"

"Know about it? It was her idea. Are you in or out?"

So much for family ties. So much for ethics. Here she

was, embarking on the same unscrupulous path her sister had followed, and her mother before that. The difference being, they were tempted by ambition and money. All she wanted was, not exactly love, but the next best thing: access to empty homes. "Sure," she answered, resigned.

Why not? Welcome to the Amazon. Come on in, the water's fine.

Over the next few years, success came her way, but it was bittersweet. The more she debased herself for the good of her sister and Rock Canyon Realty, the more referrals she received. And the more frequent the invitations from Melanie to join her for lunch, dinner or to just hang out. She refused each one, avoiding her sister at all costs. Bad enough that her naive hopes of a loving sibling relationship had met with a crushing reality. No need to keep going back to polish the sledgehammer.

At Deborah Lee's urging, she'd pose as a buyer for a competitor's listing, simply to sneak a dead rat or two out of her handbag and into the pantry during an open house. Or be the one to break into a basement and pour a few bottles of water onto the side walls right before a walk-through, so the buyer could claim faulty drainage and negotiate a big credit at closing. She'd even infest competitors' houses with carpenter ants pre-inspection, so potential buyers would reconsider their offers and perhaps buy one of Melanie's listings instead. She wasn't proud of such devious behavior, but she and Dare never lacked for a play space either.

Her sister never thanked her for her help or mentioned it in any way. Dana figured Melanie wanted to distance herself from all the ugliness, and let Deborah Lee handle her dirty work. Now that Dana had joined her on the dark side of real estate—too busy to travel and equally complicit in wrongdoing—she imagined that Melanie no longer felt the need to justify her life choices. No more jealousy or regrets over selling out. Every time Melanie topped the charts, she could fool herself into thinking realty was the only reality, that sales were the only things that mattered.

Interestingly, a lot of Dana's customers came from the scene. She concluded that despite Endie's warnings, placing her picture on her signs had been a good move after all. Think of all the potential advertising campaigns: "Dominate the Market, List with Dana!" Or maybe: "Escape the Bonds of Your Landlord, Buy with Dana Today!" In the end, she'd settled on the tagline: "With Dana, You'll Stay in the Black," so she could incorporate her name, and appeal to a larger potential clientele.

During those years, she made her weekly tours of duty to her mother's bedside, partially because it was expected, and partially to assuage her guilt over having caused the stroke. Cassandra was never particularly pleasant, but to be fair, she didn't treat anyone else much better, even her caregiver. Dana found herself coming more to see Lorelei, defending her against her mother's frequent attacks.

The final straw came a few months after Dana's return, when Lorelei cut her hair and died it black.

"What the fuck is that on your head?" Cassandra commented. "A dead beaver?"

Dana was amazed that even though her mother could barely speak, she could manage to conjure up insulting imagery. And so unnecessary and hurtful. Lorelei had obviously been feeling much better about herself since the coif. So much so, she'd pulled back the curtains in her patient's room and let some light seep in.

"Mom, leave Lorelei alone. She's done nothing to hurt you. In fact, she's willing to put up with your crap twenty-four hours a day, which is more than I can say about anyone else around here."

Cassandra mumbled something about Dana not knowing what she was talking about, but the rebuke was effective. She didn't insult Lorelei again, at least publicly, for a few weeks. Meanwhile, Lorelei started bringing Dana lemonade every time she visited. At least someone in the house was on her side.

And life went on that way, month in and month out, until Melanie exposed the Merriweather Stevens hoax and the bottom fell out. Thankfully, Dana's business remained fairly unscathed by the scandal, especially since she'd never relied on pity to secure clients. Her buyers were usually fellow pervs who wanted to work with someone who wouldn't pass judgement as they checked basements for dungeon potential.

After the incident, two major changes occurred. First, Reid lost his job and had much more time during the day to play, usually as an excuse not to work on his novel. Second, and more importantly, Dana made a vow to herself. No more underhanded dealings on behalf of Deborah Lee or Melanie.

By that point, buyers and sellers were hiring her on a regular basis, and she found the satisfaction of helping them more important than the few extra dollars that bolstering Melanie's business brought in. In fact, she was able to afford a new, two-bedroom apartment that she and Endie would share whenever he and Grayson had a spat, which was becoming more and more frequent.

Even Deborah Lee, try as she might, couldn't force Dana to give up her newly adopted standards, especially considering all the revenue she generated.

"Aren't you afraid she'll fire you?" Endie had asked.

"Ha! You'd have to be stone cold and blue to get fired from Rock Canyon Realty," she'd responded. "And even then, they'd triple check your pulse to make sure you didn't have one last deal left in you."

That's when Dana went clean, determined to prove to herself, to Melanie, and to every other agent in the county, that real estate could be an ethical pursuit.

CHAPTER 33

March 2nd

THE CELL PHONE'S RING BROUGHT Dana back from her journey down memory lane. The Caller ID read Endie.

"Ah, the only man in my life who isn't confusing the shit out of me. How are you, hon?"

"Not so good. Are you free?"

"I stopped charging years ago. What's wrong?"

"I'll tell you in person. Can you meet me around 9:00 am? The usual?"

Twenty minutes later, after grabbing the last unoccupied table at Eggs Over E Street, she was sitting down for Saturday brunch opposite a sullen-faced Endicott, looking red-eyed and gaunt.

"What the hell happened to you? What's going on?"

"Grayson left."

"Again?" Grayson had a habit of making empty threats and dramatic, passive-aggressive plays for attention. She was taking this all with a grain of salt.

"This time, it's for good. No ultimatums. I came home and found his closets and drawers cleaned out. He left a note."

"What this time?"

"Same as always. I'm working too hard. I'm never around. When I am around, all I talk about is real estate. His note said, and I quote, 'Other queens, I could compete with. But I won't compete with Queen Annes for your attention.'"

"He sounds pissed. But of course, not so pissed that he couldn't make a bad pun. I respect that. Do you want me to talk to him?"

"Uh, no. That's about the worst thing you could do. He blames you for all of this."

"Me? He blames me? You have got to be kidding!"

The people at the surrounding tables glanced over. She lowered her voice.

"I didn't get you into real estate. Hell, you were a Realtor when I came back to Gresham."

"But you were the one who got me hooked up with Rock Canyon Realty. Your mom. Your sister. All that commuting. All the extra work."

"All the money..." she pointed out. "He seemed to enjoy all of *that*."

"He's got his own IT company. He didn't need any extra money. He's got plenty of his own."

Dana took a deep breath. "Now what?"

"I don't know. I won't miss the hissy fits. Cleaning up after he'd throw his martini glass at the wall during a fight. I won't miss his hair-trigger temper."

"And I won't miss his moods, his gloomy solitudes, his blunt abrasive style..."

"What?"

"Sorry. Lyrics from *Pippin*. Anyway, I don't blame you. He definitely had a violent streak."

"I'm not worried for me. I'm worried for you."

"Why me?"

"He's vindictive. All the stuff we pulled on Cassandra. He knows how to hack, how to screw people digitally. What if he pulls that on us?"

"You think he would actually do that?"

"Hell hath no fury…well, you know the quote. I think if he's angry enough and has free time, who knows what he's capable of?"

Fuck. The last thing she needed now, with the police out combing the streets for suspects with vendettas against real estate agents, was to be revealed as someone who had perpetrated a fraud against one of their finest. But she hid her trepidation behind a mask of bravado.

"I'm not that concerned. After all, I've got someone in my corner who knows his way around law enforcement."

"Wait—OMG! Not that adorable detective who's investigating the murders?" Endie was never too preoccupied to miss out on some racy gossip.

"Yeah, him. But this isn't about me right now, it's about you."

"No, hearing about someone else's romantic escapades gives me hope."

"Don't go rooting around *my* sex life for salvation. I told you, this guy is vanilla. Though he is very cute…"

"Ooh, you're like a schoolgirl with a crush!"

Dana cringed at the thought.

"When are you seeing him again?" Endie had obviously missed out on his second calling as a manicurist at the local beauty parlor.

"I have no idea. Unless you have any leads on who's killing our co-workers. Then I'd have an excuse to call."

"Sorry, no leads. Unless it's Grayson, acting out, blaming the whole industry for our break up. Then you'd better watch out, missy."

"I can handle Grayson. With all the shit I have on him.

I could put him away for years."

"True, if you wanted to put yourself away along with him. You were the inciting cause, as his lawyer will say."

It was true. They were all guilty of fraud, and she knew that no jury was going to agree that the ends justified the means—or that Cassandra had it coming—no matter how manifestly true that was. Especially considering the final result. But Dana owned her role in the fiasco and believed that Grayson should as well.

"So you *are* blaming me for this."

"All I'm saying is that we got involved because of your need for revenge."

Maybe she was overreacting due to lack of sleep, but the whole accusation was infuriating her. Endie was hurting, she got that. But the plan had been consensual, and they had enjoyed every minute of working it. Plus, Endie had profited plenty from working at Rock Canyon Realty. He was driving around in a Corvette, for Christ's sake.

"Fuck that." She shoved her chair back and stood up. "No one is going to say anything or do anything to anyone. And don't go putting all this on me. You don't make an omelet, eat it, lick the plate, and then sue the chicken for laying the eggs. Things got messy. No one suffered for that more than me. You know that better than anyone."

She threw a ten-dollar bill on the table to cover the meal that hadn't yet arrived, and thundered out before she said something she'd regret later.

CHAPTER 34

March 5th

DANA FINALLY HEARD FROM DARE via email, rescheduling their rendezvous back at the house on Devendorf, the site of their memorable game of Bondage Bingo. He tried to make some excuse about Faith since, no doubt, others at the club had let him know she'd seen them together. Dana wrote back, reiterating that they wouldn't meet to play—only to talk, clear the air—and that she needed a favor. She held back on any sarcastic comments about whatever and whomever he'd been doing in the interim. She had no desire to decimate any last chance of an alibi for at least one of the three real estate murders.

After the interchange with Dare, she enjoyed a few minutes texting back and forth with Aidan. Like a horny teenager, she scrutinized the scroll on her phone over and over, searching for any indication of his true feelings.

Thissie: Spill it, Copper. What's the word? Any arrests?

Cummings: Only some complaints of aggravated mischief. I assumed it was you.

Thissie: Me? Isn't aggravated mischief when you destroy property?

Cummings: Yes, they were my complaints. You've totally ruined my train of thought. I can't concentrate.

Thissie: (in my best southern accent, batting my eyelashes and waving my fan) Why Officer, how you do make me smile.

Cummings: I'm glad someone's smiling. Do you have an alibi for me yet? Lasky is on my back about it. I know you're innocent, but he doesn't.

Thissie: I'm working on it. Hopefully, I'll have something today.

Cummings: Okay, good. Please call me when you've got it. Maybe you can tell me about it over dinner. You free? Dare free?

Thissie: Ha, ha, ha. Truth is, I'm over it. Tired of everyone else being Dared too.

Cummings: Good girl. I'm glad. Not just for my own selfish reasons, but because I think you're too good for that. You sell yourself short.

Thissie: Short sales are my specialty.

Cummings: Stop kidding around. I mean it. Someone like you should be put up on a pedestal and cherished. Not beaten down and dragged through the mud.

Thissie: It was oil.

Cummings: Whatever. Stop changing the subject. You know what I mean.

Thissie: I do. Thank you. It's difficult for me to talk about things like this.

Cummings: I think the problem is that you don't really hear people when they acknowledge your value. You're too busy deflecting. It's like you're wearing this impenetrable suit of armor made of puns and humor.

Thissie: I've never really thought of it like that, to be honest.

Cummings: I want us to spend enough time together to

get to know the real you. I'm betting you'll like her too. She looks pretty good from this angle.

Thissie: I have to sign off. I have so many comebacks for that line, my head's going to burst right open.

Cummings: Okay, funny girl. Slowly but surely, I'm going to get you to lower your shield and like yourself. I fear it may take years, but I'm up for the challenge.

Thissie: Gotta love a man who's up. I'll talk to you later.

Cummings: Sure. Leave tonight open.

Thissie: Absolutely. Bye now.

Her smile grew bigger every time she reread the exchange. She couldn't remember anyone ever telling her to stop trying to be funny and just be herself. Or to like herself. Even Harrison would join in her puns and self-deprecating humor, laughing and joking along, until depression would overtake him.

Aidan appeared to enjoy the humor but deep down, he seemed genuinely interested in helping her change. *But aren't you supposed to like someone for who they are and not try to change them? Then again, shouldn't you want to reach out and help someone in pain?* Was she in pain, legitimate pain? Psychic pain? Was she really that emotionally barren? She didn't have any answers, but for someone who was supposedly sterile, a lot of naughty ideas were sprouting up where Aidan was concerned.

Speaking of psychic pain, her mind turned back to Reid, and to his upcoming final appearance, at least in her world, as Dare. They were set to meet at 10:00 am, which was perfect, since it was Tuesday, broker open house day in Rock Canyon. She planned to only stay long enough to convince him to give her an alibi. If she got out of there in an hour or less, she'd still have time to tour and preview some of the new homes on the market. Broker opens meant free food, lottery tickets, wine raffles, maybe even neck and back massages. Listing brokers often spent hundreds of marketing dollars to boost open house attendance; any visiting broker might have the right buyer for their property. At the very least, touring would distract her from daydreaming about her sexy, albeit vanilla, detective.

Endie had sent a make-up email, inviting her to *his* open house on Julianne Lane, and assuring her that he would do all possible to appease Grayson so his ex-lover wouldn't out them as criminals. She appreciated the gesture, especially since Endie was planning to outdo all of his fellow hosts by serving tiny Beef Wellingtons, inspired by his idol, Gordon Ramsay. She made a mental note to hit Julianne first, before all the 'Wellies' were gone.

The driveway was vacant when she pulled up to the house on Devendorf, which was not surprising since she was usually the first to arrive. Even when she did arrive late, there were usually no other cars present since Dare always tried to park a good distance away. But she certainly didn't expect what she saw as she opened the front door. Dare was sitting on an easy chair in the middle of the room, wearing nothing more than a pair of purple Speedos and a matching mask, holding up a flute of champagne. There was a naked girl kneeling on either side of him and one behind him. It was like some perverted family portrait.

"What the fuck is this?" she asked with genuine annoyance. First, he knew that she had no bisexual inclinations. Second, she'd been clear that she didn't like playing with others. And third, he had brought these girls to *her* listing. Dana had no idea who they were, or who they might know. It wasn't being outed as a submissive that was of concern, but she had absolutely no intention of losing her license because of some *ménage à cinq* fantasy.

"I thought we'd play a little game today," he said, with a tiny smirk. "I like to call it: Best of Two Possible Evils."

The presence of others definitely put a crimp in her plans. She quickly assessed the situation, searching for a way to turn it to her advantage.

"Okay. I'll play, if I can call the stakes."

"Wow, you really did fail sub school, didn't you? You're the bottom. You get no say here."

"My stakes or I walk. Your call."

Dare glanced at the girl kneeling at his left and then to the one at his right. "You're honestly going to walk?" He was clearly amused by her stance in light of her utter lack of leverage.

She crossed her arms, tapped her foot and waited. She'd drawn a line in the sand. He either respected her or he didn't. With Aidan's advice about deserving better, she felt emboldened.

Dare seemed impressed. Or maybe so eager to go through with his scene that he was willing to compromise.

"What are your stakes?"

"One favor."

"Which is?"

"This time you have to trust *me*. It's something that I really need or I wouldn't ask you. After all, in all of our years together, what have I really ever asked for?"

He took a moment to consider. "That's fine. You do me a favor and then I'll do one for you. Seems fair. Once you play our little game. And assuming you win."

"I have to win?"

"Of course. Don't you always? I can't very well go

around rewarding you for losing, can I?"

Fuck you. "No, Sir. What do I have to do?"

"For a start, get rid of the clothes. You *know* we don't play in business attire."

She obediently disrobed, practically kicking her blouse and trousers across the floor.

"Okay, a little attitude adjustment is in order, Thissie. Play nice or you're not going to get what you want."

"Sorry."

"Could you be a little less terse?"

Could you be a little less of an asshole? She took a deep breath. The sooner this was over, the sooner she could get her alibi.

"Yes, Sir. My apologies, Sir." She prayed she'd slip into subspace. Quickly.

"Okay then. Best of Two Evils. A derivative of another game I call: Push the Limits. See, I know your limits. No sharing in scene. No girl-on-girl action. No canes. No knife play. And I've respected those limits, haven't I?"

"Yes, Sir."

"I think I've been more than patient, but today, I'm kind of curious to see which of those limits is harder. You're going to have to make some choices."

"And exactly what choices do you mean?"

"You'll find out in time. First, I want you to meet my two friends here. On the right, we have Chiara. Say hello, Chiara."

The girl kneeling to Dare's right—California girl, gorgeous, long blonde hair and flawless body—smiled obediently and whispered, "Hello" on demand. Then she went back to staring at the ground.

"And then on my left..." He reached down and drew the other girl's head up by yanking a fistful of hair, "This is Jaseree. Say hello, Jas."

Jaseree was even more beautiful—Indian, luxurious flowing black locks, also perfectly proportioned. She moaned, acknowledging her pleasure at having her hair pulled, and murmured a soft, "Hi."

Dana instantly hated them both.

She didn't know which was more upsetting: the fact Dare had plucked these girls right out of central casting just to poke at her competitive nature, or that despite her growing anger, Dare had still managed to make her jealous.

"Thissie, you're embarrassing me. Aren't you going to say hello to our guests?"

"Hello." A tone that was curt at best.

"Not very hospitable, Thissie. We'll have to work on that. Oh and meet Grace."

Dare tilted his head back to gaze up at the girl standing behind him. Grace had short, curly brunette hair, a voluptuous physique and a length of red rope draped around her neck. She walked from behind Dare's chair, across the room, and stopped so close behind Dana that she felt the sub's hot breath on her bare shoulders.

"Ask Grace to tie you," he commanded.

"I don't want this."

"I know. You never do. But there *is* something you want, right?"

"Yeah."

"So ask her extra nice and you might get it. Afterward."

Dana didn't think Dare understood how much this game was disturbing her. Or maybe he did understand, and he simply didn't care. Either way, unless she complied, her alibi would prove to be as elusive as he was stubborn.

"Fine. Grace, tie me. Please."

"Nicer."

"Pretty, pretty, pretty please."

Dare snapped his fingers once, and she tied Dana's wrists tightly together behind her back but did not move away.

Two more finger snaps. Chiara and Jaseree started massaging his feet, gently and methodically. Their fingers then slowly inched their way up past his ankles to his calves. Dare's eyes stayed glued on Dana, studying her reaction, which was not a positive one. Meanwhile, his deadpan expression tried to hide his reaction to the actions of the dynamic duo, but the growing bulge in his underwear showed her more than she wanted to know.

"Ask Grace to massage your breasts, Thissie."

"No."

"Okay, then." Two more finger snaps.

Dana winced as the girls' hands traveled from his calves up to his thighs, prompted by her refusal. Their long, expert fingers caressed and massaged the skin that was normally hers to touch. Next the girls stood and turned their attentions to his earlobes, sucking on them as their fingers explored his nipples, slowly circling and caressing each one. Dana watched Dare's erection grow even larger.

"Why are they here?" She scowled. "Why aren't I enough? Why have I never been enough?"

"Because you never commit 100%, Thiss," he said with a shrug.

"You don't believe in commitment, remember?"

"Physical commitment like monogamy? No. But emotional commitment to a scene? Trust? In power exchange, it's everything. I've waited years for you to quit the jokes and the sarcasm and truly submit, but it's never happened. I'm tired of waiting. So these lovely ladies are alternatives. Either you will give me what I want or they will. Let's see what's more important to you—the favor you want or the control you crave. It's all really up to you."

She stared at him in disbelief.

"Excuse me? I couldn't hear you."

"Okay, Grace can massage my breasts.. But please, don't…" Her voice trailed away.

Dare tilted his head slightly, as if considering her capitulation. A moment passed.

Four snaps of his fingers, and both Chiara and Jaseree left the room. When they returned, one was carrying a cane, and the other, a very sharp hunting knife. They walked back to Dare and presented him with the implements. He nodded, and they walked over to Dana. She was now flanked by an armed naked girl on either side, and Grace, naked but unarmed, standing right behind.

"We're beyond the breast massage now, Thissie."

"What does that mean?"

"It means I'm getting tired of these refusals. You're here to serve, not to argue. It's going to take more now to convince me of your resolve to obey me."

"What then?"

He smiled but said nothing. Then he nodded at Chiara.

"Stay absolutely still," he ordered.

As if out of her deepest nightmares, Chiara took the knife, and began tracing tiny circles around Dana's nipple. The tip grazed her areola, but did not cut the skin. Yet it was still terrifying, causing her pulse to race, her heart to palpitate wildly. This was no longer fear play, it was real torture, and it took every ounce of self-restraint not to pull away or scream.

"Say thank you to Chiara for her kind attentions,

Thissie."

"Thank you," she forced out, practically choking on the words.

"Let's move this along. We can continue with knife play, or you can ask politely for the cane. What's your choice, darling?"

"You're asking me to invite you to beat me with that cane? Is that it?"

"No. I'd much prefer to watch you being struck."

She shuddered at the thought. Nothing much scared her in scene except for canes and knives, a fear she had held for as far back as she could remember.

"I've never been hit with a cane," she pled.

"There's a first time for everything."

She stood, uncharacteristically speechless. She couldn't bring herself to obey.

As if sensing her reluctance, Dare broke the silence. "No one is ever going to accuse me of not being fair. I'll give you a third choice. You can bring each of these lovely girls to orgasm. Orally. While I watch. If they say you've done a satisfactory job and I'm sufficiently amused, I'll grant you your favor."

At that moment, something snapped. Maybe last year or the year before, this would have been the hottest scene ever. But right now, her visceral reaction was overriding her usual desire for play. *I don't need to do this. I don't need to be with someone who invalidates my fears and doesn't respect my limits. I'm worth more than this.* And at that moment, she said something she'd never said before in her entire life.

"Safeword."

"What?"

"You heard me. Safeword. Untie me. I want out. Now."

"But your favor…"

"Fuck the favor. I don't need it. And I don't need this. I just want to get out of here."

Ignoring a safeword was the fastest way to be blackballed in the scene, and Dare knew it. He nodded to the girls. Chiara removed the knife from Dana's breast while Jaseree untied her. Then all three girls glowered at her, as if blaming her for ruining their fun, before leaving to get dressed. Dana made a beeline for her clothes, throwing them on without any further eye contact with Dare.

"I'm sorry, Thissie…"

She wasn't interested in explanations or apologies. She simply wanted out.

"Lock the door when you leave and put the key under the mat. I'll come back later and return it to the lockbox. Oh and Dare?"

"Yes?"

"Don't ever call me again." *Slam.*

She ran to her car, drove about two blocks away and pulled over. She was hyperventilating, dizzy, skull about to shatter. She clutched onto the steering wheel for support and rocked back and forth, but the comfort she sought eluded her. Consciousness zoomed in and out like a strobe light, visions flashed before her eyes in quick succession: Jaseree, the cane, Chiara, the knife, Grace, the rope, the overwhelming look of surprise on Dare's face as she safeworded. Then the screen went black.

"Pardon me, do we have an appointment today?"

Dana cocked her head, confused. She was sitting on the floor in the hall outside Dr. Lawrence's office, knees clutched to chest, rocking to and fro.

"How did I get here?"

"I assume you drove," said the doctor. "Are you feeling all right?"

"I don't know…I was…what time is it?"

"It's around 2:00 pm. I was coming in to take care of a few hours of paperwork, but that can wait. You look like you need some help. Would you like to come in for a session?"

As she rose, Dana's cell phone rang. She checked the Caller ID, half-expecting it to be Dare, begging for forgiveness. To her surprise, it was Aidan.

"Hello?"

"Where are you, Thissie?" His tone was all business.

"I'm at the office park on Noyes Drive. Why?"

"Don't move. I'm going to pick you up. We need to talk."

"What's wrong?"

"What make of car do you drive?"

"I've got a blue Honda Accord. Why?"

"That's what I thought. You know Endicott Coxwell?"

"Sure, he's a good friend of mine. What's going on? Why do you want to know?"

"Thiss, I'm sorry to be the one to tell you but there's been...an event."

"What kind of event?"

"A few hours ago, he was out putting up signs for his open house when a car plowed him down."

"Oh my God. Oh no. But he'll be okay, right?"

"I hope so. He's in surgery at Good Samaritan. But the thing is," Aidan paused two beats too long, "the car that hit him was reported to be a blue Honda Accord."

CHAPTER 35

March 5ᵗʰ

DANA APOLOGIZED TO DR. LAWRENCE and walked out of the building in a fog, so stunned by the news. She felt lost. Helpless. Should she wait for Aidan? Or head to the hospital and stand vigil? Who would want to hurt Endie? She thought about calling Grayson, but then remembered how angry he was at her. Overwhelmed with grief and frustration—and terrified that even *she* didn't know her whereabouts for the past three hours— she sat down by the side of the road and burst into tears.

About ten minutes into her crying jag, Aidan pulled alongside the curb. Even through bloodshot eyes, it was still good to see a familiar face.

"Please, please tell me that you have an alibi for *this* attack."

"Endicott was my very best friend. One of the very few I have. Do you really think I would hurt him?"

"What do *I* think? No. I don't think you'd hurt a fly. But considering you haven't had a decent alibi for the other three killings, I think it would really help."

"Well, I don't. Have one, that is. Tell me what happened to Endie."

"There's not much more to report other than I already told you. He was on the corner of Julianne and Main, putting up a directional sign for his open house. I don't know why you agents risk your life putting up signs on busy streets, but hey, I guess you know your business. A witness claimed that as Mr. Coxwell started to cross, a blue Honda sped up, hit him intentionally, and then kept going. She described the driver as having short, brown hair, just like you.

"Aidan—it's obvious that the driver must be this nutcase who's going around killing real estate agents. What motivation would *I* possibly have for hurting my own best friend?"

"Evidently more than the police originally thought. Thiss, I'm not telling you this in an official capacity, I'm telling you as a friend. I want more than anything to prove your innocence, but it's getting harder by the minute.

"Right after the accident, witnesses at the site started tweeting and posting pictures with their smartphones. Within ten minutes, the police received three phone calls. Two were from diners who reported they'd seen you and the victim eating breakfast at some restaurant on E Street a few mornings ago. They both said that the two of you had a disagreement, something about him having some information you didn't want him to disclose."

"Plenty of people have disagreements. That doesn't mean that one goes out and tries to run over the other one."

"True. But then we received a call from Mr. Coxwell's...what, paramour? A Mr. Grayson Richards, alleging you're behind the whole thing, that you've been interfering in their lives for some time and have...

what did he say? Oh yes, an unhealthy addiction to his lover. Claimed you plotted with him to destroy a leading Realtor in the community. He didn't want to say more before consulting with his attorney. Wanna tell me something about that?"

"Oh my God. It's Grayson. He's the killer! He's setting me up!"

"Why would he do that?"

"Why didn't I see it before? Endie warned that he would try to hurt me, but I told him he was crazy."

"Again, motivation?"

"My relationship with Endie predates theirs," said Dana, hedging her bets. *No need to tell the whole story when part will suffice.* "I talked Endie into working here in Rock Canyon, which put a strain on their affair. They'd been fighting lately, and Grayson moved out. Maybe he was so mad at Endie, he became homicidal. And then decided to pin it on me."

"And he killed the other three agents over the past few months ...why?"

An excellent question.

She paused and regrouped. "His dislike of brokers generalized? Endie did say he blamed the entire real estate industry for their recent breakup."

"Kind of flimsy. But if this Grayson character has it in for you, it does give us a reason to discredit his allegations. What about the other diners at brunch?"

"What about them?"

"They reported that the two of you raised your voices at the table. You especially. Something about no one saying anything to anyone and then storming off. They said it sounded like a threat."

Dana suddenly felt nauseous. As incriminating as all this sounded on its own, if her plot against Cassandra ever came out…

Aidan's cell phone rang. He listened, gave a few *uh huh*s, and one *Thanks, she's right here. I'll take care of it.* And then hung up.

"What now?"

"According to my sources, Penelope Randolph-Purser's cell phone finally turned up. Interesting timing."

"That's good, right?"

"Well, yes. But not for you," Aidan said with a pained expression. "The local cops found it tossed in the shrubbery behind a house up in Gresham. The tax records indicated the house is owned by a company called Loopholes, Inc. but when the officers interviewed the tenants, a Mr. and Mrs. Ng, they reported that they'd rented the home directly from the owner herself, a Ms. Black. I've been asked to bring you down to the station for questioning."

"That's it," said Dana. "I want to speak to a lawyer."

CHAPTER 36

March 6th

ROCK CANYON, IN ITS ETERNAL quest to compete with the far wealthier and picturesque Westminster across the river, housed its police station in a 1942 Arts and Crafts-style home that was later converted into municipal space. Since there were very few criminal offenses ever prosecuted out in the sticks, the home's bedrooms had been converted into holding cells, with bars on the windows and cut-outs on the doors so officers could peer in and the temporarily incarcerated could stare out. Each "cell" had a double bed, two end tables, a bookcase filled with novels, and an en-suite bath. In many ways, the accommodations were nicer than the bedroom Dana had shared with her grandmother back in Centralia.

Like its makeshift jail, police and court procedures in Rock Canyon were equally idiosyncratic. The county followed its own set of rules and no one from the outside ever bothered to interfere.

Officers led Dana to a soundproofed room in the basement designed for detainees and their lawyers to confer. The décor was sparse: a large butcher-block table surrounded by a trio of chairs that screamed yard sale chic. Apparently, the competition with Westminster only went so far.

Waiting for her at the table were Aidan, in his official capacity, along with Jaycee Green, Rock Canyon's one public defender, all of 24 years old. Dana and Jaycee had only had a moment to converse before meeting with the detective, just long enough for Jaycee to advise her new client to keep quiet and let the attorney do all the talking. Especially around the police.

"I hope you appreciate that Ms. Black is here willingly, in an effort to cooperate," said Jaycee. "My first thought was, with Mr. Coxwell being black and gay, has anyone considered the possibility that this was a hate crime?"

"We have no reason to believe that, no. If that were true, it would have been the first of its kind in Rock Canyon in a very long time. We're pretty sure this is the fourth in a series of Realtor attacks that has been going on since November," said Aidan, all reserved and police-like.

Delicious.

Focus, Dana, Focus.

"And you have reason to believe my client is involved? She is a real estate agent herself, after all."

"With a personal connection to Mr. Coxwell, a reported recent argument between the two of them, and someone leaving the scene matching her description, we feel there might be a connection."

"Let's be clear. Are you formally charging my client with anything, Detective?"

"No, we only want to talk right now. We still have to run the fingerprints on the phone we found on Ms. Black's property. We also need to check out the tire tracks left by the vehicle in question and compare them to the treads on Ms. Black's car. If and when Mr. Coxwell emerges from his post-surgical coma, we hope to speak with him as well. Until then, we have nothing to formally link her with this crime."

"Do you have anything to associate her with any of the other murders?"

"Only that she has no alibi for any of the dates in question."

Dana signaled to Jaycee and then leaned over, cupped her hand against her cheek so no one could read her lips, and whispered into the lawyer's ear.

"I do have an alibi…but I don't think the person in question is going to come forward to confirm it."

"And who is that?" she whispered back.

"My brother-in-law."

Jaycee gulped.

"Detective…could you give me a few minutes of privacy with my client?"

"Sure." Aidan pushed back from the table. "When you're ready, hit the intercom and let me know, okay?"

They waited until Aidan closed the door and then a few beats longer.

"Now what did you say, Dana?"

"I said I was with my brother-in-law, but it's not what it sounds like."

"With? As in sleeping with?"

"Yes."

"And who is your brother-in-law?"

Dana squirmed in her seat. She knew how awkward this was going to get. It was a fairly small town, after all.

"Reid Wright," she said to the wall.

"Reid Wright, the reporter? Or the former reporter, rather? Melanie Wright's husband?"

"The very one."

"Your sister is Melanie Wright, the broker?"

"Yes."

"Why doesn't anyone know this? Is Detective Cummings aware?"

"Melanie and I didn't think it was important to announce our connection to the world. So no, he doesn't. Not that I'm aware of, anyway."

"Oh good, and good that it's not as bad as it sounds. Because it sounds like you're secretly sleeping with your sister's husband…the same sister who received a note threatening that her turn to die was coming up shortly. Her being rich and all? That would give you one hell of a motive for either setting her up as the murderer or murdering her yourself."

"I suppose you could see it that way. But the thing is that Reid and I started sleeping together years before I knew he was my brother-in-law. I lived away from Rock Canyon for a long, long time. I hadn't seen my sister since I was six, and I certainly hadn't met her husband."

"So when did you find out?"

"Right after my mother had her stroke."

"Oh that's right…this would make you Cassandra Beckett's daughter. Great genes there—jury's going to think you're a regular Mother Theresa. Let me get this straight…you were sleeping with Reid before the murders started, right?"

"Yes, a few years before."

"But after you found out that he was your sister's husband, you continued to sleep with him?"

"Who are you, my priest?"

"Excuse me, but these are questions the prosecution is going to ask. You'd better have answers for them. So again, you were still involved, even after discovering his identity?"

"Yes and no. It's complicated."

"It always is. Let me make it very simple for you because the D.A. is going to make it very simple, once he gets you up on the stand. Are you still sleeping with him?"

"No. Not as of a few days ago, anyway."

"What happened?"

"We broke up. Another reason why I don't think he's going to throw away a perfectly good meal ticket to rescue me."

"I hear you. How do you propose I defend you if you can't give me an alibi?"

Dana reflected for a moment.

"Part of these accusations are from Grayson Richards. We go way back. He knows that I would never hurt Endie. In fact, my original theory was that he might be the one behind the hit-and-run but as Aid—Detective Cummings pointed out, a lover's spat really wouldn't explain the three murders that preceded it. This accusation is his way of lashing out. Since I'm not under arrest, can I get out of here? Let me go and talk to him. I'm sure I can get him to retract his allegation."

"Have the police spoken with him yet?"

"I don't think so. I think he was waiting to get lawyered up so he wouldn't get in trouble."

"In trouble for what? And what were you and Mr. Coxswell arguing about at that restaurant?"

Oh God. This was going to sound even worse.

"I had a lot of issues with my mother growing up. I wanted to get even with her for having dumped me on my grandmother and then never throwing us a dime."

"And…?"

"And, you know that whole rental fraud incident back in 2007? Right before my mother's stroke?"

"Don't tell me…you were behind that?"

"Well me…and Endie. And Grayson, who likes to hack into computers during his down time. Endie was afraid that, now that they had split up, Grayson might decide to come clean, get me into trouble. The very thought of it made me angry, and that's why people at the restaurant heard me tell Endie that no one was going to say anything to anyone. Maybe that sounded threatening, but it wasn't meant to be. Anyway, I doubt Grayson is going to talk to anyone until it's certain he's got immunity."

"Let me make sure I understand this. Not only did you have motive to kill your sister to get at her husband and her money, but you've also committed real estate fraud, implicating your own mother while inconveniencing nearly 50 families in the process?"

"You're taking it all out of context," she mumbled.

"Which is exactly what I'm thinking the murderer might have said. Anything else you'd like to add?"

"Not really."

Dana figured that mentioning she was part of the local BDSM community and that she suffered from recurring blackouts couldn't help her cause one iota, so she remained quiet.

"Dana, if I were you, I'd email Grayson right now and tell him to meet you somewhere and get this all cleared up. Otherwise, I'm not sure how I'm going to defend someone who's seemingly spent years helping the prosecution build an airtight case."

Sensing Jaycee was far wiser than her 24 years might suggest, and grateful that the Rock Canyon Police Station had Wi-Fi, she immediately shot off an email:

Grayson, I'm not sure where you're living now but we

have to talk. The police think I could be responsible for Endie's attack, but in your heart of hearts, you know I would never harm him. We're both hurting right now and I think we need each other. Where are you staying? Let's meet and talk.

It took a few minutes before her phone dinged with a response:

I'm over at my old apartment at 427 Henderson Drive. 3A. You're right, I am hurting. Come tomorrow around 4:00 pm.

She showed Jaycee the email, who then called Aidan back in.

"Is my client free to go?"

"She's a person of interest. We still have more questions."

"She'll be back by 6:00 pm tomorrow afternoon. She has some important affairs to deal with."

Aidan addressed Dana directly, tired of talking through an intermediary. "Listen, I can't keep you here, but I'm advising you to return as soon as possible. There's a lot more we need to discuss, and it will go better for you if you cooperate fully."

"I understand, Detective," Dana answered, wishing their budding relationship hadn't degenerated from Harlequin romance to police procedural. "You have my word."

"Now if I only had your alibi," she heard him say as she walked out the door.

CHAPTER 37

March 6ᵗʰ

AS AIDAN LEFT THE INTERROGATION room, Captain Lasky summoned him into his office.

"Got anything for me, Cummings? A confession, perhaps?"

"Nope. Not yet. Maybe tomorrow." Aidan hoped his nonchalant manner masked his growing unease.

"Why tomorrow?"

"That's when she'll be back, tomorrow afternoon."

"What? You let her go?" Lasky's tone of voice bespoke both fury and disbelief.

"We couldn't hold her. We really have nothing on her. No one took down the license plate at the crime scene, and there are plenty of blue Accords out there, driven by women with short, brown hair. Not to mention that anyone—man or woman—could disguise themselves with a short, brown wig. We showed the witnesses pictures of potential assailants, including Dana's photo from her real estate ads, and no one could make a definitive identification. For now, we're in a holding pattern."

"And all of your poking around? Didn't that turn

anything up?"

It turned up so much, my head is still whirling. Forsaken, both physically and emotionally, she's had every reason to give up, abandon faith in this world. She lives in the shadow of her sister, the most successful agent in town, but hides the fact they're related. To maintain romantic distance from others, she hangs out with a loser who not only cheats on her every chance he gets, but treats her like a human punching bag when they are together. At her grandmother's gravesite, she vowed revenge on "all of them." And then, no alibis, for any of the murders.

And yet, he had this feeling, deep in his gut, that she was innocent. And his gut never failed him. After all, wasn't it Charles Darwin who said, 'The very essence of instinct is that it's followed independently of reason'? Not a bad premise, even if Darwin was a Brit.

"Cummings, did you hear me?"

Spilling the beans on Dana could certainly mean a cushy spot back on the police force. And if Dana did indeed turn out to be guilty, that was one thing. But he had to be absolutely, positively sure, before he shared even one of his discoveries.

"Cummings?"

"Aye, Sir. Nothing yet. But. I still have one last lead to follow up."

Cassandra Beckett's McMansion was as intimidating up close as it was from a distance. Tudor-style, oversized mahogany front door. He rang the bell and then waited, the peals reminding him of his alter boy days, eons ago. He couldn't remember the last time he'd stepped foot inside a church.

The woman who answered the door was short, squat,

disheveled and thoroughly annoyed about having her afternoon disturbed. She eyed him with skepticism.

"Yeah?"

"Good afternoon, Ma'am. My name is Detective Aidan Cummings. I'm investigating the real estate murders…"

"Oh, you must want Melanie Wright. She lives next door. The big colonial."

"Thank you, but I was hoping to speak to Cassandra Beckett."

"I wouldn't worry about her. She hasn't been a broker for years."

"I'm actually trying to gather some information about her daughter."

"As I said before, Melanie…"

"No, Ma'am, her *other* daughter."

The woman froze, blinking twice.

"Maybe you'd better come in, Detective…"

"Cummings. Thank you. And you are…?"

"I'm Lorelei Simpson, Cassandra's caretaker," she said in a far more welcoming tone. "Why don't you wait in the library? I'll see if Cassandra is up to speaking with anyone."

Lorelei led him into a small room lined with bookcases, and then left, shutting the door behind her. He walked the perimeter, studying the titles of her collection—all real estate business books written by industry icons, such as Gary Keller, Floyd Wickman, and Mike Ferry. There must have been about fifty how-to books in total, all promising a financial catapult to the top. Occasionally, there'd be an old, framed photograph, serving as a bookend. Cassandra and the mayor. Another with the governor. A third where she was honored by the Rock Canyon Chamber of Commerce.

And then, toward the back, some personal photos. One

of Melanie and Reid's wedding, which he'd already seen online. Another on some tropical island. And then…he stopped dead in his tracks. A Mardi Gras party photo of Melanie, decked out in glitter and beads, and her husband, wearing a brightly colored mask over his eyes. That's why he'd looked so familiar in the wedding photo. Reid was Dare!

Oh my God, she's sleeping with her brother-in-law. Who stands to inherit millions if Melanie happens to get murdered along with the other brokers. The missing piece—motive. Everything's beginning to fall into place. The question is, whose motive was it, Dana's or Reid's? Or both?

Lorelei plodded back into the room. "I have bad news, Detective. Unfortunately, she's not feeling up to speaking with anyone today."

"That's fine." His head was reeling. "I'll pursue other avenues."

"If it isn't inappropriate, could I offer one piece of advice?"

"Of course, Ms. Simpson. What would that be?"

"Don't waste time on Dana. She's a lovely girl. Comes and sees Cassandra as often as she's able. She has enough problems as it is, what with those blackouts and all. Don't burden her with a lot of questions and weigh her down even more."

"Blackouts?"

"Yes, it's not public knowledge but when she gets stressed, she blacks out. Can't remember where she's been or what she's been up to. She's shown up here, once or twice, babbling like a crazy woman, but we've always calmed her down, taken care of her. She's seeing a therapist now and I know, any day, they'll get to the bottom of it, and she'll be right as rain. Please, I beg you, don't cause her any additional stress. I don't want to see my Dana have any setbacks."

"Thanks for the heads up, Ms. Simpson. I promise you, we'll treat her with kid gloves."

Aidan hurried to his car. He had a hunch it was going to take more than gloves to save Dana. But what? He knew one way to find out.

CHAPTER 38

March 7th

IN THE SPAN OF 48 hours, Dana's status had regressed from Dare's play partner to ex-girlfriend, and from Endie's grieving, inconsolable friend to police person of interest, seeking vindication from a former co-conspirator. She sat at home all morning, trying hard to come up with something, anything to say to Grayson that would sway him from pursuing his line of attack.

Her cell phone rang several times during the day. The Caller ID read Melanie. The office. Melanie. A client or two. She didn't answer any of the calls, determined to lay low until she knew where she stood with Grayson.

She carefully selected her outfit (*What exactly does one wear to get someone to recant an accusation, anyhow?*) and racked her head, wondering how to approach this.

He probably blames me for the attack on Endie, seeing how I was the one who urged him to join Rock Canyon Realty in the first place. It follows that I put him in danger's path. But Grayson has to know that I wasn't the one at the steering wheel. I only wish I knew where I'd been during those three hours, between bolting from Reid's surprise play party and showing up at Dr.

Lawrence's door.

As she drove up to Gresham, she reexamined the pertinent facts. Someone was obviously framing her. Why else would they have written the pun on the boxes that crushed Kerrianne? Or attacked Endie, disguised as a Dana look-alike, and driving a car whose color, make and model resembled her own?

Maybe someone read my emails. If so, they would have known about Endie's whereabouts from the reconciliatory note he'd sent me, which included the invitation to his broker's open. And if they could access my email, why not my online calendar as well? That would have clued them in on my whereabouts on Tuesday...and during all of the other murders too.

But who knew her passwords? Only Endie. And possibly Harrison. Had she ever changed them after the breakup or had she been too damn lazy?

More likely that someone hacked in. And, once privy to her schedule, committed the attacks at times when she'd be hamstrung for an alibi. There was only one person in her sphere who wasn't only a hacker, but also held a grudge against her. And who undoubtedly knew all about her relationship with Dare, thanks to their mutual, incurably-gossipy friend, Endie.

She pulled off onto the shoulder, her blood pressure rising.

What am I doing? Am I walking into a trap? Is Grayson intending to knock me off next? Or am I letting my paranoia get the best of me?

This is when she would have called Endie to ask for his advice, to let him talk her down. But Endie was in no position to help now. She closed her eyes and meditated for a moment while the car idled.

Calm down, Dana. You've always been a survivor,

relying on your wits, your intuition. What are they telling you now?

Grayson is no killer. He's full of himself, and he loves to posture and make ultimatums, but beneath all that bluster is someone who just needs to be acknowledged. I've been so preoccupied with my own issues that I really haven't been there for him. Maybe that can change now. Maybe he and I can forge a bond born of shared concern for our friend.

She opened her eyes with a renewed sense of purpose, put the car into drive, and resumed the mission.

It was 4:05 pm when Dana pulled up outside the apartment building, a four-story brick edifice which was typical of most of Gresham's uninspired architecture. She strode through the lobby, deserted since most people weren't yet home from work, and took the elevator up to the third floor.

There were only four apartments on each level, and Grayson's was on the far right. She rang the bell. No answer. Knocked twice. Again, no response. She jiggled the doorknob and to her surprise, found it unlocked.

"Grayson?" she called out as she entered. "It's Dana."

The sparse living room had all the earmarks of newfound bachelorhood. One brown leather couch, facing a television perched on a coffee table. A small round wooden dining table with one chair. Most of the furniture in the old house must have belonged to Endie.

"Grayson?" Silence.

She knocked on the bedroom door, then slowly opened it. What she saw made her fall to her knees and retch. There was Grayson, lying sideways on his bed, his naked body soaking in a pool of blood. There was a bullet hole in the middle of his head, a handgun on the floor, and what appeared to be a giant rat, crammed into his mouth.

On the wall above his bed, someone had left a message scrawled in blood: "Only rats talk to the police." She let out one scream, and then everything went black.

CHAPTER 39

March 7th

"THISSIE, THISSIE. WAKE UP."
Dana opened her eyes and saw Aidan, kneeling beside her, shaking her shoulder.

"Where am I?"

"You're in Grayson's apartment."

She lay quiet for a moment, weak and disoriented. Then she remembered. "Aidan, did you see—"

"Yes, Thiss. I've called it in."

"What are you doing here?"

"I figured you might do something risky when you left the station yesterday, so I decided I'd better keep an eye on you."

"I didn't do this. Someone's setting me up."

Aidan ran his hand down the side of her head, stroking her hair.

"I know, sweetie. I know you didn't. Relax. You've had a bad scare. Would you like some water?"

"No, I'm okay. Why would someone kill Grayson? He isn't a real estate agent."

"No, but he could have taken back his accusation and cleared your name. If I had to guess, I'd bet that when the forensics team gets up here from Rock Canyon, they'll find your prints on that gun."

"What do you mean?"

"I mean I agree with you. Someone's trying to set you

up. They thought that by killing Grayson, the police would assume you did it to shut him up. Who else knew you were coming here?"

"No one. Well, except for my lawyer. Maybe Grayson said something?"

"I guess we'll never know. But whoever's behind this never counted on a detective friend keeping his eye on you after you left the precinct. And also thought we'd be stupid enough to believe you'd implicate yourself by leaving that note on the wall. If the forensics team determines that Grayson was killed sometime between the time I picked you up yesterday and now, you'll be in the clear. For this murder, at least."

"Thank God you believe me."

"Just because I believe you, doesn't mean that the captain will. Thissie, I think it's time you told me where you were when those murders were committed so we can clear your name."

She covered her face with her hands and started to cry. "I can't."

He sat down, pulled her into his strong arms, and cuddled her, rocking back and forth.

"Why not? What's so bad?"

"You won't…like…me…anymore," she spluttered, in-between sobs.

"Yes, I will, have a little faith in me, would you? Whatever it is, we'll figure it out together."

They sat there for several minutes. She couldn't remember the last time a man held her so tenderly, or for so long.

She pulled away slightly and gave him the response he'd been waiting for.

"I was with Dare."

"I figured as much. Why can't he give you an alibi?"

"He won't. He's married…to Melanie Wright."

"The agent who received the death threat?"

"Yes. You interviewed her. She pays the bills and he's not about to throw away his only means of support."

"Well, that explains that stupid mask anyway."

"There's something else."

"What?"

"You have to promise that if I tell you, it's as a friend. Not as a detective."

"I can't promise you that. But I do swear that I will protect you any way that's legally possible. Again, have a little confidence in me."

She told him the whole story, exactly as she had told it to Jaycee Green the day before. It poured out, and as it did, she felt a great weight lift from her shoulders.

"I can't say I'm thrilled about the fraud, Thissie, but it doesn't pertain to the murder case, and that's the only thing I'm here to investigate. You have to get Reid to confirm where you were on the dates of the second murder, so you're above suspicion. And he is, as well. Then we have to figure out who would want to frame you."

"I know Reid won't help me if he thinks he's going to be out on the streets. I think I have a way around it, though. Maybe I should speak to Melanie. If she knows, he has nothing to gain by holding back. It's just… as much of a bitch as my big sister can be, I don't want her to hate me."

Dana gazed into Aidan's sweet, glistening blue eyes. "I've never admitted this before, but I don't know if I'm strong enough to do this on my own. Would you come with me?"

"Absolutely. As soon as the forensics team finishes up here, I'll make sure you get home safely. Then tomorrow, we'll head over there. Together. It will all work out, I promise."

Dana wished she could be as sure.

CHAPTER 40

March 8ᵗʰ

KNOWING HER SISTER WOULD BE busy all day with clients, Dana met Aidan at 8:00 pm at the Beckett-Wright compound. Melanie's car was out front. Reid's was nowhere in sight. She wasn't surprised. Friday night was a big party night at the clubs.

She inhaled deeply and rang the doorbell, Aidan by her side, gently rubbing her back in support. To her surprise, Lorelei answered the door.

"Dana, thank goodness you've turned up," she said, embracing her. "Everyone's been going nuts around here." She nodded at Aidan. "Detective."

"You know each other?"

"Yes, Detective Cummings came over the other day to ask Cassandra a few questions, but she wasn't up to it."

"Oh. I didn't realize."

"After what happened to that nice boy from the agency—I used to work with him, you know—and then nobody being able to reach you, your sister was beside herself. I came over to make her some dinner. Thank you for bringing our girl back to us, Detective."

Dana quickly surmised that the allegations against

her hadn't reached the media, nor had any information leaked out yet about Grayson's murder. At least that was something.

"He didn't bring me back, Lorelei. He came with me. There's something I have to tell Melanie. Could you get her for me?"

"Of course. She's upstairs. Anything for you."

A few minutes later, Lorelei announced that Melanie would be right down, and asked if anyone would like some lemonade. They politely declined, and she retreated to the kitchen.

Melanie descended the staircase a minute later, joining them in the foyer. She appeared tired and pale.

"You okay?" Dana asked.

"No, I'm most definitely not okay. I'm sick with worry. Endicott—that's four, you know. Four murders—either attempted or successfully completed—and my turn is supposedly coming up any day now. And then I couldn't find you. You wouldn't answer your phone. What's being done to protect us, Detective?"

"We're trying to get to the bottom of it, Mrs. Wright. And to that end, we're trying to clear Dana here because she doesn't have an alibi for the times of the deaths. We were—"

"Oh, how absurd. She was with me, of course."

"All four times? Including Tuesday?" Aidan seemed stunned.

"Yes." Melanie stood there, arms crossed, holding her ground.

"You never mentioned that when we spoke over the phone after the Randolph-Purser death."

"I don't remember you asking me, Detective."

"You're going to go on record with that? That she was with you all four times? Even the day before yesterday?"

"Yes, of course. Dana was helping me with some paperwork when Endicott was setting up his open house. She has…memory lapses. Ever since our father died. So maybe she forgot. Give me whatever papers you need me to sign, and I'll sign them."

"But…" Dana interrupted, breaking her wide-eyed silence.

"No *but*s. You were with me. I'll swear to it. Is there anything else, Detective? Because if not, I'd like some private time alone with my sister."

"Dana, do you want me to go?"

Dana was equally dumbfounded by Melanie's willingness to hand out false alibis and perjure herself. She was dying to hear what her sister had to say.

"I'll be fine. I'll call you tomorrow?"

"Sure. Call me. We'll take care of that other thing. I'll let myself out. Thank you."

As soon as the door closed, Dana was ready to pounce.

"Why did you do that, Melanie? Why did you lie for me and say that you knew where I was?"

"Because I *did* know where you were. And what goes on in this family stays in this family. No need for the world to know. So, are you finally ready to tell me about you and Reid?"

Dana's mouth dropped open. If she was floored before, now she was doubly so. "You knew?"

"Oh for God's sake. I've known for years. I do have him watched, you know. To make sure he doesn't do anything stupid that could kill my business. What I didn't realize…not until he brought you back here after Mother's stroke…is that you were Thissie, the same girl he'd been playing with at the clubs all the time we thought you were in Europe."

"I can't believe you …" Dana mumbled, wondering

what else her surveillance team had uncovered. "You're not mad?"

"At you, no. Except that you're a damn fool, because he's also fucking half the other girls in town."

"Half minus one. I ended it the other day. Why aren't you upset?"

"Because you didn't do it on purpose. It's clear you didn't realize who he was when you met him. I told you, when he plays elsewhere, it keeps me from having to deal with all of…those games. That's your thing, not mine. I am curious, though. Why did you lie to us about being in Europe?"

It was clear she didn't know about the Destroy Cassandra plot. Dana was grateful for small favors.

"I was so angry at Mom for abandoning me. And you for never calling or visiting. Once I started college, I wanted to start life fresh. Make it on my own. And then for a long time, I really was on the road, as a travel writer. So part of it was true. But I apologize for deceiving you. Thank you for the alibis. Even though I'd already told him the truth."

"You're welcome. And I doubt he's going to throw me in jail for lying to the police. If he believed your story and was hoping that I'd get Reid to corroborate it, I've gotten you both off the hook. Reid's a coward. He's not going to back you up. But for now, he's a convenience, and I really don't want to disturb anything. I'll take care of him when the time is right."

They heard a dish fall in the kitchen and Lorelei start cursing. "Don't worry, Ms. Melanie. I'll clean it up."

"Please tell me that wasn't one of the *Flora Danica.*"

"I'm sorry, Ma'am. I'll pay for it."

"Indeed you will," Melanie said under her breath.

They turned their attention back to the issue at hand.

"Someone's trying to frame me," said Dana, "and I'm going to find out who it is."

"Maybe that cute detective will help." Melanie grinned. "I can see that he cares for you."

"I have to admit, I hope you're right."

"In the meantime," Melanie continued, "be careful. Don't take any chances. No showing property or putting up signs or going on listing presentations on your own. I'll go with you if you want. No putting yourself into any unnecessary danger. I couldn't bear losing you again. Promise me." She opened her arms and hugged her little sister. A long time. *This is certainly my week for hugs.* She almost hated stepping away.

"I promise. Thank you, Melanie. I'm so sorry. I'm afraid I've had you all wrong."

"What do you mean?"

"All that dirty business you had me take care of for you when I joined the agency. I thought you were getting back at me because you were jealous of me country-hopping while you were stuck home working."

"I don't understand. What dirty business?"

"All the stuff Deborah Lee made me do, up until the Merriweather thing. The rats she made me leave in the pantries of your competitor's listings, all that garbage."

"What? I never would have asked you to do anything unethical. I'll kill that bitch, having you get down in the mud like that. No, all I've been doing is trying to help you. Sending you money for college. Throwing business your way. Any potential client that my spies had seen at one of your clubs? I told them to work with you instead."

"You paid for college? Gloria told me that the money came from the government, to get her to move out of Centralia."

"I don't know anything about that. I did send the

money, but anonymously. I couldn't risk Mother finding out."

"And the clients? You were feeding me? I thought they were coming in from my signs."

"That's what you were supposed to think. And maybe now, they are. But not a few years ago."

"I can't believe it. Why did you do that for me?"

"Guilt, mostly. What Mom did, bringing me here while ditching you in Centralia after Dad died, was unconscionable. Me not insisting on going out and finding you when I had enough money to take care of you myself? Even worse. I've been trying to make it up to you ever since you got home. Had I known years ago that you and Thissie were one and the same, I would have done it a lot sooner. My bad."

Dana shook her head in disbelief. *I've had everything so wrong. My sister might put on a hard-nosed, all-business façade, but behind that, she's someone who authentically cares about me, to the point of being willing to perjure herself. And now there's a man in my life who seems more interested in building up my self-esteem than using me to work out his sexual demons.*

With the exception of the attack on Endie, Dana realized that things were finally looking up. Her world was filled with possibilities. Well, as long as she could figure out who was out to get her. Before they actually did.

CHAPTER 41

March 9ᵗʰ

DANA MUST HAVE BEEN MORE overwhelmed by the events of the previous day than she'd realized, because she slept like a dead woman until the phone woke her at 9:06 am.

"Uhhh?"

"You sound half-asleep."

"I can see why you made detective. Nothing gets by you, Cummings."

"How do you feel?"

"I'm not sure yet. I'm not awake, remember?"

"Can you at least share how things ended with your sister after I left?"

"Yes. She can verify where I was. And if you need a real alibi, I don't think she'd have any problem going after Reid and pressuring him to give you one as well. Should I ask her to do that?"

"I don't think that's necessary quite yet. Time of death for Grayson Richards came in at around 3:30 pm. I was watching you practically from the time you left the station until you showed up at his door, so unless you have a clone or twin, no way you could have done it. I spoke to the captain and told him I thought someone's trying to frame you."

"Does he believe it?"

"For the moment, yes. I explained that I expected the fingerprints on Penelope Randolph-Purser's phone and the gun that was used to shoot Grayson to match. But we need your fingerprints and a copy of your tire treads so we can compare them to what we already have. If the fingerprints are the same, he's not going to be too surprised. You and I will have to put our heads together and figure out how someone got ahold of them. But if the tire treads are duplicates, then we might have a real problem."

Yes, we might. Dana knew that the Accord had been outside her listing at Devendorf while she'd been inside with 'Dare and the Alternatives.' But what about the three hours that followed? Dana wondered how long that particular blackout would continue to haunt her.

"Could you please bring your car by the station around 4:00 pm? We'll check out the tires and unofficially fingerprint you, so we can see what's what. As a thank you, I'll take you out somewhere nice for dinner. We can celebrate you no longer being an official suspect."

"Sounds good. Count me there." She hoped her confident tone masked her anxiety over the outcome of those tests. Maybe she should have checked with her attorney before agreeing. It came down to a huge leap of faith. In light of her blackouts, just how sure was she of her own character, her motives, her innocence? The tire treads might hold an answer she wasn't positive she wanted to hear.

"What will you do in the meantime, Thiss? I don't want you putting yourself in any danger."

"I was thinking about stopping by the hospital to check

on Endie."

"I'm not sure if that's such a good idea. We've been discouraging any brokers from visiting."

"Why? Do you think the murderer will be waiting outside with a machine gun to mow us all down?"

"We don't know what to think, so for now, we're erring on the side of caution. I'd prefer you kept a low profile."

"Wow, you sound exactly like Melanie. She doesn't want me to do anything remotely productive unless she's there beside me."

"It's good advice. Listen to her. Listen to me. Christ, listen to someone for once in your life."

"Aye, aye, Herr Detective. Anything special you want me to wear to dinner?"

"Wear a smile. That's what always makes me want to kiss you and I haven't seen much of one on your face lately. Catch you later."

She hung up, glowing. And wondering what she could do to make him want to do more than just kiss.

Dana spent the rest of the day at home, as ordered, doing whatever she could to distract herself from the upcoming tire tread check and what it might reveal. Normally, she would have poked around on *Fetlife* and some of her other favorite online BDSM sites, but for some reason, she went uncharacteristically vanilla and binge-watched the episodes of *Jeopardy* and *Breaking Bad* that had been piling up on her DVR. Obviously Aidan's influence, she decided. *What's next? A knitting circle? Scrapbooking? A cookie swap?*

Then, she killed half an hour searching for the perfect dress for the evening…something that was innocent and provocative at the same time. She settled on a little black number with a V neckline, shirred at the waist to emphasize her best features. Red pumps to add a dash of spice. And to top it off, her good luck charm, a necklace featuring a silver, heart-shaped locket pendant, encasing a tiny picture of her dad she'd found hidden among a pile of old papers in her grandmother's house. She glanced in the mirror and practiced the smile Aidan seemed to like so much.

Not bad. Not bad at all.

Aidan met her at the station with an appreciative glance and made sure the fingerprinting went smoothly.

"This is really unofficial, correct? I didn't check with Jaycee. She'd probably kill me."

"You know you can trust me, right?"

"I'm afraid that word isn't in my vocabulary."

"Then I have my work cut out for me, don't I?"

She checked her email while he finished up his paperwork, occasionally wiping her sweaty palms against the coarse upholstery of the waiting room sofa. Then they headed out, leaving her car behind for the forensic examiners. She stroked her pendant and prayed to her father that the treads wouldn't match.

"Where are we going, Detective?"

"I thought VisionNary. What do you think?"

VisionNary was a new experimental restaurant on the outskirts of town that everyone had been raving about. A joint venture between a local chef, an optometrist, and the American Federation for the Blind, it was designed to help people relate to those who were vision-impaired by allowing them to eat in an environment simulating blindness.

"How did you get a reservation on such short notice? I thought they only have what, six tables?"

"The sous chef is one of my sister's…clients. It pays to have connections, Thissie. I thought you knew that."

On the drive over, Dana remained keenly aware of the

few inches that separated her body from his, how badly she wanted to again feel his gentle touch. It took all of her willpower to stay focused on their conversation and keep her hands to herself.

"Thiss, have you given any more thought to who could have gotten ahold of your fingerprints?"

"How would they even do that?"

"It's easier than you think. Whatever you touch, even a door knob, leaves a print that anyone can copy and duplicate if they want. All they need is access to a high definition camera, an overhead transparency, some graphite powder, and wood glue."

"Oh, why didn't you say so? That narrows it down. It's not like I don't open doors around town every day of the year for a living."

"No need for sarcasm."

"Occupational hazard. How about the witness who saw the car that ran over Endie? What did he say?"

"It's a she, an 80-year-old lady, who wears glasses she admits are outdated because she can't afford new ones. She claims that she saw a woman with shoulder-length hair driving the car. She couldn't give any more accurate detail to our sketch artist."

"Well, that sucks. Anyone can wear a wig. Did you check the car rental places around town?"

"We're in the process of doing that now. All the rental places within fifty miles of Rock Canyon. Thissie, tell me, how long was your Accord out of sight?"

"Wow...I don't know. I guess I parked over on Devendorf at around 10:00 am to meet Reid. I got your call around what, 2:00 pm? So around four hours."

"You were in your car at 10:00 am. You're sure?"

"Yes, absolutely." Of that, she actually was certain.

"Good. That's the time Mr. Coxwell was run down, so

there's no way someone could have hotwired your car, used it to run him over and then have returned it without your knowledge."

"He was hit at 10:00 am? Precisely?"

"Yes. We have the witness, remember?"

Dana threw her head back in joy.

It wasn't me. Thank God, it wasn't me.

It had been one thing for Melanie to provide her with an alibi, but that never ruled out what she'd been doing in the hours prior to each murder. The blackouts before each incident. This news confirmed her innocence, at least for Endie's hit-and-run. And Dare's innocence as well. She could finally stop worrying and enjoy the evening.

"You say something?"

"Just…thank goodness for witnesses."

"Agreed. So who has it out for you, Thiss?"

"A bunch of people, I suspect. When I started in real estate, I followed my broker's directives and hurt a lot of people: home sellers, buyers, other agents. I guess I have as much to apologize for as any of the other agents this killer has been gunning for."

"Does anyone stand out in particular? Maybe someone outside of real estate? Someone from the clubs? You'd said that you didn't make many friends when you and Dare became a couple."

"Club folk? Hmm. Hadn't thought of that. I wish I could say that no one in the scene knows my real identity, but thanks to the picture on my signs all over town, it's no secret anymore. Still, I don't usually play in Rock Canyon, and that's where all my signs are posted. I wouldn't worry about the jealous subs at the clubs. They stopped despising me as soon as Dare resumed sharing the wealth. I guess they're Faith's problem now."

"How about any ex-lovers?"

Cute. Aidan's fishing for information about my past love life.

"There was really only one. But Harrison and I haven't seen each other for years. He doesn't even know where I live since I moved to Rock Canyon. I doubt he's involved."

"There's clearly nothing more we can do about this tonight. Let's put this aside and enjoy each other's company, shall we?"

"Can you do that? Disconnect yourself from work like that?"

"I can if you can."

"Right. Like the woman who asks her fiancé if he will love her unconditionally for the rest of their lives. And he answers, 'I will if you will.'"

"Exactly. And perfect timing. Here we are."

As in almost every other aspect of Dana's life these days, things were not always as they first appeared. The only clue that this very ordinary looking venue was a Zagat-rated restaurant was the uniformed valet parking attendant waiting outside. Aidan threw him the keys and swept her inside.

The entrance foyer was dimly lit, and the maître d', whose name tag read Louis, asked for their phones, watches, and anything else that could give off light, so he could deposit them into a private locker. Louis then showed them a menu and took Aidan's credit card to prepay the meal.

Dana wondered about the logistics of eating soup in a pitch-black space, and opted for Caesar salad instead. And Chicken Cordon Bleu seemed like a good choice, something she could pick up with her fingers, in case she couldn't negotiate a knife in the dark. Dessert? An obvious choice. Cake, not ice cream. For Aidan, it was the opposite. Vichyssoise, Steak au Poivre, Sorbet.

"How do we get to our table if we can't see?" she asked.

A gentleman came out wearing dark glasses. Louis put Dana's hand in Aidan's and Aidan's hand on the gentleman's shoulder. "Kingston will lead you. Kind of the blind leading the blind."

I bet he makes that joke at least six times a night.

Kingston led them into the pitch-black dining room. About twenty steps in, they stopped, and he took Dana's hand and put it on the top of what felt like an upholstered bench. "They're all semi-circular booths. Slide in, miss, and then you after her, sir."

Grateful for the anonymity guaranteed by darkness, she awkwardly squeezed between the bench and the table and pushed across to leave room for Aidan. The cushion *cruuunched* as he sat alongside. She gingerly felt around the table, trying to locate her silverware and water glass without breaking or spilling anything.

The most interesting thing about simulated blindness was how loud everything sounded. The other diners' discussions, the *tink, tink, tink* as their silverware hit the porcelain, everything was amplified ten-fold. She made a mental note not to discuss anything personal.

Then a thought crossed her mind, causing her heart to palpitate wildly. "Aidan..." she leaned over and whispered, into what she hoped was his ear.

"What is it, Thiss?"

"We're in a dark room with knives. And there are people we think may want to kill me. Was this really the best choice of restaurant?"

"I thought you liked fear play. Are you scared?"

"Maybe, a little."

"Don't you think I can protect you?"

"Not if you can't see what's coming."

He put his arm around her and drew her close. "Sounds like I'm going to have to keep you surrounded."

His hand clutched the back of her head and held it firmly while his lips found hers. Soft, full, luscious and eminently kissable, she decided. Their tongues started to dance, eagerly darting in and out as they explored each other's mouths. She ran her hands up and down the front of his chest and the tops of his thighs. His hands traveled along the sides of her dress but respectfully bypassed her more sensitive areas.

"You're such a gentleman," she murmured in-between kisses.

"In public, yes."

"And elsewhere?"

"If you're good, maybe you'll find out."

"I'm always good."

"Of that, Thiss, I have no doubt."

Wait a minute. I DO have doubts. I have no idea if I'll be any good sexually if no kink is involved. I've lived in a world of power exchange, of struggling through sadistic challenges, usually followed by rough sex while bound. How could someone like that negotiate an old-fashioned, vanilla, boyfriend-girlfriend relationship? One that I haven't experienced in...forever? Could I find anything appealing in an encounter that didn't involve bondage and pain?

Aidan must have felt Dana stiffen and sensed her change of attitude because he didn't protest as she gently pushed him away, reclaiming her distance.

"What's wrong, Thiss?"

"The thing is, Aidan...I don't know if I can do this."

"Do what? Date a detective? I wouldn't worry too much about that. I am very careful, and exceptionally well-trained."

"No, it's not that. I'm sure you're top notch. It's the… vanilla thing."

"Oh. Are you afraid I'll be too tame and boring for you?" He reached over and grabbed a handful of hair and slowly pulled back until her head was facing upward. "I can handle you, I assure you," he threatened softly, menacingly.

"No," she whispered. "I'm afraid because…I don't know how…this…all…works. I didn't do the high school heavy petting thing. I went straight from virgin to perv. Kink all the way. I don't know if I can…please you without it…and I can't deal with the guilt of not satisfying you."

"Whoa, back up." He let go of her hair and pulled her back into a close embrace. "This is not about you performing some series of tasks, like a rat in a maze or a trained seal. And I am certainly no taskmaster. This is about me, being attracted to you. Your smarts, your wit, your beauty. Your damn puns. And wanting to be as close to you as possible, wanting to stay up all night talking about our dreams, our disasters, our triumphs. Wanting to make you feel desire and then satisfying that desire with deep pleasure. And this is about me hoping you'll feel the same way. Does that sound so scary?"

"Your food, sir, madam," announced the waiter. Dana got the distinct impression that they hadn't been as quiet or discreet as she had hoped.

"Let's eat," she suggested, postponing the remainder of the conversation as she moved away. He didn't argue.

He's such a good man. Smart, ambitious, gorgeous, caring, and he seems to truly like me. For me. Not for what kink I am willing to consider. Not for how much pain I am willing to endure. Am I really so short-

sighted, so gun-shy, that I'd pass up a chance to be happy without even trying? Even if it might be difficult or I might stumble once or twice along the way?

Her attempts at using her fork and knife proved futile, so she resigned herself to eating with her hands. It was a very messy proposition, as messy as the relationship she was now contemplating. And as with all difficult things in life, Dana decided to deal with it head on, and with humor.

"Aidan, I have another problem."

"What's that?"

"I...I feel overdressed." Her provocative pout was regretfully wasted in the dark.

"Excuse me?"

"The parmesan dressing. It's all over my face."

"*Oh mo Dhia.* My plan was to get you underdressed!"

He moved in close and began licking the gooey substance from her cheeks, her eyelids, wherever she had smeared it. *Who said chivalry was dead?* The pitch-black setting gave them license to cross over the threshold from civility to lust. She ripped off chunks of Chicken Cordon Bleu and fed him by hand. He managed to cut his steak and slip slivers onto her tongue.

In-between courses, they licked each other's ears and necks and wrists, even though none of those areas had come into contact with food. But they were being very thorough, and it was no surprise that they were thoroughly turned on by the time the cake and ice cream were served. They decided they were too full to finish their meal and decided to head out.

Aidan summoned the waiter a little too loudly, and they were led quickly to the foyer to gather their belongings. Dana gave up a silent prayer of thanks that no one in the restaurant could see the aftermath of their private food fête.

The valet couldn't bring the car fast enough. About a mile down the road stood a six-story building with big sign announcing the law firm of Dorfman, Plotkin and Associates.

"Have you ever seen their parking lot? It's amazing," The twinkle in Aidan's eye was captivating, even in the dark.

"Eh. I heard it's no big thing," she teased back, trying to sound nonchalant.

"It's big enough, I promise you. Wanna peek?"

She feigned a bored sigh. "I guess…"

Aidan wasn't having any of that. He pulled into the parking lot, and jumped into the back seat.

"Couldn't we get arrested for this?" she asked, scrambling to join him in crowded quarters.

"Be a good girl and I might let you try on my handcuffs."

She eyed him, askance. "I thought you had no interest in the scene."

"And you're bored by vanilla. Yet, here we are. Isn't it amazing what a little open-mindedness can do?"

CHAPTER 42

March 10-11th

LUXURIATING IN AIDAN'S KING-SIZE BED, Dana took up so much space that when he returned from fixing dinner, it was clear she'd left him no place to sit. He harrumphed loudly. She opened one eye and gave him the once over, debating between moving over and jumping his bones. She chose the former. They both needed to recharge, after a hard day of working up a sweat. Well, several sweats, to be precise.

"Cute and you can cook too. Who'd have guessed?"

"I don't know about all that, but I am an excellent re-heater." He placed the tray on the nightstand and nudged her over even further with his knee. "I've got pizza from Wednesday night and General Tso's Chicken from Thursday. What's your pleasure?"

She reached across, grabbed his thigh, and bit it gently. "I thought by now, you would have figured it out."

"That kitchen's temporarily closed. Restocking. But we do have this excellent selection over here."

She turned her attention reluctantly to the food. "I'll take the pizza for now. But I want the other for dessert."

"We'll see, Miss Greedy. We'll see."

He handed her the pizza and grabbed the Chinese food for himself. They ate in silence, content to be in each other's company.

"Aidan, I had fun today."

"Me too." He leaned over and kissed her cheek. "You're a pretty good dinner date."

"Pretty good?"

"Okay, okay. An adequate dinner date. Sheesh."

She punched him in the arm, causing one of his General Tso's infantry to fall onto the bed. She glanced up at him and quickly leaned over and licked it up.

"Good girl."

That "good girl" was so different than the ones she'd come to crave in the scene. Being with Aidan was different than anything she'd experienced before. There was no cruelty, no humiliation. No tests of endurance. Rather than dull, as she had feared, it was actually freeing. He allowed her to be herself, to touch him where and when she chose without permission, to ask for what she wanted without judgement, without reproach.

I could get used to this.

"Do you want me to drive you back home tonight, or do you want to stay over?" he asked.

"I'd like to stay, if I won't be in the way."

"You'd never be in my way, but I'm going to have to get you up around 6:00 am so I can get into the station early."

"I can do that."

She stood, wrapped herself in a sheet, grabbed the empty plates and silverware, and walked them over to the kitchen sink.

"Thiss…?" Aidan called out.

"Yes, hon?"

He followed her, sans sheet.

"Are you…is this…? All those concerns at dinner. Are you comfortable with moving forward?"

"I don't know." She smiled. "What's your definition of moving forward?"

Aidan walked over and embraced her from behind, nuzzling her hair.

"I mean, doing what we did last night about one hundred million more times."

"I dunno, Aidan. I really don't like parmesan dressing all that much."

He reached down and whacked her hard on the ass. Not bad for a novice, she decided. This man had potential, and he was clearly willing to meet her halfway. Sexually, anyway.

Aidan's cell phone interrupted their domestic bliss. Annoyed, he walked over to the counter where it was recharging. "Cummings. Uh huh…right, I assumed they wouldn't." He covered the receiver with his palm and whispered, "Tire tracks don't match. Exactly what we figured."

Then he turned his attention back to the phone. "Yes, yes, I'm listening. What? When? Did anyone see anything? Any note? Fuck. I'll be there right away… No problem, I know where she is. I can tell you for an absolute fact, she isn't involved. I'll bring her too. Thirty minutes. Goodbye."

"What was that all about?"

"God, I don't know how to tell you this."

"Tell me what, exactly?"

"It's Melanie."

"What about her?"

"She was doing a public open house today. It was supposed to end at 4:00 pm, and her assistant expected her back in the office by 5:00 pm. She never showed;

she never called. The assistant went to the house to find her. 620 Grove? Door was unlocked. All her sales paraphernalia on the counter. Her car in the driveway. No Melanie.”

Dana grabbed the counter for support. “And no note, you said.”

“No note. I’ve got to head over there. You want to come?”

“Of course I want to come. That fucking lunatic has got my sister!”

They arrived at the house at Grove around 9:00 pm. It was stuffed to the ceilings, overladen with antique furniture and knick-knacks, and teeming with police officers, all searching for fingerprints and clues.

If this had been any other real estate agent who disappeared, Aidan would have been the only one called in.

She dialed Cassandra’s house, and after a few rings, Lorelei picked up the phone. “I wanted you and Mom to know that I’m here at the house on Grove and I’m helping them figure out what happened to Melanie.”

“Oh, thank God, Dana. Your mother’s worried sick. Is there any news?”

“None that they’ve found yet, I’m afraid. But I’ll stay with them and brainstorm until we come up with something. I’m sure she’ll be okay. We have to stay optimistic and send positive energy out into the world.”

“Cassandra wants to know if Reid is there with you, because he isn’t here.”

Dana surveyed the crowd, trying to determine if he’d come in while her back was turned. “No, no sign of him. Does he know?”

“No, we haven’t seen him either. I wonder if he got

snatched as well."

"I doubt it." Dana figured that Reid was out enjoying a typical lost weekend at the club. "He's only tangentially connected to real estate, after all. Like an in-law. Related through marriage."

"No one knows anything? Not even about that nice young man that used to work with me when I was with the agency? End, something?"

"Endicott, and no, nothing on that front either."

"Please keep us in the loop. Your mother is beside herself."

That can't be pretty.

"I will, I will. I promise." *Click.*

Aidan came up from behind. "Any thoughts on how we can locate the homeowners?"

"Well, they obviously still live here. Let me see if I can use my smartphone to pull up the house's tax records and get their names. Then I might be able to use one of my real estate apps to track down their email addresses and cell phone numbers."

A few minutes later, Dana had their first lead "The house belongs to Claudia and Steven Gallup. Cell number 555-4210."

"Could you get them on the phone and ask them to come back home?"

"Sure." Dana felt practically deputized, which was a good deal better than feeling as helpless as she had up to that point.

No answer. She left a message asking the Gallups to call Detective Aidan Cummings or the Rock Canyon police at their earliest convenience, along with both phone numbers.

The investigation was still going strong at 1:00 am but the home owners hadn't called back. With nothing to do,

Dana collapsed on a yellow Victorian rosewood sofa, and an exhausted Aidan joined her.

"There's no point in both of us staying up all night," he said. "They're done with your car so let me take you back to the station so you can pick it up and drive home. That way, at least one of us can get a good night's rest."

They were both deep in thought on the drive back. "Want me to follow you back to your place to make sure you get back safely?"

"No, I'll be fine."

When they arrived, he gave her a distracted peck on the cheek, and just as she started to leave the car, his cell rang. He listened for a minute, said okay, and then hung up.

"They found the homeowners. They were up in Portsmouth, but they're heading back. I gotta run. I'll call you if anything turns up."

She watched him speed away, mourning both the potential loss of her sister, as well as the first real happiness she'd felt in a long, long time.

CHAPTER 43

March 11th

DANA DROVE HOME AND ATTEMPTED to stay awake and wait for Aidan's call, but fatigue won out. She finally awoke at 10:02 am the next morning and immediately hit *1* on her speed dial.

"I've been trying you for hours, Thissie. I was worried sick."

"I'm sorry. I was so tired, I guess I didn't hear the phone. What's going on?"

"Not a lot. No one's heard anything from Melanie, no ransom note, nothing. No answer on her cell."

"So no progress."

"I wouldn't say that. There's one potential lead. The Gallups said something about having nanny cams in the house, so they could spy on buyers touring the property. If they're on, and if they happen to be in the same room where Melanie was taken, we might have something. But they couldn't remember where they were, and with all this junk lying around, we're having a hard time locating them. So we're waiting on the owners to return."

Dana looked over at her clock. "How long does it take to get back here from Portsmouth?"

"About five hours, but they managed to get a flat tire, and that's what's been holding things up."

"Terrific. Did you reach Reid? Does he know?"

"Yup. He finally answered his cell phone. Showed up ragged and unkempt, like he'd just woken up. He didn't have any information that could help us. Frankly, he seems on edge, as if he's waiting to call the insurance company, and ask how much money he's got coming his way…should anything happen."

"Oh God, don't say things like that. Nothing is going to happen. It can't. I've finally gotten my sister back. I refuse to lose her. Not now."

"I'm sorry, Thissie. That was cold. I'm not thinking clearly. I haven't had a good night's sleep since, well since before dinner with you the other night."

"Should I come back to the house? I can help you search for the nanny cams."

Dana climbed out of bed and headed over to her closet to pull out something to wear.

"You can if you want. But honestly, the place is overflowing with detectives as it is. And I don't think you being in the same room as Reid is going to do any of us much good, do you?"

She stopped shuffling through her outfits and plopped down on the floor outside her closet, torn between what she wanted to do, and what made the most sense.

"No, you've got a point. Will you call me if anything happens? And if I come up with anything at all, I'll call you?"

"Sounds good, Thissie. Stay home. Be careful."

"You too."

As soon as she disconnected the call, the phone buzzed, an alert that there were voicemail messages that had gone unanswered while she'd slept. Dana checked the scroll. Four calls, all from her mother's phone number.

I'm having a bad enough day as it is; do I really need to deal with my mother's nonsense too? I wonder if Cassandra would be this distraught if I had been the one who'd gone missing?

Knowing the answer, she ignored the three next calls that came from Cassandra's number, deigning to hit redial only after she'd showered, dressed and finished lunch. A frantic Lorelei answered on the first ring. "Dana, are you okay?"

"Yes, I'm fine. I'm afraid I missed your calls. I've been so upset about Mel—"

"It's your mom, Dana. With all the stress of what's been going on, she started having chest pains. The ambulance came hours ago and took her to Good Sam. Maybe it's nothing; I don't know. But I wanted you to be aware."

"I'll be right there. Thank you, Lorelei."

She started to grab her coat and bag and then hesitated, questioning why she'd agreed to go to Good Sam instead of back to the house on Grove.

My mother won't give a damn that I'm there, standing vigil. And honestly, she wouldn't lift an eyebrow if the tables were turned, and I was the one being rushed to the ER.

But she wasn't her mother. She still had a modicum of humanity, and she felt compelled to do the right thing.

She grabbed her purse and raced out to the car. Key in ignition, turn, nothing. Tried again, still nothing. *Perfect.* She searched her phone for the number of a taxi service and asked for rush pickup. They promised they'd be there in less than ten minutes, and told her to stand by the curb.

Living in a quieter part of town, there weren't any

other cars whizzing by that she could flag down to hitch a ride. She waited as patiently as she could, using the time to run through Cassandra's Mother of the Year highlight reel. There was the day she'd left her at Gloria's for good, without a hug or kiss goodbye. The visits she'd made to Dana in Centralia, only to divert her attention to her clients yammering over the phone about their inflated mortgage rates and delayed closings. To the last few years, when she'd barely look up from her television program to give her visiting daughter the time of day.

What the hell? Why go to Good Sam when I could be by Aidan's side, helping him find the one family member who actually cares about me? Fuck Cassandra. Fuck her and her big house and her cell phone and her chest pains.

Dana decided that when the car service did show up, she'd tell them to take her to the house on Grove instead. But sending bad energy out into the world has its downside. Because at that moment, she felt a thump at the back of her head, and the ground came rushing up to meet her.

CHAPTER 44

Dungeon: March 13th - Captive
(The Present)

MY CAPTOR TELLS ME IT'S only been a day or two, but I feel like I have been bound here for weeks. The thirst is overwhelming, leaving my throat feeling lizard-skinned and scabby, my strength thoroughly depleted. My wrists and ankles are raw and bloody from trying to escape the leather shackles. My face is no doubt burnt and possibly scarred from boiling water. Through it all, only one goal has kept me going—to stall, to delay long enough for someone, anyone, to figure out where I am, and come to my rescue.

I have ruminated long and hard over the actions of my past, as requested by my kidnapper. The dozens of people I've no doubt hurt, though none out of malice. Each exploit accompanied by some meaningful rationale: the need for business success. Validation. Duty. Self-preservation. All compellingly justified in *my* mind, but no doubt just noise to the lunatic who has imprisoned me.

Who could have it out for me so badly? Who could hate me so intensely that they'd not only torture me, but kill others to mask their steps? Who knew my whereabouts and daily routine well enough to know where and how to abduct me?

Had I finally become such a thorn in Reid's side that he wanted me gone for good? Was Deborah Lee so deeply in debt that she could no longer afford to split incoming commissions with me and my recently departed colleagues? And all the others—snubbed vendors, disgruntled clients, shunned lovers. These days, I suppose anyone with half a clue could electronically hack into someone's digital agenda and track them down. How do I thin down this herd of possible assailants?

Through this entire ordeal, there's been only one person I've yearned to see—my sister. Torn from me when we were both so young. All communication thwarted, with no clue as to why. This was our chance to reunite, to be the real family I've always craved. Why did it have to be stolen again from me now, when we were on the verge of something so special?

The room fills with a buzz as the mic comes back on.

"Got a little musical interlude for you. Music to jog your memory by."

I hear the faint and familiar notes of a favorite tune from years gone by. And as it plays on, the snippets from the nightmares that have haunted me for almost three decades—the party hat, the cake, the door knocking— all comes flooding back in one giant, horrendous, tidal wave:

The finale to the soundtrack of Pippin fills the family room, decorated with crepe strands of pink and white and a big Happy Birthday banner hanging from the fireplace mantle.

"Think about the sun...sun...sun...sun..."

My father runs over and nudges the needle over. It

always sticks on the word 'sun.'

"Stupid skip. I think your mother must be inside this record player," he says. "She's always going on and on about wishing for the son." He picks me up and lifts me high into the air. "But I wanted another little girl. And I got the perfect one, didn't I? Six years ago, the lord answered my prayers and brought you to me. And now we're going to celebrate your birthday with a big cake!"

We both giggle and hug and sing along with the record as we do almost every night, the lyrics filled with pictures of perfect flames and angels.

"Daddy, tell me again, who was Pippin?" I ask, putting on my party hat.

"He was the son of Charlemagne, the head of the Holy Roman Empire. You'll read about him in history class one day."

"He was really important, right?"

"Charlemagne? Oh yes."

I take my finger and run it against the chocolate frosting on my cake and then suck the sweetness off with glee. "And what's this song about again?"

"It's about Pippin thinking about jumping into a box of fire."

"Why would he want to do that? That would hurt."

"Well, Pippin was confused. He spent his whole life searching for things to do that would give his life meaning. All the people singing? They were bored. They want Pippin to hurt himself so they can watch."

We hear a banging on the front door. I ignore it, not wanting the party to end.

"Daddy, let's not talk about that anymore. It's sad. When can we cut my cake? I want some cake."

"Okay, sweetums. One sec. Let me see who that is, knocking at the door."

"No, Daddy, they'll go away. Don't leave me—we're having fun!"

"It will only take a minute," he assures me as he walks into the living room.

I hear murmurs. First soft mutterings which quickly escalate into shouting interspersed with mumbling, low and threatening. "She was mine...We were in love...you fucking brainwashed her... she was going to leave... pregnant again......I don't like people touching my things!" Thud. Thud. Crash. Moan.

Terrified, I run into the next room screaming, "Stop, don't yell at my daddy!"

As I enter, I see him on the ground, curled up into a ball, clutching his legs. A strong arm grabs me and pulls me to the opposite side of the room. The other hand is clutching a cane, but throws it to the floor.

I struggle to break free, but the grip is too tight. "Let... me...go. I...need to...help...my...Daddy!" I cry, twisting back and forth.

The person holding me reaches into a coat pocket with the other hand and pulls out a knife and I feel it against my throat. It is cold and sharp and scrapes my neck.

"Don't move, honey. You could get hurt," my father calls out, still clasping his knees. "It will be okay, I promise."

My captor takes the hand not holding the knife, reaches into the other pocket, pulls out a gun, and tosses it over to my father.

"I was going to do it, but I think it's far more appropriate if you do."

"Daddy, don't! Don't!"

"Do it. Do it now, or I'll slice her throat. You'll watch her bleed to death, and then I'll shoot you myself."

"Daddy, no. Don't. It's okay. I will die. Not you. I want

to die. Kill me."

My father shrinks into himself, so small, helpless, resigned. Tears brim in his eyes. He tries to feign a brave smile. "Be good, Princess. I have to go now. Remember, I'll always love you." And with that, he lifts the gun to his head and pulls the trigger.

My ears ring and pulsate from the deafening blast. Nausea overwhelms me as the acrid smell of sulfur flirts with the coppery scent of spilt blood. The shooter pushes me down to my knees, and I crawl over to sit next to Daddy, remaining frozen and dazed as I silently watch the red river pour from the top of his half-headed body.

The assailant walks over and spits twice on my father's corpse and then kicks him between his lifeless legs. I can see the killer clearly now: heavy set, long red hair, cruel eyes. She turns toward me and shrugs.

"You ruined my party; I ruined yours. Fair's fair, I guess. Right, kid? Anyway, say a word about this or about me to anyone. and I'll come back and kill your sister while you watch. Are we clear? Good. Happy Birthday!"

CHAPTER 45

March 13th

"LORELEI!" DANA SCREAMED, AS BEST as she could, the revelation of a betrayal so deep forcing the words from a throat cracked and aching with thirst. "Lorelei, I know it's you!"

The intercom came on. "Finally figured it out, eh? Good for you." No voice distorter this time. It was all her.

Dana heard the *clunk, clunk, clunk, creak* as her captor entered the room.

"Where is Melanie? Why did you kill my father? Why are you doing this?"

"I thought you remembered."

"Some of it, yes. But I really don't understand."

"That's fine. You want your sister? Let's bring her in here and we can have a lovely family reunion."

Lorelei ripped the blindfold from Dana's eyes, the duct tape tearing off skin along with it. She'd been in the dark so long, the overheads burned her retinas. When she did manage to coax her eyelids apart and tilt her head forward, she saw Lorelei dragging a chair into the room, leaving it about three feet in from the entrance and closing the door behind her. Tied to the chair sat Melanie, bound and gagged, wide-eyed with terror.

Dana slowly recognized where they were. The rear section of their mother's house. The part that had been closed off since Cassandra's stroke because there was no need to heat so much unused space. This formal dining room used to be a business write-off on her mother's taxes. She was strapped to the long, oak boardroom table where Cassandra once held private closings. She was sure her captor had noted the irony when formulating her plan.

As soon as Lorelei removed the ball gag from her mouth, Melanie immediately started screaming for help.

"You're wasting your time. Your mother soundproofed this room when she built the house, so no one could hear what was going on inside."

"Let us out of here, you fucking bitch!"

"Now, now, flattery will get you nowhere. Girlies, let me tell you how this is all going to go down. It's only fair, since you're the main actors in this little play.

"First, we have Dana—the traumatized, blackout-ridden, therapy patient. Clearly unstable. Dana kidnaps rich, successful Melanie…so jealous of her big sister, Cassandra's favorite. So in love with her sister's husband. So eager to get her hands on all that inheritance and simultaneously exact a little revenge. And conniving enough to murder three other agents and run down a fourth, just to mask her steps. She shoots her big sis dead. Maybe through the nipple. Whaddaya say, Mel? And then, crazed with guilt, maybe flashing back to when she witnessed Daddy Dearest die the same way, Dana shoots herself in the head. Neat. Clean. No more real estate agents fearing for their lives. Everyone is happy."

"No one will believe that," spewed Melanie.

"Especially because I was with Detective Cummings when Melanie was kidnapped," Dana rasped through parched lips, hoping that by throwing a wrench into Lorelei's plans, it would buy them some additional time.

"Everyone will believe it, especially once they find all these lovely smut-filled emails between Dana and her lover, Reid. Or should I say Dare? Along with all the details of the plot she and her gay little fops hatched to destroy two careers, both yours and Cassandra's. Didn't know that she was behind the whole rental fraud thing, did you, Mel? Your little sister's no stranger to plotting conspiracies; she'd been planning to destroy you for years."

Melanie's eyes opened wide. Dana tried to grunt out an apology but the words wouldn't come.

"So no one is going to be surprised that Dana, who was off fucking her new beau, Detective Cummings, had colluded with her inheritance-hungry, perverted-partner-in-crime, Dare, to lure his wife out of her open house at Grove with some tale of an emergency back at home. Which explains the lack of any signs of struggle. And why Melanie left her car behind."

"He helped you?" Dana struggled to eke out.

"Nah, last time I saw him, he was at home, sleeping off a little Roofie-enhanced cocktail I prepared. Look Ma, no alibi!"

"But why? Why kill anyone? What has anyone done to you?" screamed Melanie.

"Let me tell you a little story," said Lorelei. "A story of two young women in New York City in the fifties. One is a nursing student, the other a budding actress. They meet through the personals section of a newspaper because what they liked to do wasn't as acceptable back then as it is today. Like you and your fucking orgy clubs, *Thissie.*

"Anyway, they meet. They fall in love. They move in together and live happily for years. But the actress, she lets ambition get the better of her. Meets someone who she thinks has a lot of money and a lot of connections. She gets pregnant, and so she has to marry him. Moves to the suburbs. But she swears to the nurse that she doesn't really love him, it was an accident. She promises that nothing's really changed—once she has the kid, she'll move back to the city, make it on Broadway, divorce him and come back to her."

Melanie and Dana stared at each other in shock.

"Good plan…until Mr. Big Shot invests big and starts losing his shirt. And his little bride has to leave mommy duty for real estate, the only decent-paying job she can find without a college degree. She starts making real money and again, we rekindle the idea of being together. Until Daddy fucking knocks her up again with Baby Number Two. That's you, Dana. Fucking Baby Number Two. So that's your sin. What I've been patiently waiting for you to confess to and repent for. You were born, and with it, all my dreams of being with Cassie died."

"You're with her now, aren't you?" Dana whispered with the last of her strength.

Lorelei stomped over and slapped her hard against the cheek. "Shut up, you fucking whore, and let me finish my story." She seized a cane that was leaning against the back wall and brandished it threateningly at each sister. "You got anything else to add?"

Both sisters remained silent.

"Good," Lorelei continued. "Even with you born, Cassie keeps making promises. And working harder. And harder. Until there just wasn't any time for me anymore. I confront her. She tells me it's over. She's pregnant with Baby Number Three—a boy this time. She's always wanted a boy, she confesses. She's not going anywhere.

"So I made it easier for her to leave. Amazing how a husband's suicide ends a marriage, and a couple of cane hits to the stomach causes a miscarriage. I think great, everything's going to go back to normal. But then she runs out in the middle of the night. Fucking disappears. And it wasn't like it is now with the Internet letting you find people so easy. I didn't know where to start. Turns out she left you with your grandmother, and took Melanie with her. Guess it's easier to stay anonymous when someone is asking around for a single mom with two kids and you've only got one. Your mom was no dummy; that's for sure."

"But you found her," Melanie pointed out, in spite of the previous warning. Lorelei was so engrossed in reliving her past that she didn't pause to reprimand her.

"Thanks to Deborah Lee Decker. I went to the library and requested the phone books for every town within a hundred-mile radius. I sent letters to every real estate company, inquiring about one Cassandra Beckett. Wrote that I admired her so much that not only would I pay a finder's fee to anyone who told me where she was working, I offered to intern for that company free for six months. It took a few years, but Deborah Lee finally contacted me and invited me to come down and join Rock Canyon Realty.

"I have to admit, Cassie wasn't very happy to see me, and she threatened to leave the agency unless Decker fired me. Deborah Lee asked her how many clients would stay her clients once it came out that her husband killed himself out of neglect and how she abandoned her own child to live amidst the cancerous coal fumes of Centralia. That's when Cassie relented and let me stay."

"That still doesn't explain why you had to start killing real estate agents." Melanie was clearly egging Lorelei on.

"Yeah!" was all Dana could manage to add. The longer they kept this lunatic yapping, the more time there would be for the detectives to find the nanny cams, recognize Lorelei, and head over to the house, hopefully with a SWAT team in tow.

Clearly incensed by the interruption, Lorelei walked over, grabbed the ball gag she had removed from Melanie, and despite her struggles, shoved it into Dana's mouth, adjusting the straps tightly. She picked up the cane again, smiled at Melanie, and asked, "Now, dearie, do you have anything to add?" Melanie shook her head.

"In for a penny, in for a pound," she continued. "You might as well hear it all. Not as if you're going to live long enough to tell anyone. Your mom and I co-existed for years at the agency, but it wasn't very pleasant. She was careful to throw herself into her work and not date, knowing that I wouldn't take any romance lightly. And every time I saw or heard about you girls, I hated you more and more. You, Melanie, because you were the spitting image of your mom, overworking, sacrificing everything including those around you, in pursuit of the holy dollar. And you, Dana, because when Melanie talked about how you were off in Paris, it reminded me of the free-spirited lifestyle Cassie had to abandon when she got saddled with you kids. I knew one day I'd get rid of you both, I just wasn't sure how or when.

"Cassandra spent so many late nights at the office, I was sure she'd work herself into an early grave. And that's when an idea hit me. I started doctoring

Cassie's coffee pot at work, adding in tiny amounts of phenylpropanolamine and anticoagulants each day. Ms. Lorelei's special brew, something to up the adrenaline.

"And then, things started to go badly in the world of real estate, thanks to little Dana here. Fraud accusations splashed across the newspapers. Fingers pointed at Cassie. More stress than usual. Her blood pressure went through the roof. Precisely what I needed to push her over the edge, so she'd stroke out."

Oh my God. I didn't cause the stroke? All this time, blaming myself for my mother's illness, and none of it had really been my fault.

"Moving back in with Cassie after the stroke was so easy. I thank you for that, Melanie. Even though your fuck-off husband was off trying to locate *Thissie* here, you were sooo desperate to get her off your hands, I think you would have hired Satan himself if he'd applied for the job. Took back my rightful place beside her in bed. Not like Cassie could protest much. Especially when I told her that if she said anything to anyone about getting rid of me, I'd kill her daughters even more violently than I'd killed her son. While she watched. But just in case, I kept her hopped up on ketamine whenever I had to close my eyes at night or leave the house for any length of time. That way I knew for sure she wouldn't be wheeling off and calling the police.

"Things were working out great until Mel here started talking about moving us out of the house. Assisted living, you suggested. Taking her away from me forever. Couldn't fucking leave things be, could you?" She took a step closer.

Melanie's eyes opened wider, her whites laced with spiny lines of bloodshot-red, and shook her head wildly, unwilling to risk saying a word and again face the cane.

"That's when I came up with this plan to get rid of you both. Stop all this interference. No one likes real estate agents, I realized. No one would miss real estate agents. And Dana here, you made it so easy for me. Not recognizing me when you first breezed back into town. Of course, keeping the room dark helped, until I had time to change my hair color and cut. Putting those lovely fingerprints all over my glasses of lemonade. Checking your email on my computer. Updating your calendar. Letting my spyware copy all of your browsing history, capture all of your passwords. I could see who you were meeting, where and when.

Once I figured out you were fucking your own brother-in-law in that oh-so-special way, I realized you'd handed me motive and opportunity on a silver platter. Made it easy to schedule my murders to coincide with times you wouldn't be able to scare up an alibi.

"I could read your online journals. The blueprints of your fraud. Even your upcoming meeting with Grayson, where you were going to commiserate over your comatose pal, *Endie*. You wrapped up every part of my plan with a big red bow, from falling for the lie about your mom being in the hospital right down to parking your car in the garage the other night so I could sugar the tank without being seen. Thanks for that."

Dana considered trying to say, "You're welcome," through the ball gag but thought better of it. It might have added on some extra time, but she didn't really want to risk getting beaten again.

"The one thing I didn't foresee as I was setting you up, Dana, was that you were going to go and confide in your sister. That was a surprise, made me speed up my plans a bit. Which brings us to today, which is perfect, since it's your birthday. The day of your daddy's death will be the anniversary of yours as well." She started to unfasten the ball gag. "I'm going to give you one last chance to say the words I've been waiting for, Dana. Apologize. Apologize for being born, and maybe I won't make you watch me cut Melanie over here into little pieces with a chainsaw instead of shooting her in the head."

"You bitch, she's not the one you want to apologize. The one you want to hurt. I am," screamed Melanie. "I'm the one that was born first. I'm the one that Mom loved, way more than you. And I'm the one who's been trying to get her to fire you from day one. You're nothing but white trash. A mistake. If she'd wanted to be with you, she would have had an abortion from the start."

Melanie's cruel comments must have rung true because Lorelei's face became distorted, as if something had snapped inside her skull. She dropped the cane, bowed her head and squeezed her eyes closed, perhaps warding off her private demons. A moment passed in silence. Dana prayed her captor might pass out and give the two sisters an opportunity to escape.

But to Dana's dismay, Lorelei regrouped, stooped down to pick up the cane, and wielded it viciously at Melanie. "No one will be surprised that Dana beat you to death instead of shooting you. Cleaner for me too, one less set of fingerprints to take care of. And it will hurt more if you don't see when it's coming."

She walked behind Melanie, her back toward the door, and started to strike. Melanie screamed as the cane came down again and again, slicing into her neck and shoulders. Rather than beg for mercy, she added insult upon insult, further incensing Lorelei. Dana didn't know if she was also stalling for time, or trying to get her tormentor so exhausted, she wouldn't have time to assault sister number two.

Lorelei was so consumed with administering her brutality, she didn't notice the door slowly open behind her. Dana did. She watched as if in slow motion. Lorelei lifted her cane for probably the twentieth time when an expression of surprise and pain spread across her face. She faltered with an "Arghh," stumbled a few steps to the left, then pitched forward and fell on her face. Wedged into her upper back was a 14" heavy kitchen knife, blood bubbling up at the site of entry.

"No one touches *my* things," said a nightgown-cladded Cassandra to her ex-lover's lifeless body. Then she turned toward her daughters. "Fucking Beaver Head left the intercom on and the door to the study open. Took me ten goddamned minutes to roll over here."

For the first time in almost thirty years, Dana was actually happy to see her mother. Cassandra hobbled over past Melanie's slumping body and came to her side. "Dana, please understand. I couldn't risk having the two of you living with me. And I couldn't take a chance on you wanting to come home. I had to make you hate me. What I did was for your own good."

Dana wanted to answer when they were interrupted by the thunder of steps, and in ran Aidan, flanked by three other officers, all brandishing their pistols. The taller one quickly took inventory, and reported into his portable radio: "Emergency situation in hand at the Beckett-Wright compound over on 1 Mallory Drive. We have two victims. We need two 105's, step on it. We also have a DOA—send in the crime scene unit and notify the ME."

"Guess we didn't need the nanny cam footage after all. Appears you took care of things yourself," said Aidan. "Why did I ever doubt that for a minute? You ladies are a force to reckon with!"

He unbuckled Dana's ballgag and restraints as another officer freed Melanie from her chair, and a third led Cassandra back to her wheelchair, which sat just outside the boardroom door.

"You okay?" whispered Aidan as he helped her sit up. She threw her arms around his neck and held on for dear life. The detective summoned one of the officers to get him a glass of water, and he held it up to her lips as she took baby sips.

" Melanie…"

"We already have an ambulance on its way. Why don't we drive you over to Good Sam as well? I think they will want to examine you, maybe keep you overnight for observation. Then I'll take you home and do the same."

"Perv," she mouthed, followed by a weak smile.

"You wish," he replied, helping her off the table and into his waiting arms.

EPILOGUE

March 13
(One year later)

DANA PRETENDED TO BE SPEECHLESS as Endie escorted her into Cassandra's living room and about forty people leapt out from behind columns, chairs and couches to yell, "Surprise." Aidan had told her about the birthday party a few weeks back, fearing that she might have some lingering post-traumatic stress that would be aggravated by any sudden shocks. She had assured him she could handle the party and even the fact that it would be held at her mother's new digs.

The house smelled of new furniture and fresh paint, Cassandra having moved in only a few weeks prior. It was a much smaller, more modest home, closer to town, easier for her new caretaker, Adelaide, to reach by bus. No way would Cassandra ever again consider a live-in aide; she preferred her privacy and knew that her daughters would be more than willing to stop by if she needed nighttime assistance.

Melanie hugged her sister warmly and led her over to Cassandra, seated in her wheelchair next to the pile of gifts in the corner. Dana bent forward and gave her mother a peck on the cheek. Aidan had easily talked the

D.A. out of pressing any charges against her for her role in Lorelei's demise; it had clearly been a case of self-defense following years of intimidation by a psychopath.

Mother and daughter were still hard at work mending fences: Cassandra was doing her best to make amends for years of neglect, and Dana had vowed to repay the $300,000 fraud loss. Forgiveness was easier now that each could understand and appreciate the other's motives, especially all that Cassandra had sacrificed over the years to keep both daughters safe.

Melanie's boyfriend, Scott Krompic, a tall and beefy-faced mortgage broker with a crew cut and ruggedly handsome features, tackled Dana and squeezed her tight. She liked Scott. Especially because he was devoted to Melanie. As it turns out, he had been romancing her for the past ten years, albeit in the shadows. Now that they were living together, Melanie was much happier, and even occasionally took some needed time off. They'd recently returned from a week in Morocco.

"How's the romance going?" asked Melanie, pulling her sister into the kitchen, away from the crowd.

"Things are good. My classes are interesting. Aidan's getting a promotion, and we're talking about moving in together."

"I like that boy."

"I do too. I've definitely traded up."

"Haven't we both," Melanie agreed.

Neither had seen Reid for about nine months, not since the day they'd both barged into Kinky Winks, Gresham's newest club, while Dare was in mid-scene with Faith. Dana had stood on the sidelines as Melanie walked over and pulled off his mask, handed him a petition for divorce, and then served subpoenas to the club owners and the Dungeon Master. She twirled the mask in the air, threw it to her sister as a memento, and then they both left without a word. Needless to say, he granted her an uncontested divorce, settling for a one-time alimony payment of $100,000. "A small price to pay to be rid of a large mistake," Melanie had rationalized.

Dana had made some changes as well. After recovering from skin graft surgery to repair her burnt cheek, she'd left Rock Canyon Realty and its dictatorial manager, Deborah Lee Decker, and hung her license at Melanie's new brokerage, Do Wright Realty. Since Melanie had no time for administrative duties, she'd turned all that over to her new office manager, Endicott Coxwell, who, though fully recovered from his hit and run, was still mourning the loss of Grayson, and therefore grateful for the less hectic nine-to-five position.

Dana handled fewer clients than before but Melanie paid her a generous ninety percent split on all of her transactions, which easily covered her living expenses. When she wasn't showing or listing homes, she was taking classes down in the city at John Jay, learning everything she could about criminal justice.

As traumatized as she was by the *Realtor Retaliator* incident, Dana did experience one positive outcome. When she and Aidan joined forces to interrogate suspects, she'd realized that law enforcement was one way to satisfy her need for fear and danger in a non-sexual way. Now with her memories unblocked, her PTSD symptoms had diminished and the blackouts were almost gone. It seemed like a good time to embark on a new career.

Though she was probably too old to join the police force as a rookie officer, Dana envisioned a behind-the-scenes role, helping out Aidan, now a bonafide detective on the Rock Canyon police force, in a research or administrative capacity. After all, she did know her way around a loophole or two. Perhaps she could make inroads in ways that strictly-by-the-rules officers could not. Plus, having been around real estate agents for all of her life, she pretty much understood the inner workings of the criminal mind.

Aidan pulled his girlfriend back into the living room and over to the buffet table. He picked up a mini-quiche, held it up to her lips, and smiled. "Love and quiches for my baby."

Everyone groaned except for Dana. She remembered the first time, back at VisionNary, when he had hand-fed her, and felt a stirring in the same place that she had back then. "Can we get out of here?" she asked, under her breath.

"Not a chance. First you have to go through the torture of opening all these gifts and blowing out all the candles on your cake."

They walked over to the triple-layer cake sitting on the mahogany sideboard under the newly painted portrait of her grandmother Gloria. It dominated the left wall of the dining room. Dana and Melanie had commissioned one of the finest portrait artists in New York City to capture the essence of Gloria, based on a photograph taken during happier times, before their grandfather had left to fight in WWII. It was Gloria at her finest—wistful, loving and indomitable. They ordered two extra copies, so that each sister could hang one in their respective homes.

Aidan poured everyone a glass of champagne and held his up in a toast. "*Lang may yer lum reek,* as my grandmother would say."

"And in English?" Endie called out.

"Long may your chimney smoke. In other words, may you live a long and healthy life. English enough for you, Endie, ya bleeding numpty?"

Dana counted the candles and tilted her head quizzically.

"Why 37 candles, Mel? I'm only 36!"

"One for good luck, silly," she answered, as the rest of the crowd laughed and applauded.

Dana plucked out a candle from the middle, held it up for all to see and then dramatically broke it in two. "Thanks, but that's not necessary." She grinned broadly at Aidan, Melanie, Endie and even Cassandra—all the people she now had the courage to love and believed loved her in return. "Thanks to you, I'm already the luckiest person I know."

A NOTE FROM THE AUTHOR

THANK YOU FOR READING EXPIRED Listings. Positive reviews are the lifeblood of a novel's success. If you enjoyed this story, please consider taking time to post a review on your favorite bookstore's website, your blog or on social media pages. And again, thank you.

For information on upcoming releases,
please follow me at:

Amazon author page:
http://www.dmbarr.com

Punctuated Publishing:
http://www.punctuatedpublishing.com

Goodreads:
https://www.goodreads.com/author/
show/15424118.D_M_Barr

Twitter:
http://www.twitter.com/@authordmbarr

Facebook:
http://www.facebook.com/authordmbarr

ABOUT THE AUTHOR:

WHO IS D.M. BARR?
By day, a mild-mannered salesperson, wife, mother, rescuer of senior shelter dogs, happily living just north of New York City. By night, an author of sex, suspense and satire.

My background includes stints in corporate communications, marketing, travel journalism, meeting planning, public relations and real estate. I was, for a long and happy time, an award-winning magazine writer and editor. Then kids happened. And I needed to actually make money. Now they're off doing whatever it is they do (of which I have no idea since they won't friend me on Facebook) and I can spend my spare time weaving tales of debauchery and whatever else tickles my fancy.

The main thing to remember about my work is that I am NOT one of my characters. For example, as a real estate broker, I've never played Bondage Bingo in one of my empty listings or offed one of my problem clients.

But that's not to say I haven't wanted to...